THE ARES
WEAPON
A Space
Colonization
Sci Fi Thriller

Casey & Michelle.
Thanks for your friendship
Oct 1, 2016

This book is a work of fiction. Names, characters, places and incidents either are products of the author's imagination or are used fictitiously. Any resemblance to actual events, locales or persons, living or dead is entirely coincidental.

For Mom. This would not have happened without your encouragement of many decades past. I wish I could have accomplished this during your lifetime.

Claim your free ebook of short science fiction stories by going to

Contents

THE ARES WEAPON

Book 1 in the Mars Ascendant Series

D.M. Pruden

CHAPTER ONE

He regarded the dead body of the ship's captain. He'd not executed anyone for some time and realized how much he missed it.

Agent 324 didn't plan to execute him on the bridge of his own vessel. He intended to space him along with the rest of the crew. Every aspect of this mission seemed to need his personal touch which he resented up to now. After pulling the trigger, he found he again enjoyed the rush of endorphins through his system.

The ship rocked and an explosion reverberated through the hull. He unsuccessfully tried to use his cortical implant to call his lieutenant. Recalling the CI inhibitor they activated when they boarded, he turned on his vocal link.

"What's going on down there?"

"We've met with some armed resistance, Sir," came the response in his earpiece.

"What's exploding? I don't want any damage to the ship."

"They are using heavy ordinance against us. Some of the ship's Rangers are holed up in engineering."

Agent 324 frowned. He knew from the outset capturing the armed Terran military vessel would be a challenge. His plan went well until a few minutes ago. If the alarm hadn't sounded, he could have disposed of the entire crew without firing a single shot. Fortunately, he anticipated a more vigorous resistance from the veteran Terran Rangers. While formidable warriors, their tactics proved predictable. They would make a final stand in the most critical section and prepare to destroy it rather than let it fall. It was a tactic from another time. While that war ended almost a decade before, the old ways were somehow always favoured.

"Pull your team back past the nearest emergency bulkhead." He pushed the body off of the console. Using his own sleeve, he wiped off enough blood so that he could use the interface.

"We've pulled back to junction C8. We have wounded men to get out of there," said his lieutenant over the static filled comm link.

"I'm taking care of them now." His hands played over the controls. He sealed off the engineering section, isolating the Rangers and his own wounded men. After a moment to double check the readouts, he pressed the button to evacuate the atmosphere. As the pumps churned, he regarded the body again.

He'd almost fooled the Captain. They boarded in a stolen Terran transport with falsified clearance codes. After much discussion, he'd almost duped the Captain that their orders were legitimate. Then the man recalled the admiral whose name was all over the orders was lying in hospital in a coma. At that point, the only recourse became to shoot him and go to plan 'B'.

His flawed intelligence annoyed him. His own spies in the admiralty should have caught the error. He intended to clean house when this ended. He couldn't afford any more screw ups. He'd lost the vessel that was his real target already and came along on this mission to ensure its success.

A red light lit up the console indicating a complete vacuum in engineering. He pressed the sequence to pressurize it once more. The ship now under his control, he went to the communications interface. Within a few moments, the worried face of a young woman appeared on the screen.

"How is everything going?" she asked.

"We experienced a minor glitch, but everything is back on schedule, Kiri."

She exhaled with visible relief. He thought her concern for him touching and wondered if it might not become annoying after too long.

"Altius wants an update," she said.

"Tell the freak all is proceeding according to plan. He needn't worry himself," he said, not trying to hide his annoyance.

"I tried. He isn't buying anything I tell him since the Helios incident."

He scowled at the screen, weighing his response. Though he hated Felix Altius, the man held the ear of Regis Mundi, which made him dangerous.

"Tell Altius I'll report to Mundi on my return to Luna."

"He won't like it, but I'll try. When will you be back?"

"These assholes damaged the ship, so we'll need some time to limp back. A week, perhaps? See how long you can put it off. Any update on the personnel replacements we need?"

"Our agent believes he found an engineer, but not a medical specialist."

"Find a way to inspire him. I need those people sooner than later."

She sighed. "I'll remind him. Hurry back."

She signed off, leaving him unsettled. He wondered if he finally took on a job beyond his capabilities. Before he could become too engrossed in self-doubt, his lieutenant signalled him.

"Engineering is secure. They managed some damage, but I think we can make it back to Luna for repairs with no problem. What do you want me to do with the survivors?"

"We don't take prisoners. Space them along with any bodies. I don't care if you kill them first or not."

CHAPTER TWO

Requiem touched down with far more grace than I expected. Lunar gravity made the pilot's job somewhat easier. That he was completely sober for the first time since forever made it seem easy. Though still surprised he had managed it, I remained quiet in my seat, keeping the thought to myself. At a time, not long ago I might have teased him about the landing, but not today. We weren't exactly on friendly terms at the moment.

Fair or not, the majority of people aboard were pissed at me. We had all been on each others' nerves more than usual for most of our two hundred and sixty-four days together. I thought we were lucky to arrive back at Armstrong without a murder committed. This crew, like those on most of the merchant freighters didn't exactly attract people without sketchy pasts.

Even though my degrees from the Terran Academy of Medical Sciences all proclaimed that Melanie Corrine Destin had met all of the requirements to graduate, Cum Laude, my presence aboard a ship with a bunch of miscreants was the true testament of my character. From my point of view, given my history, this was where I deserved to be.

As ship's medical officer, my job entailed seeing to the wellbeing of everyone on the round trip from Luna to Mars. That amounted to fixing the boo-boos one expects to find on a ship this old where half of the real trick is to keep it from exploding. Over the previous five years, I'd made myself popular by being generous with the dispensation of alcohol, along with a selection of other pharmaceutical distractions requested to endure the boredom.

That was before Sato Corporation introduced prohibition. Now I'm just another grumpy crew member who knows how to stitch a wound. Isn't it amazing what a first rate education can do for your career prospects?

Of course, I couldn't blame our new owners for being fun-busters. Even I had to admit the steady decline in maintenance and safe operation of the ship was a cause for concern. It was a miracle we could complete a single planetary orbit without falling apart. This last run had been the first where I felt reasonably confident I would return home. Despite everything else, *Requiem's* crew knew how to do their jobs well when required. Our asshole of a captain forced them to rise to the challenge. He was an effective commander, though as a person he proved himself a dick.

The dismissal of Chambers, our old commanding officer, had been a personal tragedy for me. The new captain, Aaron Tanza, was not only a company man but a martinet. He all but directly accused me of stealing supplies and would have replaced me if there had been another qualified physician available before the last departure. He practically stalked me and took weekly inventory against the medical logs to ensure none of the medications went missing. My income for this trip took a drastic hit by his interference with my little side business.

"Enjoy shore leave, Doctor Destin," beamed Tanza as I passed him at the airlock.

"Thanks, I intend to." *Up yours, Asshole.* I was sure he ogled my ass as I walked past him.

The only positive note, if one could call it such, was that Tanza's attitude towards me was far more friendly by the end of the run. He seemed somehow duped by my performance, which gave everyone double the reason to hate me as a turncoat and company stooge.

Schmaltz pinged my cortical implant to tell me he awaited

me off the ship. I joined him at the exit door to the massive underground hangar. The ship's engineering officer happened to be the only person onboard who still spoke to me.

"Can you believe that putz?" He fell into step with me and we strode down the corridor to the tram station.

"He's a company man, Schmaltzy. What were you expecting?"

"I hoped he'd lighten up at some point." He chewed on the ever-present unlit stogie between his teeth.

"Two hundred and sixty-four bunk inspections. Two hundred and sixty-four mess inspections, engineering inspections, sanitation inspections. I'm surprised he didn't count our bowel movements."

I smiled mischievously. "Whose to say he didn't ask me to keep track?"

Schmaltz jerked the cigar stub from his mouth. "He did? No way!"

I laughed uncontrollably.

"You're an asshole, Destin!"

"I know, but I couldn't resist it. The look on your face is the most fun I've enjoyed in months." I wiped tears from my eyes.

"You're a regular comedienne." He tried to frown but ended up grinning at the joke. "How about you buy me one of the two hundred and sixty-four drinks you still owe me, Doc?"

"Oh, that sounds like a hell of a good idea. Lead on."

I surveyed the hangar facility service terminal. The irregular schedule of the trams ensured a crowd of returning crews always waited for one. If possible, the place appeared more run down than the last time I'd been here. I wondered what the city council did with all the tax money they extorted from us.

"Quite the shit hole, eh?"

"You expected them to update things while we were gone? This is Armstrong we're talking about," I said.

"It would be a pleasant surprise to come home and be able to, oh, I don't know, take a shower more than twice a week. Am I asking too much?"

"Move to the poles where all the water is. C'mon, if we don't hurry we'll be waiting another hour."

We ran to the crowded car and pushed our way past the herd hanging around the openings in the hope of exiting first when the tram arrived at the customs module. We elbowed a space for ourselves to stand in the centre of the car as the doors closed and the train jerked into motion. Dust caked wheels squealed in protest before settling into a quieter rhythmic thumping. The smell of unwashed bodies hung in the poor airflow of the hundred-year-old tram car. Most of the haulers didn't carry enough water for showers. I tried not to think about how much my own body added to the ambience.

As we jostled along the track, we all fought to maintain our balance in the lunar gravity. It always took me a day or so to regain my moon-legs after such a long trip. Why the majority of the freighters insisted on running their ships at 0.9 Terran gravity remained a mystery to me. Almost all the crews were born and lived here and everyone thought it a damned nuisance to readjust at the start and finish of every run.

A fine dust coated the outside of the windows, obscuring the view of the historic memorial commemorating humanity's first steps here more than three hundred years before. The original lunar lander and flag long ago decayed under the relentless barrage of micro-meteorites. The present monument, the third one on the landing site, neared the end of its days.

"When do you suppose the council is going to replace that old thing?"

"They've been debating it since I got to Luna. Five years now? Who knows how long before then." I replied.

"They can keep talking if you ask me. Better they spend the money on a new water pipeline from Irwin or Artemis."

"Like that will ever happen."

Having killed the conversation, I returned my attention to the interior of the car. The tram contained a motley bunch, as always. Some of the faces may have been familiar, though nobody acknowledged anyone else.

Schmaltz moved close to whisper in my ear.

"Who do you suppose is working Customs today?"

I smiled at him.

"Why? Is there something you don't want them to ask you about? You'd better hope Toby is on. He's the only one left who'll consider your baksheesh anymore."

"Hmph. He's the only one who isn't hoping to get promoted out of this hole. The rest of those toadies would rather bust a nun for smuggling rosaries than let anyone believe they got their palms greased."

I frowned at him and lowered my voice another level.

"Don't let the Morality Police hear you saying shit like that. We don't need any attention."

Schmaltz bit down on his unlit cigar and nodded, reverting back to silence for the remainder of the ride.

As things turned out, most of the customs agents were of the amicable variety and nobody got busted this time. I didn't declare anything, so after a brief, routine interview, I linked my CI into the system and downloaded my declaration to the database. I didn't worry it would flag anything. My installed implant hack always told them a nice story.

After they cleared me, I moved into the arrival terminal and waited for Schmaltz, who joined me after a couple of minutes.

"That was relatively painless." He talked around the unlit stogie in his teeth.

"No cavity searches today?"

"It was one time. Can't you leave it alone, Destin?" He marched ahead of me. I hurried to catch up and we boarded the monorail for the twenty-minute ride to the main city complex.

"Line, 'em up, Louie!" I announced as we strode into O'Brien's Pub. I scanned the dimly lit room in search of familiar faces. Spotting three of *Requiem's* crew trying to ignore me like a group of offended school girls, I added, "And refill whatever they're drinking."

"Feeling rich today Mel?" asked Schmaltz.

"Hell no! This run cost me money, thanks to that asshole

Tanza. I just don't like everybody hating me." I nodded to Louie as he placed three shots of tequila in front of each of us. I looked back at my other crew mates and they waved their thanks for my generosity. Short memories are a necessity on a small vessel. I made a silent note to track down the remaining crew before shore leave ended.

While I ordered a refill, Schmaltz stared in silence at his empty shot glass collection.

"What's up, Schmaltzy? You're uncharacteristically morose. Don't try to tell me it's because of my restricted in-flight bar service. I know you keep a private stash in the engine room Tanza never found."

A sheepish smile spread across his ugly face. "You knew about that?"

"Everybody knew about it."

He shook his head as Louie put more tequila in front of us.

"They're a good crew, Doc. They all watch out for each other. I'm gonna miss them."

"What the hell are you talking about?"

"I've been offered a position as chief engineer on the *Polaris*. They contacted me during the return. I went to school with the captain and..."

"Hey, you don't owe me any explanation. I'm happy for you." I lied. Schmaltz was the only real friend I had made since my arrival on Luna.

"Really? Thanks, Mel. I didn't know how you would take it. If the offer had come while Chambers was still skippering I wouldn't have taken it, but..."

"Yeah, I know. It's not as much fun anymore without him."

We sat in silence for a minute, each digesting the situation.

"Listen, I could put in a good word for you. You're the best sawbones I know and a damned good friend."

"Thanks, Schmaltzy. I appreciate the thought, but the truth is, once they do their digging, they'll decide to search for someone else. Tanza only kept me because he was in a bind and couldn't find a replacement who would work for what I do. In all honesty, I can't afford to lose this gig."

Schmaltz placed a hand on my shoulder. "I'll still put in a good word anyway." He burped, ruining the moment.

I smiled at him, downed my drink and ordered another round to celebrate Schmaltz's good fortune. This was going to be a long night.

At some point during the evening, I realized I was drunk. It's not that I hadn't intended to end up inebriated; that was my single-minded purpose from the moment *Requiem* touched down. It annoyed me how little effort it required. Schmaltz fared no better and we both slouched next to each other in a booth at the back of the bar, engaged in a conversation that would not be recalled by either of us the next morning.

I sighed and tossed the last of my money on the table as a tip. "Easy come, easy go. I'll hustle up some more."

"C'mon, Doc. I'll see you safely home."

"Naw. I'm in the next section. I'll be fine."

"Are you sure you don't want me to walk you home? You don't exactly live in the upper Tens. I don't feel right about letting a lady wander home alone. Why are you still living down here?"

"My place has the luxury of being affordable. The neighbourhood can be a little edgy, I'll admit, but nothing ever happens that I can't handle. Go home to the little woman, Schmaltz. She's probably been keeping your side of the bed warm."

He smiled stupidly as he reflected on my words. "Okay, Doc. G'night. You go straight home."

I gave him a sloppy kiss on the cheek and watched him stagger off to his anticipated booty call.

"Nowhere else to go," I muttered to myself as I stumbled in the opposite direction.

My uncertain steps banged down the metal staircase to the apartment level. I tried without success to descend quietly and not wake those who needed to rise shortly for their fourteen-hour shifts. This was a working class neighbourhood for those with employment. For the majority who couldn't find work, it was the least expensive place to crash before resorting to the charity shelter, or worse.

I wondered who I would find when I opened my door. Many of the apartments were leased by spacers like me who spent months away. They often arrived to discover squatters in their place. Generally, they were tolerated as long as they didn't steal anything and the place wasn't trashed. Things rarely got ugly because most people played by the rules and moved on when the real tenant returned. A few occasionally made trouble, but I'd been lucky so far. I sometimes worried I might one day return to someone taking up permanent residence in my humble lodgings.

The corridor was dark, partly out of a poor effort to simulate a Terran night cycle, but mostly because the expired lighting panels didn't get replaced. The dim red glow of the few still functioning fire and CO_2 detectors cast enough light for me to pick my way over the occasional body of somebody sleeping one off.

I silently counted the doors from the stairwell as I felt my way along the wall. Most of the numbers were rubbed off, so I kept track of how many I passed. Though I tried to maintain my unit number on my door, it never remained in place. It disappeared regularly with whatever creative graffiti offended the landlords enough. The corporation could respond quickly enough if somebody slighted their name in writing, but couldn't seem to find the resources to put in some lights.

Confident of my count, I stopped at my apartment. The ancient panel lit up in anticipation of my manual entry code. The bastards who owned all this didn't update for CI access. That was okay since most down here chose to deactivate their implants for various reasons.

Something stirred in the shadows and I jumped back, startled, as a figure emerged into the light. It moved between me and the door and I suddenly wished I had taken Schmaltz up on his offer to walk me home.

CHAPTER THREE

I dropped my rucksack and backed away from the figure stepping out of the shadows. My heart beat a tattoo as I glanced back down the corridor, wondering if another assailant followed behind me.

Can I make a break for the stairs?

The adrenaline blasting through my system would carry me to them but the chances were still good I would trip over any one of the derelicts sleeping things off.

Would anyone even wake up if I fell over them? Would they come to my rescue if I screamed?

The stench of spilled booze and urine in the hallway filled my nostrils and I realized I couldn't expect help. Fights and screaming happened all the time down here. I was on my own.

"Melanie!"

How does he know my name?

The voice seemed vaguely familiar. The lousy lighting obscured his face.

"Who are you?"

"I'm Charlie."

He stepped forward to allow the one functioning light in the corridor to shine fully on him. I stared at the Eurasian man, unable to place him.

"Remember? From med school?"

At those words his face forced its way into the recollections of my drunken brain.

"Charlie Wong!"

The man smiled. He presented an older version of the Charlie I remembered. He seemed stockier, though I couldn't be sure because of the jacket he wore.

"What the fuck are you doing creeping around my place?" I said in a stage whisper, remembering the time and the thin doors and walls.

Taking my cue, he replied in kind, "Looking for you. I learned you made port today and..."

I waved him silent and moved past him to key in the access code. The door slid open and I led him into the apartment. I keyed on the lights and made a quick inspection of the place to ensure I didn't surprise any squatters in residence. The faint odour of something rotting in the kitchen told me whoever squatted here departed some time ago. At least they didn't trash the place, keeping to the "rules".

I lead Charlie into the cramped central room and cleared a tattered novelty throw pillow from the couch. He cautiously picked his way into the room, making as little contact with anything as possible. I invited him to take a seat, embarrassed about where my life brought me.

"Can I offer you anything? Oh, I'm sorry, I don't think I..."

Charlie's smile showed off perfect teeth. "No thanks, I don't need anything."

I perched self-consciously on the edge of a mismatched chair across from him and absently hugged the pillow. We sat in silence while Charlie examined my home. He made no comment, returning his gaze to me.

"Sorry, the walls are pretty thin and my neighbours don't like it when..."

"It's okay. I understand."

Though we are the same age, he appeared far younger than his thirty-five years. He'd put on some serious muscle since I'd last seen him, and his face was filled out a bit. I fidgeted, ashamed for not recognizing him given the amount of time we spent together in those days.

"As I said, I came here looking for you."

"How did you find me?"

"Oh, you didn't make it easy, I'll tell you that."

I blushed and looked away.

"That should tell you something."

The silence awkwardly hung in the air. I was making a mess of this visit but had no idea how to make it better. I didn't deal with people in Charlie's social class anymore.

"I don't pretend to understand why you vanished like you did. I appreciate you have your reasons, but..."

"But what? I don't owe you any kind of explanation for what I've done, where I've been or why."

Now Charlie struggled to find words. I don't think he came prepared for my defensiveness. In all honesty, I didn't realize why I became suddenly so chippy about things. It wasn't like I had settled into domestic bliss here. My place was essentially a flophouse for me and anyone else when I wasn't here. I only held the lease.

It was strange to see him struggle like this. He always filled the awkward moments with his razor wit and quick, glib replies. I decided to take him off the hook.

"What do you want, Charlie?"

He seemed relieved by the change of subject. "I want to offer you a job."

I dropped the pillow and pushed myself back into the chair. I stared, dumbfounded, at him. Of all the answers I anticipated, that did not even come up for consideration.

"What the fuck?"

"Don't sound so surprised. You're a damned fine physician."

"Was, Charlie. That's all ancient history."

"Top of the class, as I recall. You even beat me, the Asian keener." He grinned in his self-depreciating way as if still embarrassed by his intelligence. True, my marks had been better than his, but I sweated blood for those grades, mostly so as not to disappoint my benefactor. Charlie goofed off a lot and made it look as simple as eating with chopsticks.

I plodded to the kitchen. The smell of the rotten food grew stronger and gave me something else to focus on. I stood with my back to him while thoughts raced through my head. This would be so much easier if I were sober. Right now I was too emotional and couldn't trust myself to speak without weighing every word. He hadn't even asked why I'd left. At least, he remembered enough about me to not push that button.

"Why are you on the moon trying to hire losers? You're supposed to be running some big hospital now, aren't you? Wasn't that the family plan?" I was ashamed for being a bitch. I kept my back to him. It was easier.

He sighed heavily. "I did the whole follow-the-family-plan thing, Mel. It wasn't for me. Truth is, I haven't practiced medicine for years. I'm a businessman now."

I waited for him to grin with that 'gotcha' glint in his eye. His face was deadpan serious. "Your daddy must be some pissed off with you. Did he cut you off?"

"Pop's been dead for five years."

Charlie's eyes betrayed no deceit. I could always tell, though why anyone would lie about such a thing was just weird to consider. It must have been the booze or something and I felt like the lowest form of life for entertaining the idea.

"I'm so sorry."

Charlie waved away my apology.

"It's okay. You couldn't have known."

"What happened?"

"It was a freak accident. His private shuttle broke up on re-entry on a return trip from Luna."

I sat on the couch beside him and placed a hand on his knee. "I remember how much you admired him."

"After Pop died, I just couldn't find it in me to continue on in medicine. I took some time off and travelled; just tried to figure out my life, you know? When I got back home, some associates of his approached me with an offer that was hard to ignore. I work for Rego Corporation now, Mel. I succeeded Pop as Director of Acquisitions."

"Wow, that's quite the change. As long as I knew you, you despised your Dad's employers."

"Chalk that up to wide-eyed youthful naivety and idealism. I thought going into med school would put me as far away from Pop's world as I could get. It wasn't until he died that I understood I was doing it all to get his attention. After that, I had no way to make up for the hurt I'd caused..."

I took Charlie's hand and we sat in silence. A muffled alarm clock went off next door. Neither of us spoke until the spell was broken by somebody shutting it off.

"I'm sorry I reacted the way I did. What job are you talking about?"

Charlie smiled broadly.

"We are putting together an exciting recovery expedition. An amazing discovery has been made on Titan. Initial reports suggest it might have alien origins. We want to send a team in an outfitted ship to recover the artifact before our competitors can beat us to it. I had the entire group assembled, but then our physician backed out and I needed to replace him in a hurry. Your name came up and imagine my surprise when I realized you were the same Melanie Destin I went to school with."

"I'm confused. How would my name have come up?"

"I forgot to mention that we are launching from a base on Luna. Believe it or not, there aren't too many doctors with space-faring experience around here who are competent. You are well regarded by my sources. When I heard it was you, I had to find you and ask you to join."

"I...I'm flattered, Charlie. Really. Especially after all this time. But I don't think I am the person you want."

"What are you talking about? We both know how good you are. Before you left Terra you were on the fast track. And you loved it too."

"That was before the attack."

Compassion crossed his face. "You lost a lot. I never got a chance to say how sorry I was about Carlos."

I waved his comments away and fought to keep the tears from flowing. Seeing my distress, he changed the topic.

"You can't be getting much of a challenge patching up spacers on freighter runs. I definitely know you aren't paid what you are worth. Think about it Mel. One expedition and we can pay you enough to get you out of here." He gestured to the apartment.

I'd felt like a ping pong ball in a tornado since Charlie's arrival on my doorstep, but that comment hit me like a kick in the guts.

"What the hell do you think is wrong with my life? You think I want your money? That I'm not happy here?"

"Mel, I didn't..."

"Maybe I choose to be here! Maybe I'm right where I belong! I didn't ask you to find me and I don't need or want to be rescued from my pathetic life, and you sure as hell aren't my fairy god-mother"

"I'm sorry. I simply meant..."

"You meant for me to feel ashamed of my life because I didn't live up to your expectations."

"Mel, I didn't mean to imply any disrespect..."

"You didn't mean to show disdain either, but I saw you gingerly pick your way across my floor. I noticed you look carefully at the couch before you sat. What's wrong? Are you afraid you might catch something?"

I stormed to the door.

"I think you need to go now."

He slowly walked to the open door. The sound of crying children and arguing parents echoed down the corridor.

"I didn't mean to ..."

"Please leave, Charlie. Pretend you never found me."

Regret written on his face, he stepped outside and the door shut behind him.

I stared at the door for a full minute before a tear ran down my cheek. I stumbled into the bedroom, fell onto the bed and cried myself to sleep.

CHAPTER FOUR

"I was told you had everything under control."

Few people could intimidate him. Regis Mundi was one of those few. The head of the Corpus Rego, or Dominus, as he preferred to be called, did not take the news of failure well. Nearly eighty years old, he wore a toga *palmata*, richly embroidered and decorated with a palm leaf pattern along the hem. He sat straight-backed with the posture of a man half his age on a replica of a *sella curulis*. The low dais it rested on at the end of the large audience chamber gave Mundi enough of a presence to make people uncomfortable. Agent 324 understood that discomfort led to unintended disclosures, and he planned to avoid any such mistake.

At Mundi's side hovered his personal servant, Felix Altius. While his appearance was that of a slight, effeminate man of indeterminate Mediterranean ancestry, his true origins were much more exotic. A synthetic human, grown in a vat somewhere in the vast complex, he appeared perfectly at home in the ankle long tunica his Dominus required him to wear. Agent 324 afforded the freak only a cursory inspection, preferring to maintain all of his attention on Mundi. He could ill afford any distraction and he admonished himself for giving any thought to the servant.

Despite Mundi's affectations to the forms of imperial Rome, falling on one's sword for defeat had yet to become a custom. Not that he would have done so in any case. He prided himself on being a survivor, and from his perspective, the project was far from a failure.

"Our agent met an unexpected end and could not complete his mission, Dominus." He addressed Mundi with eyes lowered, as expected of him. Though he spoke impeccable latin, he felt insecure about delivering such a critical report in the dead language; another measure designed to keep people off balance. He ignored the itch of the simple wool tunic he was compelled to put on before entering the chamber, annoyed that a man of his position within the corpus needed to participate in Mundi's historical fancy.

"We believe he succeeded in directing the ship to the predetermined landing coordinates before he died."

"You believe?" Mundi raised one bushy eyebrow. "Then why haven't you retrieved it?"

"Someone aboard the *Helios* managed to get a distress signal out. The entire inner system is swarming with Terran military."

"All the more reason to expedite the recovery, is it not? It would be a shame to waste all the resources entrusted to you for this project if the Terrans locate their missing ship first."

"They are looking in the wrong places, Dominus. We made sure of that."

"Yes, and fortunately for you, I have been assured they will continue to do so for the time being. Still, it is only a matter of time before even those fools think to search the planet. Even my influence cannot defer that forever. Tell me of your current plan."

If the Dominus wanted to intimidate him, he failed. He was well aware Mundi's operatives lurked everywhere within all of the planetary governments. Some of them were also his own double agents. He played a dangerous game, but history proved this as the only way to keep one's head when dealing with Regis Mundi. That much the mistakes of his predecessor taught him.

Lucius Antonius was the *nom de guerre* of Agent 197. He'd settled on it as his final assumed identity, convinced the necessity of masquerading as anyone else firmly in his past.

The fact he chose a latin name to impress Mundi did not prevent his termination. Mundi never received failure well.

"We have acquired another vessel. It is being prepped as we speak. We only have one more specialist to acquire and we will be ready for launch."

The older man frowned and 324 felt a smug sense of satisfaction in the knowledge that some things remained secret.

"What sort of specialist?"

"We believe the released pathogen killed the crew. We need someone who can deal with the situation. More importantly, it must be someone we can... motivate."

"That is a very specific prospectus, given your timeline. Is there no such person already in our employ?"

"Unfortunately, the only such person perished on the *Helios*."

"Such skills coupled with the required inclinations are difficult to cultivate."

"I understand your concerns, Dominus. My operative has identified a promising individual who he believes can be recruited."

"Very well, do as you will." Mundi waved his hand in dismissal and turned his attention to the pad held by his assistant.

Any agent should have been terrified at the double-edged approval just granted. 324 experienced exhilaration. He knew Mundi enjoyed little choice than to allow him to continue with what he started. Mundi's grand plan would be set back years if this project failed. Success would be well rewarded, but there existed no more room for error. While he wouldn't be falling on a sword, he would not survive to report the failure in person. He could live with that motivating risk.

With no further interest shown in his presence, Agent 324 marched out of the audience chamber. As he left, he couldn't help but be impressed by the exacting craftsmanship Mundi employed to produce all of the replica furnishings.

Mundi was certainly an oddball, but he was an obscenely wealthy oddball. His preoccupation with the ancient roman world was both amusing and disturbing. It amused because it was anachronistic and unique; it was always an education in history to visit Mundi. It disturbed because Mundi's wealth allowed him to indulge his predilection and nobody dared to question the peculiarities of the business tycoon. No one knew where the fascination would end. 324 worried Mundi shared the ambitions of emperors he so admired.

Outside, a sentry in the traditional uniform of a Roman centurion approached him with his personal belongings he relinquished on arrival. The guard was armed with a simple *gladius* sheathed at his hip. A second, similarly dressed companion warily eyed him from the other side of the doorway. Both men understood their role as bodyguards to be nothing more than showmanship. The real security officers who watched unseen from another room trained remotely controlled particle weapons on 324 from the moment he entered the building.

Dressed in his own clothes once more, he exited the sprawling complex that served as the combined residence of Mundi and the corporate headquarters of the Rego Corporation. To his recollection, the constantly growing facility accounted for ten percent of the total size of Artemis. He suspected Mundi owned far more of the city than that.

Artemis had been Mundi's pet project for the past forty years. Everything about the metropolis, from its strategic location over the Moon's largest water ice source to its final adoption as the capital of the recently liberated Lunar Republic, was planned and orchestrated in detail by Regis Mundi, making him the invisible, unelected ruler of Luna.

Agent 324 sneered at the thought of the old man's presumptions. He didn't fancy himself a republican by any stretch of the imagination. He'd spent much effort to avoid military service, choosing to support the conflict with Terra in a more commercial capacity as an arms dealer in a previous life. He believed that rulers needed to be accountable to the people they governed, a belief he shared with the patriots who died in the rebellion. He wondered what their ghosts would think of the man who now effectively ruled as the secret emperor of the world they fought to liberate.

He strode out of the palace into the central pedestrian mall known as the *Forum*. He stopped and looked up through the massive, transparent dome at the blue jewel of the erstwhile home world hanging in the black sky. Moments like this, when Terra appeared high above, he couldn't help but be awed at the engineering feat of Mundi's Artemis. The unobstructed view through the dome always gave him the impression that he walked, unprotected, under the lunar skies.

His cortical implant alerted him to an incoming message. He smiled and signalled for the ground car to pick him up. By the time he'd exited the *Forum*, the requested vehicle with his personal assistant inside waited at the curb.

He sat across from Kiri Mason as the robot car pulled into traffic and proceeded toward the connecting tunnel grid.

"You're sure?" he asked.

She frowned. "I explained in the message that I wasn't. But he's the closest thing we could find on such short notice."

He relaxed into the plush cushions and smiled. "You're far too tense, Kiri."

She passed him a sealed envelope. He emptied the contents onto his lap. He picked up the passport and absorbed the details.

"Hello, Erik Dunn. Nice to be you."

He returned the other items into the envelope and handed it back to her.

"And the other arrangements?"

She stared at him critically before replying, "They're complete. But they cost more than we thought. I'm not sure we paid enough for their silence."

"After the launch, you can see to that."

She nodded, but her brow remained furrowed.

"You worry too much, Kiri."

"He's not even a close match."

"It will be fine."

She looked out the car window. The only things to be seen

were the flashes of light from the passing cars in the tunnel.

Dunn leaned toward her. "Kiri, I'll be fine."

"Lucius used to say that all the time. He, at least, took a latin name. You practically flaunt your rebellion as if there were no consequences."

"Would you feel better if I took a permanent identity, like Lucius, and operated from the sidelines? He died because his agents betrayed him. It's best to handle things personally. You know this."

Dunn frowned and pushed himself back into the seat cushions. He crossed his arms and joined her in looking out the window. Kiri was right to worry. There was more at stake here than Lucius ever tried to put into play. He hoped is assurances were not empty.

CHAPTER FIVE

I woke with a pounding headache to the screams of little Ahmed, next door, protesting his nap time. The chronometer insisted the time was early afternoon and I'd slept the day away. With a groan, I rolled onto my back and stared at the filthy ceiling, wondering how big spiders grew on the moon as I contemplated the cobwebs in the corner. I wanted to lie still for a little longer, but the pressure on my bladder convinced me otherwise. I sat on the edge of the bed and the pain of an ice pick stabbed behind my eyes. I fought to keep whatever remained in my stomach down. I swallowed around the coarse grit sandpaper in my throat and wrinkled my nose at something stinking up the room. I fell back and sniffed the sheets. The fresh scent of cheap detergent told me of my 'guests' consideration, so the foul odour defaulted to be my contribution.

A trail of dirty clothes in my wake, I somehow located the toilet and gave my poor bladder some welcome relief. More comfortable, I stepped into the spotless shower stall. I marvelled at the cleanliness of the bathroom and resolved to learn who'd squatted here and invite them back.

The allocated water ration ran out far too soon, and I keyed in an expensive top up for another five minutes of hot water. After what happened with Charlie, I decided to indulge myself. The shower helped the headache somewhat, but I would need some pharmaceutical support if I intended to be functional with what remained of my day.

Wrapped in a fresh smelling towel, I padded into the tiny kitchen to find anything to eat. The odour of rotting food reminded me even the best of guests are not perfect. I located and disposed of the offending unidentifiable mouldy bio-matter. Aside from the one blemish on their record, my mystery squatters kept the kitchen in better shape than I did. Unfortunately, the cupboards were bare and my belly protested.

While I massaged my temples, I made my way back to the water closet. I stopped in front of the mirror to view the horror. The morning after the night before is never a good time for self-appraisal, but it seemed I didn't want to treat myself all that nicely.

The person who stared back at me appeared worn out. If not for the generosity of the last few years of lunar gravity I shuddered to think how old I would appear. At least, there were no wrinkles or crows feet. My face seemed a bit puffy from the booze and the bloodshot whites of my eyes distracted from their pretty blue colour. I thought them to be pretty because they were the only feature my bitch mother ever complimented me on. I suspect she would have been disappointed to see them this morning.

My bobbed hairstyle didn't help my appearance at the moment, but I preferred to keep it short so it didn't get in the way during space travel. It needed a trim, blow dry and a brushing, but no grey lurked among the auburn tresses, and that appealed to my vanity. I knew I presented better under normal circumstances, so I decided to give any further critical assessment a pass for the time being.

A faded, twenty-year-old travel poster advertising the Martian cloud city, Olympia, hung in a frame over the toilet. The fresh start that everyone dreams of, but nobody gets. I wistfully regarded the picture and my thoughts wandered to a new life in the sky that surveyed the landscape being terraformed. I couldn't remember how long it served as my idea of heaven, but I kept it as a reminder to continue dreaming. Olympia remained the reason I stuck out the lousy job. I would be much closer today if Chandler hadn't gotten himself replaced.

I removed the poster to reveal a high end safe. I put my hand on the identification pad and endured the discomfort of holding my eye wide open long enough for the iris scanner to confirm my identity.

"Access code 468-987-Whiskey-Cocaine." The anachronistic voice recognition security steps caught most unprepared thieves off guard, or so my associates assured me. The expensive, state of the art vault itself was a difficult item to procure. Its installation in these humble lodgings would have raised a few eyebrows if I'd acquired it via the normal commercial channels. Fortunately, there are people who can be discrete; for a price, of course.

I stared into the safe at my depleted supply and sighed heavily. The latest trip did nothing to help me restock. I selected a potent pain killer and popped two pills. Back in the bedroom, I took off the towel and fell naked on my back onto the bed, eyes closed, and waited for the medication to act. I luxuriated in the cooling caresses of the air on my freshly scrubbed skin. For the first time in months, I enjoyed the freedom of being alone and I lay still, thinking of nothing. After a time, my mind tired of fighting the emptiness and I indulged myself with daydreams of a future life in the clouds over Mars.

Every credit I could earn, hustle and con over the past eight years went towards the dream. If Tanza hadn't been such pain in the ass the last trip would have given me almost enough to finance a Martian citizenship. One more run after that would have provided for the requisite apartment on Olympia and the funds to support me.

The noises of the surrounding apartments invited me back to the present. At least, my head no longer pounded. My growling stomach suggested the need to find some food. I got up and quickly dressed in the cleanest dirty clothing in my rucksack.

I took one last survey of the face in the mirror before I headed to the door. The poor thing needed a touch of makeup and some new clothes but was presentable enough. I went out the door to forage for something to eat and think about my next move.

I wanted to indulge in a traditional, multi-course, welcome home feast at Chianti's in the central hub, but I was far too hungry to go anywhere but the main commissary in the residence complex. The fast service offsets the basic quality of the food. Being inexpensive also helped make the meal taste better, but only marginally. This late in the day the cafeteria teamed with people coming off shift and going to work. I spotted a familiar face and sat down beside a sullen Vijay Zaoui.

"Hello, Vijay. How is Devika making out?"

He made a great effort to smile at me. "Oh, hello Doc. Thanks for asking, but not so good."

"Do you need another refill? I still have some, but I'm afraid the price is higher than last time."

He tried to maintain the goofy grin he always sported, but it vanished under the weight of his trouble. His words spilled out in a rush that his Indian accent made hard for me to understand. "No, I'm told we are beyond what the medicine can do for her. She is in the hospital and they say she will die soon."

"What happened? She responded so well to the meds."

"Yes, she did. But while you were away, she developed complications with her liver. They say it is a side effect of the medicines."

My food turned into a lump of lead in my stomach. Two years before, doctors diagnosed Devika with Carson-Epburg disease, a degenerative condition of the skeletal connective tissues common to those who lived in low gravity environments. It was prevalent among residents born and raised on Luna. Most of the time a simple genetic treatment administered a birth prevented it from developing. Devika's family, like many of the working poor, could not afford the injections and so played biological roulette in the hope that she would not develop the disease.

When they diagnosed her, she did not qualify to receive the expensive drugs that could offset the advance of Carson-Epburg because her family didn't treat her at infancy. Even when Vijay offered to pay for the treatment out of his own pocket, the Lunar Medical Authority refused to sell him the drug. With nowhere else to turn, he sought me out through the black net and I became his supplier. At the time, I had been delighted since the drugs he needed, while relatively easy for me to acquire, commanded an obscene price and netted me a tidy profit.

"Why can't they just clone her a new liver?" I suspected I knew the answer but hoped I was wrong.

"For the same reason, they would not give her treatment for the C-E," tears flowed from Vijay's eyes. "And I have not enough for it." He broke down and wept openly.

I held the grief-stricken man as he sobbed into my shoulder. A husband and three beautiful children were soon to lose a wife and mother and I was now overwhelmed with the realization that it was all because of me. Selling black market drugs to the rich and powerful is one thing. They can well afford to deal with the consequences of their decisions. But people like Vijay and Devika? What chance did they have when vultures like me preyed upon their circumstances? I felt sick to my stomach.

Giving it only a few seconds of consideration, I resolved to right the situation. Perhaps we could still save her, and, in the process, redeem a portion of my own soul. I accessed one of my bank accounts with my CI. Before I could change my mind, I transferred every credit Vijay had ever paid me back into his account.

He thanked me repeatedly, promising to repay everything, but I refused to hear of it and told him it was a gift. I took some satisfaction from the joy on Vijay's face as he rushed away to tell his family.

Watching him, I briefly felt proud of myself for the first time in forever. Then, with growing panic, I gradually appreciated the consequences of my generosity. Not only had Vijay been a regular, desperate customer, willing to pay whatever it took to save his wife, he was also one of my best cash cows and my spontaneous act of kindness had just cost me significantly.

The untouched meal on my tray no longer appealed to me and I pushed it away. Now I had to work that much harder to get out of this hell hole. Of course, there was Charlie's offer to consider. Even though I had summarily dismissed him in a pique of anger, what he was offering was worth even more now that I was apparently the Mother Theresa of Armstrong. Perhaps I could crawl back to him and apologize; ask for another shot at the job. I shook my head and gulped down the cold coffee. No, some bridges needed to be burned and people like me just didn't deserve to be redeemed once, let alone a second time. Cinderella's ball had ended long ago and there were no more chances of living in the castle.

Other resources remained to me. It would take some time, but I would rebuild my cash reserve and get to Mars on my own, even if it took another year or two.

The Tank, as the locals called it, was part of the oldest infrastructure of Armstrong, all built underground. There were no apartments, only shallow niches carved into the rotting concrete of the warren of abandoned tunnels. The unfortunates who found themselves here enjoyed no plumbing, only a bucket in the corner of their hovels. The really well off ones owned a separate one to wash in. For heat and communal cooking, discarded fuel barrels burned whatever refuse that could not be put to another purpose. My eyes stung from the smoke and the stench of sewage.

Of late this place had seen an influx of immigrants from some of the bigger cities, like Artemis. The socio-political mandate for the newly independent Luna boasted of the elimination of poverty, much of that accomplished by flushing the human refuse into places like this when their waste bins became full.

If the Tank served as hell's waiting room, then Oscar Vostok held the position of Satan's receptionist. He ruled supreme over everything and to cross him meant expulsion. Few crossed Oscar Vostok.

I'd only met him twice before. On the first occasion, he'd sought me out up top. I'd been referred to him as a good source for medicines that his people needed. We did business, and while I didn't make a huge profit, I got some feel good points for helping out.

That, of course, led to our second meeting, this time, initiated by me. I visited him here and offered him a partnership opportunity to transport some popular recreational drugs via his network to the most affluent assholes on the surface. Today I intended to collect from him on that deal.

I found him holding court in his office, as he called it. It consisted of a raised platform that overlooked the large central cavern where everyone could observe their king dispense justice. Instead of a throne, he sat on a high backed chair behind an ornate antique desk. Standing to either side of him, awaiting his whims were two of his lieutenants. They, like Vostok, were ex-Lunar militia, loyal soldiers whose meagre military pensions could not support the habits they'd acquired while serving their homeland.

On seeing my approach, a broad smile broke out on his face and he came around his desk to greet me with a bear hug.

"Doctor Melanie. So good of you to come and visit me again."

He smelled of expensive cologne and wore a dark warm looking wool coat. The rings on his fingers flashed gold in the flickering light of the fires below as he vigorously shook both my hands. His closely cropped, oiled beard shone jet black as did his full head of slicked back hair. He reminded me of the bear that frightened me the one time I'd been to a Terran zoo as a young child.

"Oscar, you are looking well," I said as I took a seat across from him at the desk. I sank down into the soft cushion and craned my head to look up at him.

"What can I say? Business has been good. You see? Now I have this most excellent desk, once owned by a tsar in old Russia. You are familiar with Russia? On Terra?"

"Yes, I am."

He beamed at me.

"So few people learn of their heritage. It is important to understand from where we come, no? Otherwise, we just become cavemen, throwing rocks at each other, no?"

Oscar obliquely referred to his rumoured military career during the war of independence. The word was that Luna ran a special operations force tasked with redirecting asteroids towards Terra. Luna always officially denied the allegations, but two major strikes on Terran cities did a lot to end hostilities.

"Do you know of your heritage, Doctor Melanie?"

"I'm afraid not, Oscar. I am a war orphan." My standard lie.

"Oh, pity. But you have emerged stronger, no? A doctor who helps people. See the people you have helped? You are a hero, here." He beamed broadly and extended his arms to indicate his little fiefdom.

I blushed and squirmed in the uncomfortable chair. I was anything but a hero, and he knew it.

"But you did not come to me to glory in the fruit of your good works, did you?" He became all business.

"No, Oscar, I'm here about our other arrangement."

He smiled beneath his moustache and looked down on me like a judge about to pass sentence.

"What arrangement might that be?" His eyes glinted, but I couldn't tell if from mischief or malice.

"The transportation arrangement? You moved some commodities for me?"

"I recall no such arrangement, Doctor Melanie. I recall you donating some items for us to sell for the good of the people." Again, his large hands extended toward the cavern behind me.

Maybe it was the chair, or the stench of the place, or simply my desperation; whatever the reason, I did something I told myself I wouldn't let happen.

"Damn it, Oscar. You owe me one hundred thousand credits." I regretted those words the moment they came out of me.

He glared at me. Then the snarl beneath the moustache curled upward into a toothy grin that showed off his gold-capped front tooth though his eyes did not join in. He put both arms on the desk, leaned forward and spoke so softly I strained to hear.

"Let me be clear. You are owed nothing. The drugs are mine and you have your life and may leave, unharmed. You understand, yes?"

I sank into the ridiculous chair and sighed quietly.

"I understand, yes."

He sat back and his eyes regained their playful glint.

"Vasily will escort you safely out." The large man on his right stepped around the desk and stood beside me.

"Doctor Melanie, it is a very dangerous place, here. It is not advisable for you to return uninvited. I could not guarantee your safety and would hate to tell the people that something unfortunate happened to their patron saint. You understand me, yes?"

"I understand you, yes."

Vasily, not too gently, helped me to my feet.

"I think we will not meet again, Doctor Melanie. I wish you well."

I held my tongue and allowed Vasily to show me the way out. I had just danced with the devil's doorman and was grateful I still lived to tell about it.

CHAPTER SIX

I admired the foxy woman who looked back at me from the mirror. I spun a quick turn and liked what I saw. I enjoyed the same svelte figure I owned in my twenties, including the firm boobs and killer ass. Lunar gravity helped that way; less wear and tear on all the potentially saggy parts. I had to admit that I cleaned up well. It took a couple of hours, but after a spa treatment that cost a small ransom and some expensive makeup, I hardly recognized myself. I presented as a sexy woman instead of a space rat.

"Where have you been hiding, Sugar?" I queried the vixen who gazed back at me. She winked but I doubted her sincerity.

What the hell was I thinking? I had given up this life, twenty years before with no intention of ever revisiting it.

When Walter Bickel found me I had thought him another one of a long line of dirty old men, out for a cheap screw with an under aged prostitute. My handlers had determined my value in supplying services to older professionals with daughter fixations and wives that paid no attention to them. The fact that I wasn't strung out on drugs like all the other girls my age and could actually carry on a conversation merely added to my appeal.

He claimed he hadn't sought me out for sex, however. Naturally I didn't believe him.

"I've heard a lot about you."

He maintained a healthy distance between us, stepping back whenever I moved in to begin my routine.

"What do you want? A show?"

"No, I'd just like to talk, if that's okay?"

"This is your hour," I told him, displaying all of the bravado of someone well on her way to the end of a short life. I jumped on top of the hastily made up bed and he sat in the cheap chair beside the cheaper desk.

"My name is Walter. What is yours?"

I regarded him as a rube.

"You ain't payin' enough to know that, Walter." I enunciated his name to make my point.

"Fair enough. What may I call you?"

"You kin call me Angela, I s'pose."

"How old are you, Angela? Fifteen? Sixteen?"

"I'm old enough," I responded defiantly. "I got ID that says so. What are you, a cop? Cuz if you are, we ain't doing nothin' that you can arrest me for, even if I was underage." I was eager to demonstrate my undeveloped appreciation of the law. Something about Walter compelled me to impress him, or at least try.

"Everything is okay, Angela. We're only talking. I'm not with the police, or social services or any church organization, so you can relax."

"Then why ARE you here?" I wasn't about to relax. The whole situation started to creep me out.

"As I said, I've heard a lot about you and I wanted to meet you for myself."

"Why? Whose bin talkin' about me? If it's Britney, you can't believe anything that drugged up skank says. She's just tryin' to mess with my business."

"It isn't anyone you know. "

Now I worried. I honestly didn't know anyone outside of the small circle of girls my pimp allowed me to associate with. Walter took notice of my discomfort.

"There is no need to worry. I have a proposal for you if you'd like to hear it."

I relaxed. He was finally getting down to business. With any luck, I could finish him fast and take a short break before the next client.

"Nothing, kinky." I started to undress. Walter shook his head with amusement on his face.

"Nothing kinky, I assure you. I want to offer you a chance for an education."

"Look, Wal-ter," I over-enunciated his name again, "I told you nothing kinky. That included your school girl fantasy..."

He burst our laughing.

"What's so fuckin' funny?"

"I'm sorry. This is entirely my own fault. I chose my words poorly."

"Well, you better get to the point or else I'm ending your hour now." I pulled my top back on and edged to the side of the bed.

"Melanie, I'm here to offer you a way out of this life, if you want it."

I froze at the mention of my real name.

"How do you know my name? Nobody knows that, not even Skids." Skids was my pimp boyfriend.

Walter must have sensed his closing window of opportunity. He ignored my question and continued with his pitch.

"You're an intelligent young lady. I want to give you a chance. I want to sponsor your education. I think you'd make a fine engineer or doctor."

I have no idea why I listened to him. My brain screamed at me to get the hell out, but something about his manner and voice drew me in. It took some fancy talking on his part, but I stayed in that hotel room and I weighed every word. He asked me to think about it.

He met several more times with me, and, in the end, something about him was convincing enough that I decided to take him up on his offer. It turned out to be the biggest break of my tragic life, a regular Cinderella story. At least for a few short years.

* * *

I checked for the time and realized I still needed to put some clothing on the doll looking back at me from the mirror. I turned my attention to the items I'd recovered from long term storage.

The choice came down to two outfits I swore I would never again wear. The older cocktail type dress imitated the styles of the mid-twentieth century. It went of fashion ages ago but showed off my ass to good advantage in a short flared skirt. The other, more contemporary outfit, while technically out of style as well, was modern enough not to draw too much-unwanted attention while still complimenting my cleavage and figure.

I had to be careful to be noticed by the right people, and not the Morality Police, so the second one became the only choice.

The dark-net account that I accessed on return to the apartment sent a signal to my CI. The number of responses to my ad surprised me. Most of the responders were perverts or poorly concealed attempts at entrapment by the MP.

Scrolling through the list, I worried I wasted my time and money in an effort to reenter a profession I'd sworn off long ago. One response caught my eye and gave me a glimmer of hope that my plan stood a chance.

The man's profile seemed promising, so I confirmed his references. Some of them were girls I knew, customers for off book antibiotics, botox, and recreational pharmaceuticals. Even though I didn't associate with them in anything beyond a business capacity, I still trusted some of them.

Their endorsement for Jake Matthiews, or whatever his real name, made him credible as a legitimate customer. Not too young; not too old; good credit reference; clean health check; moderate sexual tastes with nothing flagged as too kinky. If his deposit cleared, he might be worth the risk of a meeting.

I beamed him a reply and set up a rendezvous in Hub 10, at an upscale nightclub called Earthshine. Then I booked a room for the night in the most expensive hotel in the upper Tens.

Feet now firmly placed on the chosen path, I took one last inspection of my reflection for encouragement and resumed dressing.

An hour later found me perched on the edge of the bar stool and nursing an overpriced drink. I wiped the sweat from my palms on the cocktail napkin for the fifth time while I scanned the crowd. They were mostly middle management professionals or up and coming political wannabes in their mid-thirties to forties. The younger people didn't live in Armstrong if it could be avoided. The music in Earthshine consisted of a campy mix of the latest tunes and some retro shit that nobody really listened to, played at a tolerable volume to provide ambience, but not so loud as to force everyone to shout. Like I said, an older crowd.

I assessed the outfits worn by some of the other women in the club and decided that more than one of us sported outdated fashions. Despite the pretence at sophistication by the patrons of the Tens, Armstrong remained a backwater and most of these people wanted to get out as badly as me. The smart ones had the potential of scoring a transfer to Irwin, Artemis, Hawking or any of the other cities in the capital region. With the war over, they might even get an opportunity on Terra if they worked for one of the syndicates. The rest were lifers that tried to make the best of the shitty hand dealt them.

Right on time, my CI signalled that Jake Matthiews entered the nightclub. His picture file, discreetly omitted on his dark net profile, now came up on my CI. A handsome man, his image showed a strong jaw, deep blue eyes, trim, fit physique and close-cropped hair. He sported one of the currently fashionable temporary scalp tattoos wrapping around the back of his head.

I looked through the throng and located him near the entrance. By the cut of his suit and the way he walked to keep his balance, I guessed him to be newly arrived from Terra. Probably a syndicate executive away from home and looking for a little personal diversion between business meetings. The perfect customer. I signalled for my profile image to be released to him and indicated my location.

He emerged from the mass of people and made his way toward me. He gave me an appraising review, then, seeming satisfied that the goods were as advertised, sat down on the stool beside me.

"Angela?"

"Yes, I am. I presume you are Jake?"

"Guilty as charged." He revealed a perfect set of dazzling white teeth when he smiled.

He flagged the bartender and ordered a drink for himself and a refill for me.

"Is this your first visit to Luna, Jake?"

"Am I that obvious?"

"We call it the B3; beginner balance bounce. It's hard to hide until you are used to the gravity change."

"Hmmm, I'll keep that in mind for future reference. I take it you're a long time resident here?"

I smiled coyly and moved close to whisper and give him a good nose full of my pheromone-laced perfume. "You are not paying enough for that kind of information, darling."

"Oh, sorry, I'm afraid I'm not very experienced at this sort of thing. It...this is my first time and..."

"Shhh. It'll all be fine," I breathed heavily into his ear. "I think I have enough experience for the both of us." I moved back from him and gave him a knowing wink. Jake blushed and searched for a reply until the bartender placed the drinks in front of us.

He raised his drink and clinked it in a toast with mine. He downed it in a single gulp, then flagged for another.

"Whoa! Slow down, Tiger. There's no need to rush. You're paying for the whole evening."

Jake grinned nervously, the suave affectation he previously sported now evaporated. The second drink arrived and he sipped at it, calmer now. I used my experience to engage him in a casual conversation, laced with just enough innuendo about what awaited later to keep him on edge. I wanted him balanced between nervous and excited. With any luck, he wouldn't last too long and I could enjoy the rest of my evening by myself. He seemed nice; kind of cute, even, but not anyone I particularly wanted to spend a great deal of time with.

After a half hour of escalating flirtation, spiced with a few more drinks, 'Angela' invited him to join her in the hotel room.

We rode alone in the lift, during which time, I teased him with soft kisses and suggestive 'accidental' brushing up against him with my breasts and hands. We entered the suite and I lead him by the hand towards the bedroom. He reached around behind me to undo my dress, but I stopped him gently.

"I'm afraid there are some business details to attend to first, Tiger."

"Oh, right. Of course."

I handed him a tablet to authorize a credit transfer to my holding account. Once the payment was authorized and confirmed, I embraced him, giving him full access to the goods.

While Jake may have been a neophyte at the business of sex, he proved himself an expert practitioner of it. Despite the professional detachment I long ago learned to put up when entertaining clients, I found myself enjoying my time with him. It had been a long time since I enjoyed any kind of sexual encounter and he demonstrated enough competence to allow me to relax and flow with the experience as much as possible.

When finished, we shared a sensual shower and then took our time getting dressed.

I sat on the bed, pulling on my silk stockings when a loud knock sounded on the door. Jake, seemingly unbothered by the intrusion, walked calmly toward the door. Before I could warn him not to, he opened it and two uniformed members of the Morality Police pushed into the room.

I glared at Jake, who just smiled and blew me a kiss as he strode confidently out of the room, showing every sign of being fully acclimated to Luna's gravity. It had been a sting operation, and I'd fallen for it like a novice.

"Melanie Destin, you are under arrest for solicitation and prostitution," recited the beefy officer, clearly enjoying himself.

This day just kept getting worse.

CHAPTER SEVEN

It had been a very long time since I experienced such abject humiliation. I tried to remain stoic as the MP paraded me in restraints through the hotel lobby and into the corridors of Hub Ten.

Many of the sophisticated people who earlier in the evening snuck envious glances at me now openly displayed disdain on their faces. The officers led me, half dressed, to a waiting police monorail car.

The plodding car rumbled down the tracks at an agonizingly slow pace. About the time I believed the ride would never end, we stopped at the prisoner entrance to the sprawling Societal Protection and Education Centre, which occupied an entire Hub of Armstrong.

SPEC is a place that no citizen wants to find himself and to spend any duration at it means the authorities found you morally lacking and in need of re-education. I preferred to think of the place as a brainwashing clinic, but my opinion interested nobody.

For the past five years, I'd made a point of remaining under their radar and I went to great lengths in covering the footprint of my business activities. Yet, here and now, in my only attempt to solicit in forever, I'd been trapped like a stupid rabbit and stood on the brink of losing every speck of respectability I came to Luna to attain. Though I replayed the events leading up to this, I could not see where I messed things up. It must have been a huge fluke of luck that placed me in the crosshairs of "Jake" and on the path to Moral Correction.

Everything got much worse after my arrival. They cleared out my bank account and found the other carefully hidden ones buried under layers of shadow accounts and dummy corporations. Every credit I earned outside of my regular pay was deemed corrupt and forfeit to the government. It was the price of getting caught and I was paying it, with interest.

Following the economic humiliation, there began an invasive batch of medical tests for STI's, ending with a prescribed course of nanite injections as a preventative measure. They understood the limits of re-education and chose to hedge their bets in the eventuality of a moral relapse.

The medical workers acted surprised to find that I already possessed a previous series of nanites, given to me as a routine requirement for Terran medical school admission. Despite the fact that my bloodstream crawled with the little buggers, they thoughtlessly decided to proceed with their own treatment, giving no consideration to how the different machine species would interact with my body. No matter how vigorously I argued my case, the idiots ignored me and in the end, strapped me to a gurney and injected me with them.

I was desperately sick for the better part of two weeks as the competing nanites battled each other. God only knew what kind of permanent mess they made of my guts in their turf war. Finally, when it looked like I might die on someone's watch, they decided that I needed some attention and reviewed my blood work.

They administered a bunch of toxins to try to kill off the less established system of nanites they'd introduced. They said they couldn't do anything about my original population because they didn't have access to their pseudo-genetic code.

After a couple of days, I felt better. The attending physician who obviously got his degree by correspondence tried to tell me they managed to eliminate most of them, but hybridization probably changed a significant number of them before the treatment, so I retained a second population inside me. The good news was that they were adapted to my system, but nobody could say if they were neutral, or if they would turn around and eat out my insides over the next few years.

Not satisfied with attempting to murder me, after my recovery, I was forced to endure another week of morality education in which the evils of my way of life and the horrors it held for society at large were explained ad nauseam. My name was posted to the public record for anyone to see and I was released back to the tram station with only an ugly orange jumpsuit and a pass to get me back to my own hub.

The stares of the people eventually ceased as the car made its way to Hub Two where most people knew someone or had themselves been victimized and done time at SPEC. I drew no attention as I exited the monorail and hurried home.

Once inside, I stripped myself naked and placed the orange abomination into the incineration chute. I spent far more money than I could afford to take a long, hot shower before I crashed in bed for fitful sleep.

Waking nearly twenty hours later, I dressed and sat down in front of the terminal in the bedroom. Every bank account I owned, secret or not had been located and rifled. There were only a few credits left in one of them to pay next month's rent and allow me to feed myself. The food was not a problem as I was due to ship out on *Requiem* in a couple of days. The ongoing lease was another matter. I would have to beg Tanza for an advance. I had some cash hidden in the safe, undiscovered by the MP who most likely took one look at my address and decided they didn't want to catch anything by walking down the corridor. Unfortunately, the money couldn't be deposited to the account as that would set off a flag for an undocumented income source and trigger another round of investigations that might prompt them to bother searching here next time. I had more than enough credits to cover the long-term lease but had no way to spend them.

After five years of hard work, I had nothing to show for it but a shitty apartment and a shittier job. It would take me even longer to rebuild now that I sat in the middle of the sites of the authorities.

Out of the corner of my eye, I noticed a blinking icon indicating a message. I so rarely received messages of that kind that I didn't routinely pay attention to the interface. The log for it was dated two days prior and indicated it was from Tanza.

Not having a good feeling about it, I reluctantly played the video. His smug face stared from the screen and I could sense he was prepared to enjoy his announcement.

"Doctor Destin. I have the duty to inform you that your employer, Sato Corporation, has no further need of your professional services. Your employment is hereby terminated under the moral deficiency clause, section twenty-two, paragraph six, subparagraphs twelve through sixteen. I would recite the contract to you, but you are an intelligent woman and can read. Besides, we all know what you have done. Good luck in your future endeavours."

The message ended with a satisfied smile on Tanza's ferret face. It took all of the remaining willpower I had not to punch in the screen.

I stared at the vid screen and tried to process what happened. What fucking contract? It took me a few moments to remember the agreement I signed five years before as a formality when Chambers persuaded me to enlist as ship's doctor. I didn't recall the thing because nobody read the standard legal document imposed by the Ministry of Moral Conduct. Anyone who needed to work from Luna signed one. Nobody ever paid attention to those fucking things because not one word could be negotiated. You signed or didn't get a job. After Chambers placed it in front of me, he made it clear the contract made no difference to our verbal understanding of how things functioned aboard *Requiem*.

Even before the topic of the contract came up, Chambers himself proposed the idea of skimming pharmaceuticals, with him taking a ten percent cut. I didn't take much convincing and everything worked wonderfully for five years. Now the same innocuous document we all dismissed as nothing more than an inconvenient formality came back to haunt me like some Faustian arrangement.

Now broke, unemployed and unemployable thanks to the scarlet letter placed on my file, my destroyed life hung pathetically before me. I wanted to break down into tears and cry into my pillow for the next week, but I didn't even possess the energy for that. I could only stare at the screen in the stupid hope the whole thing was some kind of practical joke fermented in Tanza's pointy head.

Who had I ever fucked over so badly in the past karma dealt out this shit to me? I ran through the list of everyone I knew, but couldn't think of anyone screwed by me to earn me this payback. The truth is I am a trusting pushover who gets myself into these situations. I usually received the shitty end of the stick. There seemed to be an almost endless parade of people to kick me around, from my dear, alcoholic mother to her abusive boyfriends, to my own poor choices of paramours.

Up until this moment, I never thought of myself as a victim. I always thought I'd just drawn some bad breaks and the universe was not out to screw me over. Damn it, my life was on track and I was working to a plan! Victims didn't make plans, they rolled over and let people piss all over them.

I had been a few credits away from breaking away from all of the ghosts of my past and the creeps in my present and starting life on my own terms when the entire mountain came crashing down on top of me. If I wasn't a victim, I certainly presented a good approximation of one.

I shuffled into the kitchen and made a cup of tea. Taking it into my small sitting room, I sat down on my worn out couch and stared blankly into space, lost in dark thoughts. My mind turned to the vault above the toilet and the drugs I had left in my inventory.

Being a user had never been a consideration for me, even during the darkest times as a teenager on Terra before my rescue. I witnessed first hand what they had done to my friends and acquaintances. I determined long ago my life was bad enough without overprinting it with a drug habit. But in that moment, the temptation to try something and float away into blissful oblivion was stronger than ever before. I fell back onto the couch with a sigh. Too much energy was needed to open the safe.

Normally, booze was my preferred form of self-medication. While I routinely indulged in binge drinking whenever I returned from a run, the usual after effects of the morning after were enough to dissuade me from any kind of regular repetition. Something about living with a chronic boozer can make the idea of spending your life in a bottle seem stupid. I know some people follow in the footsteps of addicted parents, but something inside of me didn't let that happen. For that little boon, I was grateful. Still, if I had any booze in my place, I would have been nursing it.

Out of the corner of my eye, I saw something which didn't belong. A business holo-card lay on the floor beside me. I lethargically rolled onto my side and picked it up to examine, grateful for the unexpected distraction. The card belonged to Charlie Wong.

A smile came across my face as I recalled seeing him again for the first time in years. Then, just as quickly I was ashamed at how I ejected him from my home.

Charlie, from his point of view, wanted to give me a helping hand , but I was too fucking proud and kicked him out in a big huff. I didn't want anyone's help again. I had to be the one to lift myself out of my dysfunctional life and resented him for his success and his superior attitude.

I looked around the shit hole I lived in. Why shouldn't he think I needed a hand? Who was I kidding? I spent five years as a drug dealer and the last few weeks as a convicted hooker. I was pathetic to think I even had a chance at making my way out of here on my own. Nobody ever made it out of here. Why didn't I see it before? He was only trying to help, dammit, and I treated him like shit. Maybe I did deserve to fail.

I turned the card over and I looked at it through tear-filled eyes. Perhaps Charlie's offer was still available? He said he couldn't find a qualified doctor. I hoped I hadn't so completely pissed him off with me he wouldn't entertain the idea.

I jumped off of the couch and raced to the vid terminal in the bedroom. I prayed as I entered the contact code he would answer in person and not let the call go to his avatar.

"Hello, Mel." He sounded cheerful and happy to hear from me. I wiped my eyes, realizing how frightful I must appear.

"Uh, hi Charlie. Listen, I wanted to apologize for what happened the other night..."

"I'm the one who needs to apologize to you. My comments were totally out of line."

I interrupted him before he could get syrupy.

"How about if we agree we were both a bit at fault and leave everything as forgiven and forgotten?"

"I would like that, thanks. It will make my leaving here a lot easier. I didn't want to part from you again under a cloud."

"Oh? Are you going away? So soon?"

"Mel, I have been on Luna for six weeks and I can't find anyone here for the position, so I am going to try looking on Terra."

"If the job is still open, I'm interested. I've given it a great deal of thought and, well, I think you're right."

"Really?"

"Yes, if you'll still have me."

"Oh, Mel, this is fantastic news. You have no idea how much this means to me, and to my employers. We'll make it worth your while, I promise. You won't regret this."

"I appreciate the second chance."

"Listen, I have to go into a meeting right now, but I'll send you the agreement documents, contract, and the schedule. Oh, this is amazing. Thanks so very much."

"Thank you, Charlie."

I signed off and felt a huge weight lift off of my shoulders. As uncomfortable as it had been, taking a helping hand from a friend could end up working out after all. Yet in the back of my mind, experience told me disappointment followed and to prepare for more trouble. I told experience to fuck off.

CHAPTER EIGHT

I found it more difficult to say goodbye to my little home than I expected. Though the lease had been in my name for the past five years, I only lived in it for a total of eight months. With all my worldly possessions packed into two bags, I felt a pang of regret as the door closed on my old life.

The idea of locking the unit briefly crossed my mind. The apartment was paid for at least another month and it would take the corporation that owned it the better part of a year to figure out I didn't live in it anymore. That gave whoever next squatted here almost twelve months of undisturbed residency. Maybe the good ones from my last absence would return.

Shouldering one bag and carrying the other, I strode down the filthy corridor for the last time. An hour later, a grinning Charlie Wong greeted me at the hangar facility.

"Ready for this, Mel?"

"You have no idea."

He continued to grin and led me into Hanger 23 where a sleek, modern lunar suborbital shuttle sat prepped and waiting to launch. The ship's steward welcomed us, took my luggage and showed us inside the spotless ship. He directed us to our plush leather chairs in the passenger section. Moments later, another flight attendant offered us champagne and instructed us on the safety protocols and various entertainment features of our seats.

"Is anyone else joining us?" I asked Charlie.

"You are the last member of the team, Mel. Everyone else is assembled at the launch site and awaiting your arrival."

"I'm that critical to this mission? Seriously?"

"Yes, you are." He smiled the friendly way he always used to. It seemed like no time had ever passed. And yet, the smile did not seem exactly the same. Something lay behind it that dimmed the sparkle in his eye, so subtle I almost didn't catch the difference. Perhaps the death of his father? Whatever the cause, I regretted that I had not been around for him.

The orbiter launched smoothly and after ten minutes of silence passed, I asked, "Now can you tell me where we are going?"

"We are going to a launch facility the corporation operates on the far side, near Pirquet."

"Why so remote?"

"Helps to keep it a secret that way." He winked. "Settle back and relax. We'll arrive in about three hours."

I relaxed into the plush leather and sipped on champagne. The landscape below silently scrolled past. In all my time on Luna, I had never travelled away from Armstrong. Aside from the first glimpses I witnessed of the lunar surface when arriving from Terra, I had never seen the terrain away from the Sea of Tranquility. It floated by beneath us, beautiful and hypnotic and lulled me into a dreamless sleep.

I awakened to the ship's deceleration. A disorienting blackness filled my view outside. Only the crisp stars gave any a sense of orientation and relieved the panic that gripped me. With no earthshine, the lunar night on this side of the moon was two weeks of utter darkness.

My eyes couldn't pierce the dark as I searched for any sign of our destination. I expected some lights or signs of a base, but only black nothing lay below.

All forward motion halted and the blackness rose to devour the stars as the ship descended to the surface. The gentle bump of an expertly piloted touchdown was followed by the vibration of the landing platform's descent. When we stopped moving, bright lights illuminated the exterior and revealed the inside the underground hangar. Through the window, I saw the ceiling above us close completely.

Within ten minutes, we were allowed to disembark. Uniformed private security guards escorted us to the main facility. Once processed, Charlie led me through the labyrinthine complex to a conference room where eight other people were gathered.

Without thinking about it I sent out a query ping through my CI to identify all the occupants. To my shock, I got nothing back from anyone. That only happened when someone didn't possess an implant, or it was damaged; in other words, not very often. This site must have been using an ID blocker in the facility; very expensive and highly illegal. My new employers wanted anonymity.

Charlie greeted the two older men dressed in business suits while I perused the other people in the room. My survey was cut short when I caught the eye of an equally shocked Norbert Schmaltz.

Before we could acknowledge each other, I was pulled aside by Charlie to meet the two men. Mr. Avery Swan and his secretary, Mr. Xu Jhan politely shook my hand and welcomed me warmly. He then introduced me to my crew mates.

Clive Garrick was the pilot and Captain for the mission. He stood and greeted me in with a firm, formal handshake. About fifty years old he possessed a fit build and grey blonde hair with a matching moustache. His white skin told of a lifetime spent in the confines of spaceships.

The petite, middle-aged Eurasian woman sitting next to him with a shock of white streaking through her otherwise long, jet black hair was Shigeko Limn, the navigator, and co-pilot. She smiled amicably at me but did not rise to shake my hand.

Schmaltz offered me his hand and pretended we had never met. Behind him, with a cup of coffee in hand stood his assistant engineer, Bogdan Skorupa. The twenty-year-old was ghostly pale and his light blue eyes locked onto mine as he smiled and waved hello before resuming his seat.

Dylan Hodgson sat quietly across from Schmaltz. His close-cropped hair and too much muscle development for anyone having spent a lot of time in space flagged him as ex-military. He nodded at me, his face unreadable.

Charlie addressed the room, "Erik Dunn, the Rego corporate representative could not be here and sends his regrets. He is finishing up another assignment and will join the crew in orbit after launch."

We spent the balance of the meeting going over operational details of the mission and the tight timelines involved. The Captain, navigator and Schmaltz all gave report around the preparedness of the ship. When questions about the readiness of the medical facilities were raised, everyone turned to me. Charlie intervened on my behalf.

"Obviously, Doctor Destin only just arrived and hasn't inspected anything aboard the *Fortuna*."

"Of course, this is understood, Mister Wong," said Mr. Swan. "She may use the next hour to inspect and ensure medical's readiness prior to your launch in five hours."

Swan then addressed the group.

"I cannot emphasize enough that many other interested parties compete against us on this salvage operation. Through our intelligence network, we enjoy an advantage, but soon our competitors will learn what we know and initiate their own missions. Until the task is successfully completed, you are all under a communications blackout."

The other man, Jhan, stood attentively a pace back of Swan, recording everything with his CI linked directly into a data pad in his hand.

With no request for questions, the meeting ended and the two executives and Charlie prepared to depart. As he walked to the door, he winked at me. I crossed my eyes at him like I used to in med school when I wanted him to lose his composure in a presentation. He smiled as he went out the door.

Once they left and people began to mill about, Schmaltz sauntered over to me, nervous. Before he could say a thing, a stern Captain Garrick approached us.

"Are you still here for some reason, Mister Schmaltz?"

"I was just telling Doctor Destin that I would be happy to familiarize her with things."

Light perspiration shone on Schmaltz's forehead and he spoke rapidly in the same way he did when lying to Tanza on *Requiem*. I frowned at him, but Schmaltz subtly shook his head and glanced in Garrick's direction. I decided it best to follow his lead and addressed the Captain.

"Yes, imagine my surprise to see Norbert here of all places."

Schmaltz squeezed his eyes shut like his finger had just been caught in a door and I realized I'd said something wrong.

Garrick raised an appraising eyebrow at us. "So, you two have met?"

"We knew each other as young children back in school on Terra, before my parents were transferred, that is. Now here she is, and a doctor at that."

"That IS an unusual coincidence, Mister Schmaltz. Regardless, you can catch up after we launch. The primary thrusters still need your fine attention to get them running at spec. I will ask Mister Hodgson to escort the good doctor to the ship and give her the tour."

"Yes, Sir."

Schmaltz departed without another glance at me or the Captain. I turned back to face Garrick.

"Do you have particular concerns about the medical facility that require my attention, Captain?"

"Just make sure the bio-filters are in place and that the containment chamber in the research section is fully functional."

I almost asked about the need for such high-tech equipment on a salvage expedition but remembered Schmaltz's odd behaviour.

"Yes, Sir."

Seemingly satisfied, he signalled Dylan Hodgson to approach and left to attend to other matters.

"Doctor, I believe I'm your escort for the next little while," said Hodgson, a self-satisfied smirk on his face. I straightened my posture and gestured towards the door.

"Please lead on, Mister Hodgson."

As he guided me down the corridor, I made plans to locate and question Schmaltz soon. Something was definitely off about this job and the sooner I discovered what made the normally unflappable Schmaltz nervous, the better.

The medical facilities aboard the *Fortuna* were the most advanced I had ever seen. Everything was state of the art though some of the technology was unfamiliar to me. The familiar instruments I quickly determined to be fully operational and required no maintenance. I needed some time to research the unfamiliar equipment but didn't want to bring up the manuals and start reading while Hodgson watched from the doorway.

"Can I help you with something, Mister Hodgson?"

"Nope." He leaned against the doorframe with his arms crossed, an amused expression on his face.

"Are you not needed somewhere else?"

"Nope."

I faced him straight on, hands perched on my hips. "Why are you still here?"

"My orders are to render any assistance you require, Doc."

"Doctor."

"Huh?"

"You will refer to me as Doctor Destin, or simply, Doctor. Is that clear, crewman?"

"Yes, ma'am. Er, I mean, Simply Doctor." The grin on his face infuriated me. I gave him the dirtiest glare I could muster.

"I'm sorry. Doctor Destin. I was only fooling around."

I frowned at him and returned to my inspection of the medical supplies.

The door slid open behind Hodgson, startling him. He turned, revealing Schmaltz, cradling his left hand, crudely wrapped in a bloody bandage.

"What the hell happened?"

I harshly addressed Hodgson, "Let him come in, you idiot."

He stepped aside to allow Schmaltz entry, then resumed his

vigil at the doorway.

"I dropped a spanner into an access panel and tried to catch it. Cut my hand on the opening." He smiled sheepishly.

I carefully unwrapped the bandage and examined the injured hand.

"Hodgson. Your orders are to assist me?" I kept my back turned towards him, shielding his view of Shmaltz's injury.

"Yes, ma'am. Er, Doctor."

"Then leave, unless you can stitch a wound."

I heard the door open and close. Schmaltz sighed and his shoulders relaxed.

"He's gone."

"What the hell is going on? This cut wouldn't make a little girl cry, let alone require this much wrapping. And what is all this alleged blood?"

"Hydraulic fluid. I needed some kind of excuse to talk to you before it's too late."

"Too late for what?"

"You need to leave."

"Why? I just arrived. What are you doing here, anyway? You're supposed to be on Polaris, as I recall."

"That job disappeared. For no damn reason. They said my references didn't check out, but that was total bullshit. Before I raised a stink with them, this guy, Wong, approaches me at my front door and offers me another position. Amazing pay. Like you wouldn't believe how much. I almost told him to take a leap, but the missus tells me to take the job, so, I do as I'm told..."

"Okay, okay, I understand. Now why should I leave?"

"Because these guys stole this ship."

"Ridiculous."

"I ain't kidding, Mel. This ship used to belong to the Terran Science Corps. I was here when it arrived. I have no idea how things went down, but blood was on some of the walls and floors and it had blaster damage on the hull and in the engineering section. Me and Bogdan spent the last four weeks patching it back together."

I looked around the room and saw the high tech equipment in a new light.

"Whatever these people are after, you want no part in it. Leave while you can. Before you learn anything that you're not supposed to. Tell them you're sick, or your cat has shingles or something. Please get the fuck out of here." Fear reflected in Schmaltz's eyes and his voice quavered.

I indicated his arm with the fake injury. "I'm going to need to put some real staples in this, or else they'll realize something is up with you."

"Didn't you hear what I said? This ain't a joke, Mel. They're killers."

"And what do you think they will do to you if they find out you've snuck in to tell me this stuff?"

He looked at me, dumbfounded.

"The Captain clearly didn't want you talking to me, remember? This isn't the first time we've run with a bunch of criminals. Hell, half the companies that fly cargo out of Luna are in with one of the crime syndicates. Everyone knows that. Who do you think Chambers was involved with on Requiem?"

"This is different. Nobody on our old ship was a killer. There wasn't any blood staining the corridors when we signed up there."

"Well, there might have been if we'd have spent another week with Tanza," I grinned at him.

"Damn it, Mel! I'm serious. This is a bad situation. I know it. What kind of people can get military tech like this?"

"Obviously, people with guns, according to you."

"Exactly. They killed the crew and now we're taking this up like it never belonged to the Terrans. If they catch us..."

"Schmaltzy, if I walk away from this gig, assuming they'll let me, I will be turning my back on the only future I've got left."

"I'm telling you if you don't leave you could end up another smear in the corridor."

"So why is it so dangerous for me to stay, but you're not racing me for the exit?"

"I told you. The money is too good for me to turn down.

Listen, when the Polaris job vanished, I tried to go back to Tanza. He laughed at me. I was seriously screwed and needed the work. This one came along just in time. These guys were the only ones besides my buddy on Polaris who didn't look too closely at my credentials. I really had no other choice, Mel. You do."

Of course, Schmaltz didn't know what had happened to me since I'd last seen him. I debated over how honest to be with him.

"Tanza fired me."

"What? Is he off his nut? Well, it doesn't matter. You're a doctor. You could work for anyone else. I can't."

I didn't want to argue with him.

"Let's just say that my options aren't as many as you think."

I retrieved the stitching kit and held up a hypospray for him to see.

"Now, do you want me to freeze it, or are you going to tough it out?"

CHAPTER NINE

The med bay door opened to reveal Hodgson leaning against the opposite wall in the corridor.

"Ouches all fixed, Doc-tor?" I wanted to slap the grin off his face, but I addressed Schmaltz instead.

"Keep it clean the way I showed you and if you need any painkillers, come back. I want to examine it again tomorrow. Understood, Mister Schmaltz?"

"Er, yes Doctor." He glanced at Hodgson for the briefest of moments, then hurried toward the engineering section. I directed my attention to Hodgson.

"Why are you still hanging around?"

"I have a hangnail." He held up his pinky and grinned.

"It looks bad. I may have to amputate."

He lowered his hand and became more serious.

"If you're finished, I'm to take you to the Captain to report."

"I need a bodyguard for that?"

Hodgson chuckled. "This is a big ship and I'm to be your tour guide once this medical inspection stuff is done."

I relaxed on hearing that and followed him to the bridge where Garrick was in conversation with Shigeko Limn.

"Ah, Doctor Destin, you are here sooner than I expected."

"Yes, Captain. The facilities check out and are one hundred percent up to specifications, including the items you particularly mentioned earlier."

"Excellent. How is your first patient making out?"

My heart dropped to my stomach, but I managed to retain my composure.

"He'll live, Sir. A minor injury which shouldn't impede his duties at all."

"Excellent, Doctor. Just to be clear; we do everything strictly by the book on this vessel. Please make sure your medical log is updated with the incident prior to our launch."

"Of, course, Captain." He was even stricter than Tanza and seemed to know everything happening on his ship.

Without any further comment, Garrick turned his back to me and resumed his discussion with Limn. I stood in place for a couple of seconds before I realized my report was over and I had been dismissed. I brusquely marched off the bridge, Hodgson following right behind.

Once the door closed behind us, I stopped and faced him.

"Can you please take me to speak with Mister Wong before we leave?"

"Uh, sure. I guess."

His eyes took on a vacant look as he accessed his CI. Curious as to why his was working, I checked mine to discover it still inoperative. He informed me Charlie was in his office and ten minutes later, I was ushered into Charlie's spacious and tastefully appointed executive suite by his administrative assistant.

"Mel, I'm glad you came by. I was worried I would not be able to see you before your departure." He walked around his desk and greeted me with a brief hug. He invited me to sit and offered me a choice of drink.

"So, what do you think?"

"It's all pretty overwhelming. I mean, the spaceship is the most modern one I've ever seen. There is stuff there...well, medical is a technical wonderland, that's for sure."

"It certainly is. I almost envy you, Mel. If I had kept up my skills I would have jumped at the opportunity to go myself."

"Where did you get it?"

Charlie hesitated the briefest of moments. "I'm sorry?"

"The ship, where did it come from?"

"Rego operates a huge research wing as well as a shipbuilding subsidiary. The *Fortuna* came directly from the factory. It had been commissioned by the Terran Science Corps, but when we explained our requirements to them, they fully understood and agreed to receive the next one from the line."

"I see."

"Is there something wrong?"

"Oh, no. The whole idea of being on an expedition to recover an alien artifact is nothing I ever dreamed of."

Charlie smiled and nodded enthusiastically.

"Just one question bothers me," I said.

He leaned forward, concern on his face.

"What is it?"

"How do you know this thing we are recovering is alien? I mean, isn't that a bit far fetched?" I smiled disarmingly. He relaxed and sank back into his expensive leather chair.

"You got me there, Mel. It's the cover story we used to recruit people. What you are going after, while not as exotic, is important to the company. We didn't want word of our actual intentions to leak out and tip off our competitors, hence the little fib."

"I can understand that. So what are we after and where are we going?"

The smile vanished from his face, he leaned forward again and lowered his voice so much I needed to lean close to hear him.

"That information will be given to you after you launch."

I thought about his answer.

"Okay, I can accept that, but why all the cloak and dagger stuff?"

"What are you talking about?" He smiled nervously.

"Oh, the secret base, the misdirection, my blocked CI, the sealed orders after departure. Even having the big goon follow me around. A little extreme, don't you think?"

Charlie shook his head, "Hodgson's not following you

around."

I stood to leave. "Fine. Whatever you say."

"No Mel! Please sit?" He looked pleadingly at me as I poised above my chair. A moment of reflection later, I sat down again.

"The mission your crew mates and you have agreed to go on is of vital importance, not only to the future of Rego, but to several politically influential people. I can't tell you more. We need to keep a lid on everything around this. I'm sure you can understand and forgive me a little for my evasive answers?"

I smiled at him. "They're actually evasive non-answers, but, yes, I can appreciate your position. Forget I even asked."

"It wouldn't have been in your character to not ask. You were always too curious for your own good." His eyes suddenly widened as he realized what he had said. I glared at him through narrowed eyelids. My fingers squeezed into the leather armrest of the chair.

"Mel, I am so sorry. I didn't mean to..."

"Forget it, Charlie." I stood. "It was a long time ago and I've learned to live with the events around Carlos' death."

I walked out of the office without looking back. I could forgive Charlie for a lot of things, but he had just lied to me and reopened an old wound I thought healed. I regretted my visit with him and felt like the biggest fool on the moon. Worse, I had reason to give Schmaltz's paranoia some serious consideration. My life might well be in danger.

After the disastrous meeting, I returned to the ship under the watchful eye of Dylan Hodgson. He completed my tour and orientation to the vessel then left me at my station to prepare for the launch. The final preparations kept me too busy to dwell on Charlie, but once strapped in on the bridge and awaiting the clearance for liftoff, there was plenty of time to consider Charlie's lies.

He had never successfully lied to me before. In med school, something always tipped me off when he tried to and I'd made a habit of calling him on it. It became a running game between us. He randomly would try to lie and I would always catch him at it. He never succeeded in deceiving me. Ever. But today I caught him lying to my face twice without displaying any of his tells. The entire incident cast doubt on how well I thought I still knew my friend. It hurt to learn that I could not trust even him, given the history we shared.

I ignored the operational chatter as, normally, none of it applied to me, so it took a gentle nudge from Schmaltz to interrupt my daydreams.

"Doctor?" repeated Garrick.

"I'm sorry Captain. I couldn't hear you."

"Did the laboratory containment fields show any signs of power fluctuation during our launch?"

I reviewed the panel readouts in front of me and answered that all systems showed green. He grumbled something and returned to the routine of operations. I decided to be more careful and pay closer attention to the remaining deck conversations.

Once in orbit, the artificial gravity activated and clearance was given for us to go to our duty stations. I unstrapped and rose from my launch seat, prepared to experience near Terran G. To my surprise, I found myself still at lunar normal. I sent Schmaltz a puzzled look.

"Everyone is from Luna, so we are maintaining lunar gee." I was glad I wouldn't need to acclimate to stronger gravity. It was a logical thing to do if they wanted the team to be operating at peak efficiency from the start of the mission, rather than exhausting us during the first few days. I squeezed by Hodgson at the narrow entrance to the bridge without excusing myself. I got the impression that he purposefully made himself as large as possible just to feel me rub against him. To my relief, he no longer followed me about the ship, now having other duties to perform.

As per operational procedure, the medical centre was locked when unoccupied, so I keyed in the access code and entered. On the first arrival at the base, I briefly entertained thoughts about restarting my sideline business but dismissed the idea as soon as Garrick revealed his penchant for discipline. Given

Schmaltz's paranoid ramblings, I could imagine being spaced for such an infraction.

I made the unnecessary inventory recount and system's function check and logged everything. Despite my recent history, I knew how to behave myself when circumstances required. I managed to be an exemplary student during my sojourn at the Terran Medical Academy, much to the surprise of my sponsor and me.

The comm chimed and the speaker crackled with the emotionless voice of the first officer, Shigeko Limn.

"All hands, attend to stations in preparation for orbital intercept. Docking in T-minus five minutes. Doctor Destin, Crewman Hodgson, report to port B1."

With the real boss's arrival, I wondered if the ship could accommodate two alpha males. Though, on second thought, Garrick seemed like ex-military, so he was probably not bothered with working under a ranking officer. I smiled at the mental image of him being dressed down by the mysterious Erik Dunn like some lowly crewman. Not bloody likely to happen, but an entertaining thought, nonetheless.

I locked the medical bay before heading towards the docking port. As I descended the ladder to B deck, I spotted Hodgson ascending from C deck.

"You don't seem happy to see me, Doctor," he said.

"Wherever would you get that idea?"

I motioned for him to walk ahead of me, mostly because I didn't want him watching my ass.

We waited outside the portal in silence. Hodgson stared off into space, empty thoughts presumably filling his empty head. I was glad he wasn't chatty and hoped he finally understood my feelings for him. The floor vibrated at contact with the transport shuttle and the airlock began its pressurization cycle.

I straightened, looked ahead and moistened my dry lips in preparation to formally greet the company representative on behalf of the crew. I wanted to redeem myself for the poor first impression I had given Garrick.

The soft hum of the pressure pumps stopped and the green

light on the door panel indicated a proper seal. The shuttle door opened and I signalled Hodgson to open the door. With a slight hiss, it slid aside and a male figure moved from the shadows of the connection bridge between the ships. Erik Dunn stepped through the opening and smiled charmingly at me.

"Permission to come aboard?" he asked, almost innocently.

I stared at him, speechless. In the doorway stood Jake Matthiews.

CHAPTER TEN

Felix Altius normally wouldn't interrupt his Dominus at this time of day, especially with any potentially bothersome news. The late afternoon was reserved for Regis Mundi's period of recreation with one of his favourite concubines and to disturb him would set a poor tone for the rest of the day. The call prompting this interruption came flagged as a special case. Felix usually rescheduled callers for the next available opening. Such a deflection ensured the person would be put off for another six months at least. It was a tactic he regularly employed on those who sought to use him as a quick conduit to Mundi. Most of the fools regarded him as a mere secretary. None appreciated Altius' true role, which both he and his master preferred.

He arrived in front of the massive bronze door guarding the *vestibulum* to Mundi's private quarters. This deep inside the complex there were no guards, ceremonial or otherwise, and beyond this entrance, even the hidden security was banned. Aside from himself, only selected guests were permitted within the residence.

Felix absently activated the access code with his cortical interface and the doors silently opened to admit him. He strode through the *fauces* and past the *atrium* to the recreational *cubiculum*. Mundi laid out his private apartments in the pattern of a traditional ancient roman home with the rooms arranged in a historically accurate plan.

He paused to listen, sensitive to not interrupt at an especially crucial moment. Hearing only a brief burst feminine laughter, he girded himself and knocked on the door post of the curtained chamber's entrance. The laughter cut itself off and after a few seconds of silence, the annoyed voice of an older man bade him enter.

Felix pulled back the curtain and waited in the doorway for his master's pleasure. Though he was Mundi's most trusted servant, he remained but a servant. Mundi stood beside the large bed in the centre of the room, barefooted and dressed loosely in his *toga*. Neither of the two women made any effort to cover their nakedness.

"I trust there is good reason to interrupt us?"

Felix performed a slight bow before replying.

"My apologies, Dominus, but an urgent matter came to my attention regarding Agent 324." He looked toward the concubines.

"And you are acting according to my instructions. Yes, yes, yes." He turned and waved the women away. They quietly collected their clothing and, without dressing, slipped past Felix. He noted their identities and showed no overt interest in them, despite the subtle efforts they made to attract his attention. Though they were attractive specimens, he regarded them as works of art rather than objects of desire.

Regis Mundi sat on the side of the bed and smiled at him.

"In truth, I am grateful for your interruption, my friend. I doubted my stamina this afternoon." He chuckled, then raised his hand in a sign for Felix to give his report.

"Agent 324 assumed an identity and is proceeding outwardly with the plan he outlined but a few weeks ago." He paused to ensure Mundi's attention. Mundi nodded for him to continue.

"My spy informs me Agent 324, or Erik Dunn, as he is now known, also secretly commissioned another ship in addition to the *Fortuna*. This one is manned by his own vetted personnel, all retainers completely loyal to him."

"Only to Dunn? This is verified?"

"I initiated my own verification of this. My source only just informed me."

"What is his endgame?"

"Unclear. But I do know he located the *Helios* and I suspect he plans to betray you."

Mundi exhaled loudly through his nostrils.

"I wondered how big a prize it might take to turn him. Now we know, don't we? Pity. He was beginning to grow on me."

Mundi looked up at him for a moment, seeming to weigh a decision for as long as possible.

"I suppose you recommend his termination?"

"Not at the moment."

"Are you getting soft on me, Felix? Do you think I've grown so fond of 324 I might appreciate keeping him around for a while?"

"No, Dominus, I agree you must order his death. I simply meant he is still your only opportunity to recover the item you need. If we terminate him now, we will lose the window and the Terrans will find it first."

"So what is your council?"

"I believe once the item is recovered, he plans to rendezvous with his second vessel and take the sample for his own purposes, leaving you with two missing Terran vessels to explain. I suggest we allow Dunn to continue with his plan. I propose we commandeer the second ship and crew it with your own people. You will obtain what you sent him to retrieve, and expose his treachery."

Mundi regarded him admiringly.

"You are enjoying turning the tables on him, aren't you? I didn't think you were capable of such base pleasures, Felix."

"I am conditioned to enjoy any of the pleasures of a natural human but with more self-control." Felix allowed himself only a slight smile.

"And yet your conditioning still assures me of your complete loyalty, doesn't it? I wish I employed more like you."

"I am working towards that, Dominus." Felix bowed.

After a moment of consideration, Regis Mundi said, "Proceed with your plan. Kill all Dunn's retainers and replace them with our own."

"With respect, we need to keep some alive to prevent him from discovering our intentions."

"Yes, yes, I hadn't thought of that. Very well, do as you see fit and keep me informed. Please send in Drusilla again on your way out."

Felix Altius bowed low and backed his way out of the *cubiculum*. He smiled slightly to himself as he marched purposefully back to his office and his agent who was waiting for instructions. She would be rewarded handsomely for the information, of course, but he also hoped he would be permitted to allow Kiri Mason to live when all was finished. He always needed good agents, and she was proving herself to be most valuable.

CHAPTER ELEVEN

I stared, mouth agape at the man responsible for all my recent misfortunes.

"May I come aboard? Please?" He stood in the doorway, no sign of recognition on his face. He acted as if meeting me for the first time.

I swallowed hard, then regained my composure and, with only a beat or two missed, responded as professionally as I could. "Welcome, Mister Dunn." A bead of sweat ran down the small of my back.

He extended his right hand in greeting.

"It is a pleasure to formally meet you, Doctor Destin. You came highly recommended." He smiled as he continued with his act. Over the shock, I pushed down the almost overwhelming urge to scratch his eyes out.

"Thank you," I replied, then added as an afterthought, "Sir."

With an amused expression on his face, he nodded towards Hodgson. It took me a second to understand his lead.

"Mister Dunn, may I present crewman Dyson Hodgson?" I gestured to Hodgson who stood at rigid attention. He firmly shook Hodgson's hand.

"Mister Hodgson and I are familiar with one another."

I glanced at Hodgson before I turned back to Dunn. I don't know why the idea the two men knew each other caught me off guard. Despite the claims of familiarity, Hodgson remained still and showed no expression. I guessed that their relationship was not a warm one.

"Mister Hodgson will escort you to your cabin and give you a tour of the ship, Sir." I put too much emphasis on the formal address but I didn't care what Dunn, or whatever he called himself, thought of me. I just wanted the charade to end and wondered why I hadn't listened to Schmaltz a few short hours before.

"I trust I will see you at dinner with Captain Garrick later this evening?"

I had forgotten about my expected appearance at the Captain's mess for the first meal. I offered the most cordial response I could muster.

"I look forward to it, Sir."

"Oh, please Doctor. I don't stand on formalities. Call me Erik."

His smile was predatory, seeming to invite me to step closer to him for him to pounce. I fought to remain in character.

"I look forward to it...Erik." The name tasted like bile.

He smiled and allowed Hodgson to lead him into the ship, leaving me at the still opened airlock in disbelief at what had just happened.

I closed the hatch and informed the bridge of Dunn's arrival. I leaned against the wall, legs shaking. At least, the son-of-a-bitch didn't out me in front of Hodgson, of all people. How long would it be before the news of my humiliation made its way to the rest of the crew?

I wasn't ashamed of my previous life before I got my sponsorship to med school. I viewed that as my history. Nobody could do anything about their past, but it annoyed me that I had determined to leave that life behind and failed. On my first foray into the world's oldest profession in over twenty years, I'd bungled things up like a novice. You'd think all that was enough, but what angered and embarrassed me more than anything else was having been played. There was more going on here than Charlie's lies, and I intended to learn what.

* * *

That evening, I shared a table with Garrick, Limn, Schmaltz and Dunn in the Captain's mess. I had thought of calling in ill, claiming female issues, but realized that would be capitulating in the little game Dunn forced me to play.

While the crew did not wear uniforms, the expectation called for more formal attire, especially when honouring a guest. I had only brought one outfit that could even pass as semi-formal, and it happened to be the same one that I wore the night I met "Jake".

I was seated across from Dunn. Though he behaved appropriately towards me, I remained keenly aware of every glance he gave me and wished for some kind of coverup.

Schmaltz, freshly shaved and showered sat next to me in his fine suit. I had only ever seen him dressed in his dirty orange coveralls, his unshaved face covered in grime and the ever-present unlit cigar in his mouth.

"You clean up nice, Doc," he whispered to me.

"Said the pot to the kettle," I replied in a whisper, punctuating it with a friendly smile.

Hodgson, wearing the dress uniform of a Terran Marine Sergeant, served the table with the skill and manners of a trained waiter. Everyone seemed to have secrets that were coming out and I prayed that Dunn continued his role as a gentleman and allowed mine to remain secret.

"Did you not enjoy the soup, Doctor?" Hodgson whispered in my ear as he removed the untouched serving. The meal itself was fairly standard ship's fare, mostly pre-packaged and reconstituted in the galley's food dispensers, yet he tried to sound offended like I had rejected something he had slaved over all afternoon. I glared at him but did not reply. He smiled politely and returned to the galley.

The remainder of the dinner proceeded without incident, most of the conversation remaining polite and safe. After the dessert course, Dunn stood and spoke to the group.

"Ladies and gentlemen, thank you for the fine welcome you have given me on this, the inaugural mission of the Rego science vessel, *Fortuna*. On behalf of our employer, I congratulate you. Each of you has been carefully selected and recruited as the most qualified individuals to be found. You are destined to be here to make history." His eyes fell on me. I tried not to squirm in my seat.

"It is time to open your orders, Captain."

Dunn produced a sealed envelope and handed it to Garrick at the head of the table. He opened it and spent a few moments digesting the contents. He rose and cleared his throat before reading from the page.

"The *MSV Fortuna* is hereby ordered to immediately plot a course and proceed in the shortest time possible to the planet Mercury to recover and claim as salvage the disabled and abandoned Terran ship *Helios* and all it contains, under universal law. Dated today, etcetera, etcetera."

Garrick lowered the page, satisfaction written across his face.

"Crew of the *Fortuna*. We have our orders. Proceed to your stations and prepare for immediate departure."

Without a word, everyone left their place and exited the mess, leaving me alone with Dunn. I pushed back my chair and stood.

"I need to make sure the medical bay is prepared."

Dunn rose from his seat.

"I am sure everything there has been ready since your arrival, Doctor. May I call you Melanie?"

"I would prefer if you didn't."

"Oh?" He sounded genuinely disappointed.

I avoided eye contact as I walked to the exit.

"I really have to get to my station. Please excuse me."

As I reached the doorway, he spoke to my back.

"Perhaps Angela, then?"

The impertinence of the comment was almost a relief. I composed myself and faced him, ensuring I kept a neutral expression.

"Doctor Destin will do just fine, Mister Dunn."

He had the appearance of a cat playing with its prey.

"As you wish, Doctor." He bowed his head in a mocking imitation of gallantry.

I strode down the corridor, jaw clenched and nails cutting into my palms. This was going to seem like a very long trip.

CHAPTER TWELVE

The door opened and Norbert Schmaltz walked hesitantly into medical.

"Good morning, Mister Schmaltz." A good night's sleep and a fresh cup of coffee had done wonders for my mood.

"You wanted to take a look at my 'hand'?" He held up the allegedly injured appendage, still neatly bandaged from his previous visit.

"Come on in, I'm the only one here."

"You got rid of your bodyguard?"

"It seems once we launched, nobody cared where I went."

He chuckled. "That sort of happened to me when I first arrived. He left me alone when I started making him help in engineering."

"Something's off about Hodgson, that's for sure. I get a bad vibe from him."

"Maybe he's a spy." He winked.

"Yeah, a real spook."

I unwrapped his hand and examined it.

"You do remember it was a fake wound, right Mel?"

"I'm only checking for any infection around the staples you forced me to use."

"Well, I won't be doing that again anytime soon. It hurt like hell when the freezing wore off."

"Serves you right for sneaking around. What do you know about this mission?"

"Not much more than we were told last night. I don't think you need this class of armed ship to run a simple salvage op."

"Armed? As in weapons?"

"Oh, yeah. Big ones too. This is a serious military vessel, Mel. They are expecting some sort of trouble." He appeared worried.

I looked at the isolation chamber and the controls for the containment field and bit on my lower lip.

"What about Dunn? You two seemed familiar with each other."

"No, I only met Erik Dunn yesterday." I didn't like lying to Schmaltz.

"What do you think of him?"

"I don't like him."

"Yeah, those corporate types give me the creeps normally, but there is something else bothering me. He seems like the kind of guy who acts all nice and proper, but would throw his grandmother out of an airlock for a profit. You know what I mean?"

I nodded absently while I re-bandaged his hand.

"We should probably keep these conversations between us, Schmaltz. I don't trust anyone on this ship. The sooner we can finish this mission and return to our lives, the better."

"Don't worry about me. Bogdan is a smart kid, but I don't trust him either. Just you and me, Mel. We've got each others' backs, right?"

The door opened and Erik Dunn stood outside the entrance.

"Am I interrupting?"

"No, we were just finishing up. Please come in, Mister Dunn."

I addressed Schmaltz in my best professional voice. "That should heal up nicely, Mister Schmaltz. Keep it clean and the staples should dissolve in a day or so. Come back if it turns red or becomes painful."

"Will do, Doc." He nodded to Dunn and left.

"What can I do for you, Mister Dunn?"

"Please, call me Erik."

"How do I trust it's your real name?" I regretted the words the moment they came out.

"There, you see? Now we are finally communicating."

"What do you want, Dunn, or whatever your name is?"

"For my purposes here on the ship, for this mission, I am Erik Dunn. I will be someone else on another assignment. I am who I need to be. As to the question of what I want..." he jumped up to sit on the examination table, rolled up his sleeve and extended his left arm.

"I want you to take a blood sample, Doctor."

I was surprised by the sudden change in the conversation.

"Why? I have all your medical workups."

"You have all the medical workups for Erik Dunn. I need you to update the records." He raised his arm again.

"What happened to the real Erik Dunn?"

"You don't really want to know about that, Melanie." He gave the same predatory smile.

"What's to stop me from calling the Captain and reporting this?"

"Go right ahead. In fact, my request is unusual enough, you should." He rolled down his sleeve and stared at me. "I'll wait."

I decided to call his bluff and walked to the desk to activate the comm, never taking my eyes off him. He waited and watched while sitting on the examining table, dangling his legs like a little boy. After a moment, Garrick responded.

"Yes, Doctor?"

"Captain, Mister Dunn has come into the med bay with an unusual request and..."

"Yes, Doctor. I meant to tell you. Please comply with whatever medical requests he makes of you. Understood?"

"Of course, Sir." I deactivated the link and regarded Dunn with suspicion.

"You see? All legitimate. Well, perhaps not legitimate, but it is sanctioned." He smiled and rolled up his sleeve once more.

I retrieved the venipuncture kit from the drawer and returned to the examination table. I wrapped the rubber tubing around his upper arm and patted his lower arm to find a vein. I inserted the needle, twisting it slightly.

"Ow!"

"Sorry." I wasn't.

I handed him a gauze to hold over the wound while I labelled the sample tubes. I took my time, then placed a bandage over the gauze.

"I'm afraid you may get a bruise."

"I'm pretty sure I will," he said as he rolled down his sleeve. He hopped off the table and walked to the door, stopping before opening it.

"Have dinner with me tonight."

"I don't think so."

"Oh, come now Melanie. We shared so much more only a few weeks ago. Surely a simple meal isn't too much to ask? I would like an opportunity to apologize and explain if you're interested."

He had played the right button, piquing my curiosity like that. He likely intended no physical harm, and I was dying to hear what he had to say for himself. In the end, my curiosity overcame my sense of reason.

"All right, then. I suppose dinner can't hurt. I have to eat anyway. But only dinner."

"Of course. Shall we say 19:00 in my quarters?"

"19:00 it is."

As the door closed behind him, I decided I definitely needed some backup.

I didn't want to talk to anyone, especially Dunn. I needed time to think and some strong coffee to do so, and the mess hall remained my only option for both. My hopes for solitude vanished when I saw Shigeko Limn sitting alone. She looked up from her cup and flashed me a polite smile, the kind that says, 'prove you're not a bitch and at least say hello'.

I covered my disappointment by returning her greeting and, now trapped, elected to go inside anyway. After pouring myself some java, I joined her. Sitting anywhere else would be rude, and I didn't need any new enemies aboard ship.

"How are things, Doctor? Are you settled in yet?"

She seemed sincere enough and I admonished myself for mistrusting her without knowing anything about her.

"One medical bay is the same as any other." I reached across the table for the sugar. "Limn is a Swedish name, isn't it?"

Amusement danced in her dark brown eyes. "My father is Swedish. I'm afraid I took after my mother."

"Japanese?"

She nodded, the smile fading from her face as she raised her cup for a drink.

"Destin is a French name, isn't it? It means destiny if I'm not mistaken?"

"Yes, it was my mother's name. I didn't know my father. He was killed in the war before I was born." My mother's real last name was Watkin. Destin is the name Walter Bickel helped me come up with when I applied for Medical school. I liked the sound of it and never gave its meaning much thought.

"My father was a pacifist," she said.

"Oh, that must've been hard for you."

"We did better than most. We could have been sent to the internment camps, but he volunteered as a firefighter and we got to live with him. After the war, he resumed his teaching position. Most of my friends' parents were pacifists too. They weren't as lucky and had to go to the camps."

A wave of guilt washed over me. I'd spent a lot of time feeling sorry for my lot in life; having to scrape out an existence because my whore mother didn't want anything to do with me. But the families of registered pacifists rarely fared better, many of them dying of starvation in the camps. Those who chose to contribute to the war effort in some way by working dangerous jobs at least got fed, though their lives were far from easy.

"How did you end up as a pilot?"

"I always had an interest in flight and space travel. After the war, one of my father's former students came by for a visit. He worked for Sato Corporation and was recruiting to rebuilt the merchant fleet. I signed up without a moment's hesitation." Though her mouth smiled at the memory, her eyes did not.

"How about you? How did you become a doctor?"

I gave her my best depreciating smile. "I won a scholarship."

"A smart one, eh?" She winked.

I hid my embarrassment by taking a drink of the coffee. It needed more sugar, and the topic needed to change.

"Have you worked with the Captain for a long time?"

"Garrick and I go way back. I met him when he was in the camp. When he was old enough, he joined the military. We kept in touch but only started working together a few years ago. Mister Dunn hired him and Garrick needed a copilot he could trust. One thing is for sure, I will never need to worry about money anymore."

"Mister Dunn takes care of you then?" I almost choked calling him that.

"He takes care of the Captain who takes care of me. That's the way it works."

"I see..."

"But you already know Mister Dunn, lucky girl. You've got a direct connection to the main line, so to speak."

I took another drink of coffee and tried to come up with another direction to take this conversation.

"What is he like?" asked Shigeko.

"Who?"

"Mister Dunn, of course. He seems so mysterious. This is the first time I've ever seen him."

"You never met him before?"

"Usually, the Captain receives his orders and we carry them out. This is the first time he's ever joined us on a mission. It must be important for the corporation. This is so exciting."

Before I could say anything more, she looked up and stared into space for a few seconds. Her CI seemed to be working fine.

"I'm sorry, but I am needed on the bridge. I've enjoyed talking with you, Doctor. It is so nice to have another woman aboard the ship for a change."

She left me in the now empty mess hall with more to ponder than I originally had planned when I entered. What mission was so important that Dunn had to dupe me into joining and then, uncharacteristically, supervise himself? This evening's dinner was going to be very interesting.

At 19:00 I stood in front of the door to Erik Dunn's quarters. My throat felt like sandpaper. I activated the live link to Schmaltz. He wouldn't be able to listen to the conversation, but I could send him a distress signal if things got out of hand. I wished I had a weapon, but something told me that Dunn was the kind of killer who could handle any aggression on my part. That he was a killer I didn't doubt.

On his departure from the medical bay, I brought up the records for Erik Dunn. I was not entirely surprised that the ship's computer linked directly to the Terran Central Databank. The ID I'd been provided contained the highest level access codes, with full editing privileges, something that was not only illegal but should have been technically impossible.

It revealed Erik Dunn to be a middle-aged bureaucrat who served as a civilian technical adjunct with Terran Military Security. His medical profile showed him to be physically identical to the Erik Dunn I knew and loathed, suggesting a previous modification to the record. The DNA on file differed from the sample I took from him. This data was encrypted and only accessible by someone implanted with specifically coded nanites, something difficult to fake. I now understood why they needed me for this mission. As a medical graduate from Terra, I was encoded with the authorization allowing me access without setting off any security flags.

I briefly toyed with not making the changes, but, on second thought, realized that was not a healthy idea. Whatever the real purpose of the mission, Rego went to a lot of trouble to involve me and likely required Dunn's file modifications for it to succeed. If I didn't make them, the lives of everyone on board may be endangered.

I pressed the buzzer to announce my arrival and the door slid open. My eyes took a moment to adjust to the dimly lit cabin. Prominently, in the centre of the room a table was set, complete with table cloth, china, silverware and burning candles. Dunn stood beside the table, dressed in a well cut and expensive business suit. By contrast, I elected to wear my duty uniform and a down vest that concealed my figure. He hid any disappointment.

"Welcome, Melanie. I'm so glad you could come." He pulled out a chair for me.

"Real candles? Did you disable the fire suppressors?"

"Hardly." He held his hand a centimetre above the flame of one candle. "Holographic."

"Pity."

He feigned a hurt look. "You'd really wish me harm?"

I smiled broadly at him. "What is for dinner? I'm famished."

He nodded and took his seat opposite. The door opened and in walked Hodgson, pushing a trolly. Playing the perfectly trained waiter, he elegantly draped a napkin across my lap, repeating the operation on Dunn. He then placed a covered dish in front of me and lifted the lid to reveal a steaming bowl of butternut squash soup. I tasted it and could not hide my surprise.

"This is quite good. Have the food dispensers been updated?"

"Mister Hodgson is more than just hired muscle, aren't you Dylan?"

"Yes, Sir."

"Mister Hodgson served as the personal chef for General Adamson of the Terran Central Command before he retired." Hodgson's face remained impassive during the conversation, but I got the sense that he didn't care for Dunn any more than I. I wondered what methods were employed to 'recruit' him.

The evening continued with casual conversational attempts by Dunn. I chose to keep my responses monosyllabic and the meal proceeded quickly. When the last of the dishes were cleared and Hodgson pushed the trolley out of the cabin, the door closed and we stared across the empty table at each other.

"Well?" I asked.

"Well?"

"You promised me an apology and an explanation if I agreed to dinner."

Dunn did not try to hide his disappointment.

"Yes, of course."

He straightened his posture theatrically.

"Doctor Destin, I would like to offer you my sincere apology for the deception I played on you the night we first met. It became a necessary step required by my...by our employer to secure your acceptance of employment.

"Part of my job for this mission was to find a way to persuade you to sign on after your initial rejection of Mister Wong's offer. Your return to, shall we say, your former activities, provided me the most expedient manner of doing so. I kept the appointment under the name of Jake Matthiews and made arrangements for your arrest."

He finished, looking like he had just recited his last travel itinerary. He showed no remorse or regret in his voice. It had been strictly business and totally impersonal.

My heart raced and I wanted to leap across the table and slap him.

"How could you be sure that I would be terminated by Sato Corporation?"

"Sato is owned by Rego. They were instructed to release you."

"I find it hard to believe you need to go to such trouble to obtain a fake DNA profile. Surely other doctors are available who would need less persuasion to recruit?"

"Don't underestimate yourself. Few physicians share your credentials and...proclivities. We need you for far more than my little subterfuge. You graduated at the top of your class and possess extensive expertise in nanotechnology. Your specialization in medical school, if I am not mistaken? You have practical experience in space medicine and are someone who has, what we shall describe as, blurred lines around your ethics. Other, more critical and challenging tasks remain for you in the mission ahead."

"Such as?"

He sipped at his cognac and let the conversation pause for a moment.

"We will be arriving at our destination in forty-five hours when we will immediately locate the downed ship, *Helios*. On arrival, we will recover a biological agent. A virus."

"What kind of virus?"

"We don't exactly know." He closed his eyes while savouring the cognac.

"Why do you want it?"

Dunn answered the question with his predatory smile.

"I see," I said, almost whispering.

"Your job, Doctor, is to secure and isolate the virus and determine its properties."

"You need to learn how it can be commercially exploited," I said.

"Precisely."

My eyes remained fixed on his while I ran the scenario over in my head a couple of times. I folded my arms across my chest and sat up straight.

"Ten percent," I said.

"I beg your pardon?"

"I want ten percent of the profits Rego realizes from the virus."

Dunn laughed heartily.

"Oh, I heard you were opportunistic, Melanie, but I didn't expect this. What makes you think the corporation would authorize that kind of agreement?"

"Because you're desperate."

"I think you are misinterpreting the situation."

"Am I? You needed someone with my skill set desperately enough to go to extraordinary lengths to get me aboard a ship, hidden on the far side of the moon in a secret base, cut off from all communications. You already demonstrated your intentions are not legal," I indicated his arm, "and have gone to great efforts to acquire an armed vessel, suggesting you consider the prize very valuable and there are going to be other interested parties trying to get to it ahead of you."

Dunn's face lost all signs of amusement.

"Go on."

"I think there is no choice but to deal with me on my terms as the race to the virus is well under way and there is no time to secure an alternate person to replace me, leaving you vulnerable to...negotiations." I smiled sweetly at him.

"I could threaten your family, your friends."

"Go ahead. If you did your homework, you would know that I don't have any family, at least, none that I give a shit about, and as far as friends go, well, I'm not the befriending kind."

I thought of Schmaltz and was grateful he couldn't hear the conversation. I kept my arms tucked to my sides to hide my sweating as the seconds ticked by without a response from Dunn.

"I'm not authorized to speak for the company for a deal of that size." His face remained impassive, and he swallowed frequently.

"No, I don't suppose you are. But I think you've negotiated a substantial finder's fee for yourself. I'll take a percentage of your cut. Shall we say, oh, forty percent?"

Dunn considered the offer, then the smile returned to his face.

"Twenty-five percent."

"Done."

"I'm curious how you intend to determine whether I've cheated you in the end?"

"It's very simple, Erik. I will secure the virus and not release it to you until I see your bank records and verify the transfer of twenty-five percent of your receipts to my account."

"You aren't afraid I won't simply kill you afterwards for your impertinence?"

I gave him my own predatory smile.

"How do you know I won't infect you with it?"

The colour drained from his face and he sat back in his chair to put some distance between us. Seconds later, he recomposed himself and extended his hand to accept the agreement.

"I suppose trust has to begin somewhere, doesn't it Melanie?"

I took his offered hand. "It definitely does, Erik."

I knew that Dunn intended to screw me. I just needed to find a way to double-cross him first and stay alive in the process.

CHAPTER THIRTEEN

"Are you out of your fucking mind?"

I didn't expect Schmaltz to be happy about what I told him, but he remained apoplectic.

"Schmaltzy, Dunn bent me over a rail. I needed to do something to level the playing field."

"And threatening a trained assassin is your idea of doing that? You'll be lucky if you ever step off this ship when this is over."

"Believe me, the thought crossed my mind, but I have a plan."

"Well, it better be good or we'll both be dead."

"What makes you think you're in any danger?"

"You said he threatened your family and friends."

I raised one eyebrow at him. "Who said we're friends?"

His jaw moved, but nothing came out. I grinned at him. He scowled back at me.

"You're an asshole, Destin."

"Yes, I am," I said while laughing. He eventually joined me.

"You're right. Nobody can know about us. I hate to say this, but we've got to stop meeting like this."

"Yeah, I take your point. Okay, this is my last visit to the med bay unless I really injure myself. Don't want anybody to think anything is going on between us."

"You make it sound like we're screwing."

He blushed.

"In all seriousness, Schmaltz, we can't completely cut off communications. A lot is going on here that we don't understand and I'm not ready to go alone against Dunn or Garrick."

"So what's your idea?"

"Six hours before we arrive at Mercury, I'm going to develop some diagnostic issues with the containment chamber that you'll need to help me address. It will give us a chance to compare what we've learned and make a plan before things get busy."

"I've got to go before Bogdan starts to think we ARE screwing."

I handed him a bottle.

"What's this?"

"Antibiotics for your infected hand. Make sure you take them so they show up in your system."

He accepted the vial and left. I dutifully noted the visit and the prescription in the medical log. I was glad to confide in him though my selfishness disturbed me. I'd placed him in serious danger if Dunn got even a hint that we were more than shipmates who'd shared a kindergarten class together. In a way, it would be simpler to dismiss if we were screwing, given my history. Schmaltz could become just another customer as far as Dunn thought. But I didn't want to do anything of the kind to him or his wife. I valued his friendship too much.

It would probably help matters if I spent some time with other members of the crew. Since the launch, I had mostly kept to myself. I didn't want to endanger anyone else, but I needed somebody to take some attention off Schmaltz, and nobody deserved to serve that role more than Hodgson.

I found Dylan Hodgson in Cargo Bay 1, going through some kind of martial arts exercise. His shirt was off, revealing several old scars across his back. His muscular torso glistened with sweat. This chef saw action at some point in his career. He completed his kata and addressed me without turning.

"Anything I can do for you, Doctor?"

"You haven't been hanging around my door for a few days. I began to worry."

He chuckled and reached for his towel.

"Afraid I lost interest?"

"Something like that. I'm starting to suspect your attention to me wasn't your idea."

He gave me a wry smile as he leaned past me and retrieved his shirt. The musky scent of his perspiration sent a shiver up my back that I hadn't experienced in a long time.

"The captain ordered me to stay with you to keep you out of trouble. For some reason, he doesn't seem to trust you."

"Hmm. Imagine that. Not trusting a ship full of...people with colourful pasts."

"I don't know what you are talking about."

"I suspect you do, Mister Hodgson. There seems to be more to you than muscle and culinary skills."

"Sorry to disappoint you. I'm simply a retired soldier trying to supplement a meagre military pension."

"Indeed."

An awkward silence followed.

"Anyway, I came by to apologize for my rude behaviour towards you."

He accepted my offered hand and we shook.

"All right, Doctor. I accept your apology though it isn't necessary."

"So you were hitting on me?"

He blushed.

"Well, soldier, you need to understand that I like men who finish what they start."

"I'll keep that in mind."

I gave him my best vamp smile and walked out of the cargo bay. With luck, any potential heat would soon be off Schmaltz.

My CI sent me a wake-up signal far sooner than I wanted, but it was ten hours to our arrival at Mercury and I had a full schedule. I surveyed the sleeping face of Dylan Hodgson. Unshaven and drooling on my pillow, he had been much more dashing the previous evening.

I almost gave up waiting for him to show up at my quarters and was starting to think my seduction skills had seriously slipped when the buzzer sounded. Standing at my door was the freshly showered figure of Hodgson, complete with a bootleg bottle of wine stolen from Dunn's personal stash. His romantic gesture, as sweet as it was, proved unnecessary.

I looked past his gently snoring form at the unopened bottle still on the floor by the door. I thought it might be a good vintage, and I could certainly have used a good drink to stiffen my resolve for what lay ahead.

I considered what I was doing to Hodgson, and felt a small pang of regret. Maybe it was my underdeveloped conscience waking up. Under other circumstances, I could grow fond of him. He was a decent lover, even if he was an annoying ass. He didn't deserve to be set up like this, but I had to take the spotlight off my friend Schmaltz. Hodgson was the lucky candidate for that position. At least, he got laid.

"Wake up, sleepy head." I nudged him in the ribs. He groaned and rolled over. As good as the prospect of cuddling in bed for the next few hours sounded, I needed him gone, so I booted him out of the bed. He fell, startled, to the floor, pulling all the covers with him.

"What are you doing?"

"Party's over, soldier boy. We have a big day ahead."

He got up and stumbled around to gather his scattered clothing.

"The night didn't last long enough, Mel."

"Well, if you'd have shown up a bit earlier..."

"Aw, c'mon. I couldn't decide if you were serious or yanking my chain."

"You're a coward. No wonder you're a chef."

I instantly regretted the cutting remark. He frowned while he put on his pants. He reached into his pockets and pulled them inside out, empty.

"Sorry, I left my wallet in my other uniform."

I was surprised by how much that hurt, but I deserved it

after my thoughtless words. It was the second time he'd alluded to knowing about my past.

"Does everyone on this ship know?"

He shrugged, clearly embarrassed by his own comment.

"Look, I'm sorry. That was uncalled for."

I put my arms around his neck and drew him in for a deep kiss. His large hands ran down my back and cupped my ass.

"Make sure you come back for your follow-up examination soldier?"

"If the swelling continues, I'll be sure to come back." He winked, walked to the door and picked up the discarded wine bottle. He placed it on the table, blew me a kiss and left me naked in the centre of my cabin, feeling very exposed.

CHAPTER FOURTEEN

The two unmarked spacecraft met at predetermined coordinates in the quiet expanse between Terra and Mars. Their anonymity was harshly shed when each illuminated the other in bright light.

The smaller of them was of a sleek, contemporary design, its smooth silver exterior as much a work of art as of functionality for atmospheric flight.

The larger vessel was more modular and had the look of long and varied use. Its repainted surface showed the wear of micro-meteors and long exposure to the silent, harsh environment of interplanetary space.

Out here in the deep blackness, where no unwelcome eyes witnessed, they prepared for an intimate coupling. The ugly ship extended it's docking bridge like a proboscis towards its companion. The contrasting sensual curves of the small yacht made the maneuver appear clumsy, like the uncertain advances of an awkward teenaged boy.

It took Felix Altius months of coordination and intricate negotiation to arrange everything. Inferred obligations and overt assurances had been exchanged and agreed upon, and now, at long last, the event would take place. Despite his meticulous preparations for the encounter, he was surprised to find himself anxious now that his efforts came to fruition.

If there existed even the slightest likelihood of treachery or danger to the interests of his Dominus, he was prepared to cancel the rendezvous and begin another plan. Yet the anxiety remained; stubbornly gnawed at him; distracted him. If he was going to abort he needed to make that decision now, before the airlocks equalized. Once the final phase began, there would be no going back.

The other party risked more than Regis Mundi. The Martian politicos would not approve of this encounter, so those about to cross the docking tube operated unsanctioned and exposed. Felix was as much responsible for their well being as his master's. Perhaps, he thought, that is why he felt anxious. Mundi's world he controlled. The Martians presented too many variables for all to be considered confidently.

Left to him this meeting would never occur. Mundi wanted it more than anything he ever coveted before and it was Felix's duty to fulfill those desires.

His milky blue eyes scanned the readouts before him. Satisfied everything was in order, he inhaled deeply and slowly let the exhalation pull all the visualized doubts from his mind. After a curt nod to the yacht's captain to open the airlock, he abruptly left the bridge and strode to meet his guests.

He arrived at the access port and looked down the empty, brightly lit tunnel. The distinctive, dusty odour of Mars floated on the newly mingling air currents. Felix did not like the smell of the red planet. He visited there, once, when all this began. It reminded him of something unfinished and filled him with unfamiliar emotions. His old mentor once described them as primal promptings related to inadequacy and unfulfilled dreams. Strange how the odours of a partially terraformed world elicited such feelings in him, given his origins.

Three men and a woman made their way cautiously down the docking tunnel, thin, from malnourishment or genetic selection he did not know. They hesitated as they adjusted to the subtle difference between the gravitational fields of the two ships. On his order the artificial gravity aboard the yacht was purposefully maintained at Terran normal. It was crucial to keep them off balance both physically and psychologically during these final negotiations. It was why he insisted they come to him, a particularly niggling sticking point in the arrangements. Had he agreed to confer on their ship, they would have hoped for the same advantage. His synthetic body was more adaptable and the change in gravity would not have affected him. The negotiation tactic would have been ineffective, and therefore, a waste. Like Mundi, he detested missing any leverage which could be exploited.

He graciously ushered his anonymous guests to a comfortably appointed lounge and, to their anticipated surprise, offered them seating in comfortable, overstuffed lounging couches they could only recline on. While making them feel pampered, he wanted them to avoid assuming any kind of aggressive seated posture.

He did not attempt to ply them with alcohol; too obvious and clumsy a tactic. Instead, he tempted his guests with a wide assortment of exotic delicacies. The table offered Turkish delights direct from old Istanbul, assorted sweetmeats from an ancient roman recipe and an exhaustive selection of fruits that the Martians never saw on their spartan world. The sweet and savoury treats further tempered any resistance they might hold to his negotiating position. The room was subtly filled with the scent of flowers and fresh grass; an olfactory reminder of what they wished Mars to become.

The senior member of the delegation spoke first.

"Maestro Altius," he began with the martian formal address, "we appreciate you meeting with us on behalf of your Dominus. We are all anxious for these negotiations to conclude successfully, so I will be brief."

So that is how it shall be, is it? "But of course, Maestro Alpha." He used the agreed upon code name.

"It is unprecedented to allow off-worlders, such as yourselves, access to the level of economic influence you seek. It will be impossible for us to persuade the governing council to grant you the charter you desire. Perhaps if you contented yourself with a series of corporate licenses to open various business franchises, over time your entitlement might grow with continued residency? In a few generations, after the completion of the Effort, the successors of your Master, as citizens, would be in a better position to ask for such a charter."

"And, naturally, Mars would benefit from several decades worth of taxes and tariffs from these businesses," said Felix.

"Taxation provides for the greater good. Your business enterprises would contribute to the Effort of which you would also become a beneficiary."

Felix directed his attention to the platter of food between them and selected an especially succulent orange. He peeled it and a tart aroma filled the room.

"And how much time do you project will be required for your terraforming effort to yield meaningful results?" He popped a segment of the fruit into his mouth.

"Our current models estimate a breathable atmosphere will be in place in seven generations."

Felix wiped his fingers with a napkin. "Unfortunately, my Dominus wishes to establish a more influential foothold on Mars within his lifetime." He gracefully swung himself from a reclining position and sat upright on his couch.

"Let me be brief, Maestro. We are well aware that your projections are unrealistic. All your secret studies agree it is going to take three millennia before living conditions can be established with your current efforts."

Alpha sputtered and clumsily fought the higher gravity to match Felix's seated position.

Felix pressed on with his advantage. "Additionally, your resources to perform the terraforming and continue to provide for your citizens are limited. In short, you cannot build sufficient habitat for a growing population. Your taxable base will be capped within one or two more generations. After that, genetic diversity becomes a problem. Three thousand years is a very long time. The entire rationale of your terraforming effort will need to be reconsidered in eighty years. Mars will become another Luna. That differs substantially from the dream of the lush Eden you have sold to your populace."

He realized he enjoyed the looks of shock and outrage on the faces of the delegates as they all now struggled to sit upright. They all spoke simultaneously. Felix held up two placating hands and regained control of the discussion.

"Of course, this conjecture is strictly confidential between us. We would never consider revealing our projections to anyone."

After they calmed down enough to listen, he continued, "It is clear that the single largest threat to the achievement of your Effort is Terra, is it not?"

He now owned their complete attention and one, by one, they each perched awkwardly on the ends of their lounge chairs.

"If not for the Terran trade embargo on your world, you would have far greater access to resources from the entire solar system. As it stands now, you are confined to what you can mine and manufacture on Mars. There are a few black market operators within the asteroid belt who are willing to defy Terra but the cost is proving prohibitive for you. Without firing a single missile, they have defeated you and killed your dreams. With some planning, you may be able to avoid the costly kind of war that Luna fought to retain a semblance of its independence, but Earth has learned from that conflict and I doubt such an action would yield comparable results for you."

"We are developing the means to challenge Terra. We can end the embargo and fulfill the Effort." The stature of the slight woman who spoke belied her martial tone.

"We are aware the Terrans stole your bio-weapon." Felix's words sucked all the air from the room.

"I would not be distressing you, my friends if I could not help you."

"What are you proposing?"

"We know where the virus is. We are recovering it as we speak. Once in our possession, we will simply need to make arrangements with an appropriate party. Whomever that buyer is, be it Mars or..." He let the sentence hang, unfinished.

As expected, Alpha took the bait. "Under such circumstances, I am confident the governing council would see the wisdom of granting you the trade charter you seek."

Felix smiled amicably and stood, extending his hands towards the delegation.

"Who is hungry? Our chef has prepared a marvellous repast of roast lamb, beef and chicken with some very tasty vegetables."

He thought he heard their stomachs growl as he lead them to the dining room.

CHAPTER FIFTEEN

I took my seat on the bridge beside Schmaltz.

"Is everything in order, Doctor?" asked Garrick.

"Yes, Captain. Mister Schmaltz replaced the faulty backup battery and all the systems are fully operational again."

"They had better be."

One hour from entering orbit, the planet now loomed large on the monitor at the front. Schmaltz had nothing to tell me, any communication from the bridge he had received being purely routine. That was good news, but I was more concerned Dunn and Garrick had remained tight-lipped as to the nature of the virus, despite my multiple attempts at some clarification. Dunn evaded almost all of my technical questions and only gave me the most rudimentary of files on the pathogen. What I'd read disturbed me, both by what was contained in the file and what was missing. Basically, all I learned was how contagious and deadly the bug was; nothing I hadn't already surmised. At least, I was provided a bio-trace profile to program into the medical scanner. Theoretically, it would tell me when I encountered any of the bugs.

Limn and Garrick engaged in a subdued conversation, which I couldn't overhear, ending with Garrick ordering her to "Check that out." Dunn appeared concerned by their exchange.

"What is the problem?"

"We are getting a signal from another ship."

"What? Who?"

"We are checking now, Sir."

After several tense seconds, Limn announced, "Captain, the ship's transponder identifies the vessel as the *TSF Athena*. They are on an intercept course."

"Are they tracking us?" Garrick turned in his seat and glared at Schmaltz. "I ordered our transponder disabled."

Barely able to suppress his panic, the chief engineer responded, "I did the job myself."

"How the hell did they find us?" He did not wait for a reply and turned back to Limn for more hushed discussion.

"I need options, Captain." Dunn's relative calm contrasted strongly with the anxiety the command crew displayed.

"We're working on it, Sir."

Dunn turned to Hodgson, "What do you know about this ship?"

"*Athena* is a Terran space forces heavy battle cruiser, one of the newest additions to the fleet."

"Mister Dunn," interrupted Garrick, "I've confirmed our transponder is disabled and we can detect no signal coming from us. They might not realize we're here. We all understood it would not take long for others to find out about our prize. It makes sense the Terrans would send a military vessel."

"They'll need to spend time scanning the surface for the *Helios* after they arrive. We still enjoy a time advantage, Captain," said Dunn.

"That ship is nineteen hours out. Our mission parameters give us sixteen hours on the ground to secure the virus, assuming we have the right intel on the location. With one hour landing and launch time, we will be well within *Athena's* firing solution when we lift off from the planet."

His comment disturbed me. If we were on a legitimate salvage operation, why would the Terran's even consider shooting at us? Things weren't making any sense. I wanted to ask the question but was confident I would be shut down if I did. Shutting up and listening was my only best option.

"The ship's location is correct, Captain. It's time for some innovative thinking out of this highly paid crew." He glanced around the cabin, making sure he had everyone's attention, which wasn't necessary since we all hung on every word.

Dunn spoke directly to Schmaltz. "I am presuming you can set up a link with this ship allowing it to be controlled remotely?"

"Yes, I believe so." Schmaltz was as puzzled as everyone else.

"We will all proceed to the surface in the drop ship. There, we will secure the virus, and use the *Helios* for our escape," said Dunn.

"What about the cruiser?" I blurted out.

Dunn gave me a self-satisfied smile and continued, "The engineer will reactivate our transponder and remotely pilot this vessel away from the planet at full burn. The Terrans will have no choice but to pursue, giving us an opportunity to launch without detection. Mister Hodgson, you will rig the munitions in the armoury to detonate when the *Athena* catches this ship."

"All the fire power on this small craft won't even dent their hull," said Hodgson.

"I don't want to hurt them. I only need to keep them distracted long enough for us to escape, undetected."

I'm ignorant about military strategy, but Dunn's plan seemed sound to me. Apparently the Captain and the others thought so as well since none of them brought up any objections.

"Mister Schmaltz, Mister Hodgson; how long do you need?" asked Garrick.

"I can build and test the remote link in about half an hour," said Schmaltz.

"The biggest bang we will get is if we can blow up the engines and fuel reserves. I need a couple of hours to configure the munitions, rig the proximity sensors and set the fuse. One hour if I have help," said Hodgson.

"Mister Skorupa, and Mister Dunn," ordered the Captain, "assist Mister Hodgson. Miss Limn, help the doctor transfer the portable containment chamber to the drop ship. I will pilot us into orbit and join you to prepare for launch. Are there any questions?"

"That unit is heavy, even in lunar gravity. Our task would be easier if we could disable or reduce the grav-gen," I said.

"Does anyone have any objections to Doctor Destin's request?"

Nobody objected.

"Very well, Doctor. Mister Schmaltz, please set gravitation at one-quarter Lunar. We don't need loose objects floating around. That's it, people. We launch in one hour."

We all scrambled out of our seats and proceeded to our assignments. The containment chamber was going to be a bitch to move even at reduced lunar G, but with Shigeko's help we would be able to wrestle it into the hangar on time.

With the loss of the *Fortuna* my computer links to verify Dunn's banking activity would be compromised; a fact he undoubtedly understood when he voiced his plan. I really didn't believe he would go to this much trouble to screw me, but he was a devious bastard. How, for example, could Dunn know the other ship had not crashed unless his bosses arranged for it? If the Terrans were prepared to fire on us while we ran a legitimate salvage operation, they clearly did not view the *Helios* or its contents as anything they wanted to fall into anyone's hands.

This whole mission was turning into something nasty.

The pressure suits took longer to put on than we planned for. Already a half hour behind schedule, Hodgson finally entered the drop ship hangar. He apparently experienced a few issues around getting the detonator properly set so it could be triggered remotely. We spent another forty minutes fussing with the seals on the suits. Dunn and Garrick grew more impatient by the minute. Eventually, we all sat strapped in and ready to depart.

"Are we in scope range of the cruiser yet?" asked Dunn.

"I have put the planet between us which should delay being sighted for another hour," Garrick replied.

Without any preamble, he sealed the door and depressurized

the hangar. *Fortuna's* doors opened and the small shuttle maneuvered its way out to descend to the cratered face of Mercury below. The usual operational radio chatter filled the speaker in my helmet as we accelerated. The ship was too small to have a grav-gen, so I endured the temporary discomfort of weightlessness stoically. Thankfully, the Captain didn't want to waste any time and before too long, I enjoyed the familiar tug of my own weight as we descended, which soon grew to be uncomfortable as the full force of Mercury's pull became noticeable. Suddenly jumping to almost two times lunar gravity did not strike me as a good idea. I wondered if Dunn took that factor into his plan? We would all tire very quickly and likely not be as efficient as he and Garrick wanted.

With no atmosphere to slow us down, the descent was fast and smooth and we soon cruised thirty kilometres above the ground en route to the designated coordinates of *Helios*. We passed the terminator into the Mercury's nightside.

We had no windows, so I watched the passing surface on the screen in front of me. Just as well, as the enhanced image showed a landscape that would have been nothing but inky blackness to the naked eye. The crater-pitted ground was indistinguishable from the terrain of Luna, and I soon became bored with the monotony and drifted off to sleep.

The deceleration of the drop ship woke me and I noted I had been out for a little under an hour. I realized my microphone was active and prayed I hadn't snored. Nobody paid any attention to me, so I assumed I had not embarrassed myself.

The practice of running cargo ships at ninety percent of Terran normal gravity now seemed like a good idea, in hindsight. At least the amount of time I'd spent on them meant my muscles weren't as atrophied as a permanent Lunar resident's would be. Still, I seemed to weigh a tonne. The chatter in the cabin was minimal, which told me most of the others felt just as shitty at the moment.

Garrick set us down on the surface more roughly than I expected of him. His voice crackled in my helmet, "All right people, there she is." He indicated the enhanced view from the monitor camera to the side of the ship revealing the sleek form of *Helios*. It was about a hundred metres away and glowed eerily in the infrared spectrum displayed on the screen.

"Engineers, Hodgson and Doctor, proceed with me to the *Helios* first," said Dunn. "Captain, secure and seal this vessel and follow us in. Schmaltz, you and your assistant restart the power but hold off on life support until ordered. Doctor I, need you to scan for bio-contamination and check the integrity of the ship's containment chamber. Once all is cleared, we will establish living conditions and complete our transfer."

"What about our bio-containment unit?"

"That is a last resort in the event the one on *Helios* has failed."

"What are we going to find, over there, Dunn? What happened to the crew?" I wasn't entirely sure I wanted to hear his answer.

"We should find nothing alive. Well, nothing human." The emotionless way he said it sent a chill up my spine.

CHAPTER SIXTEEN

We trudged our way across the rocky regolith that passes for ground on Mercury. We all laboured to walk in the higher gravity. The weight of the pressure suits did nothing but add to our workload. The one-hundred metres between the ships felt like a ten-kilometre hike with a full pack. I wanted to ask Garrick if he parked so far away because he worried about getting a scratch on the paint. I decided to keep my mouth shut and continue walking.

My heavy breathing was all I heard as we arrived to stand under the belly of the huge vessel. The landing apparatus supported the hull some ten metres above us and no way presented itself for us to enter. Dunn removed a pad from the pocket of his suit and activated the controls with the clumsy gloves he wore.

An access ramp descended and he climbed up, followed by the rest of us. At the top, we were met by a closed doorway. He accessed a panel beside the door and keyed in a very long code. A small opening appeared on the wall and he inserted his left arm up to the elbow. He winced as the security system fired a needle probe through the fabric to sample his blood. I held my breath while the computer decided if the DNA matched its records. Suddenly, I did not feel as confident in my database hacking skills as I had been a few hours earlier.

The security system withdrew the needle and sealed his suit. The door slid open revealing the black interior of the lifeless ship.

I followed Dunn into the derelict's airlock and shone my helmet lights into the darkness. I removed the bio-scanner from my utility belt and interlinked it to my helmet's HUD. The typical readouts jumped up before me. With my CI, I adjusted the settings to scan for viral contamination.

When Dunn provided me with the strange detection code of the contagion, I reviewed the specifications closely. What I saw scared the shit out of me. The detector was calibrated to look for a variant of an old Terran virus, related to ebola, but a thousand times more infectious. Even wearing a space suit, this was nothing I wanted to be exposed to. Thankfully, nothing came up on the scanner. Dunn didn't need a doctor for this; if the contagion was present we were screwed. We wouldn't be able to return to the shuttle because even attempting to remove the contaminated suits in anything but a vacuum would result in immediate infection and death within hours. A functioning decontamination chamber might be of help, but only if programmed with a specialized nanite population designed for the specific microbe. I could only pray nothing escaped the containment field in the bio-lab, otherwise, we were all dead.

"Nothing is in here. I'm transferring the protocol to each of your HUD's in case we are separated. If the bio-alert goes off in your ear, it means you've encountered a released virus and you should alert me without delay. Until we clear this ship, we won't turn on life support and absolutely nobody cracks open their suit after that without my final clearance."

Everyone voiced understanding and we exited the airlock.

The *Helios* had been parked here for some time. The interior temperature read as a cozy minus 150 Celsius, only ten degrees warmer than the year long planetary night time outside.

A startled cry crackled in my speaker. It sounded like the young engineer, Bogdan.

"What is it?" asked Dunn.

"A body! A dead body!" Bogdan called out.

We made our way as fast as our clumsy suits allowed to where he and Schmidt stood. Their helmet lights illuminated a frozen corpse slumped in a chair, head lying on a table. The man appeared to be napping at his desk when he died. I ran a detailed scan of the body and the surrounding area but found no trace of any contagion. The dead crewman was a solid block of ice, so I couldn't turn it to examine the face.

"What happened to him?" asked Bogdan.

"You mean aside from the obvious? I don't know. Seems he succumbed before the environmental systems failed. There is some blood on the desk under his head, so it may have been an injury." I didn't want to mention the hemorrhagic virus. The kid was freaked out enough.

"I'm surprised there is even a body here after this long. Why isn't it cremated?" asked Schmaltz.

"We're near the North pole. It never gets too hot," answered Dunn.

"The perfect conditions to preserve something, if you wanted to," I said.

Dunn turned towards me and his helmet lights shone in my face so I did not see his expression, but I imagine he didn't like my editorial comment. I addressed the entire group, changing the topic.

"For the moment, we should finish our survey; see if we find anyone else. Touch nothing. Just record what you find. And, Schmaltz, under no circumstances do I want the life support activated until we can determine how this poor fellow was killed, understand?"

I counted the number of space suits standing around.

"Where's Hodgson?"

Everyone shone their lights about cabin looking for him. A voice crackled over the comm, "I'm headed for the bridge."

"Umm, okay," I said.

Dunn broke in, "Good call, Hodgson. Find out what you can. We can make better time if we split up. You all have the ship's schematics uploaded and available on your HUD. You two," he indicated Schmaltz and his assistant, "go to engineering and search every cabin and hallway on the way. Remember what you've just been told. Hodgson, check out the command decks, one and two. Doctor, proceed to the medical facilities. I'll examine the lower deck and cargo areas."

I shouldn't have been surprised that Dunn had the schematics for the ship. It was pretty clear by now who was responsible for it being here. But he certainly seemed as shocked as the rest of us by the discovery of the dead body.

It took about an hour of room by room searching before I finally reached the med bay. On the way, I encountered five more bodies in posed variations of a pain filled death. One, a woman, lay curled in a fetal position in her bed, a sheet pulled up over her shoulders, frozen blood covering the pillow, eyes, nostrils and mouth. Despite her horrific appearance, she appeared peaceful, as if resigned to her fate.

Medical held the real horror. Inside strapped down on examination tables were a half dozen corpses, all in the same painful death rigour. I moved into the facility and found another body restrained to the table in the isolation chamber; patient zero.

In the far corner, the only light other than my own blinked amber at me from across the darkened room. The bio-containment unit still drew some power.

Beside the lit panel, on a table, lay four innocent looking silver tubes, closed on both ends. I recognized them as secure medical transport containers for biologically hazardous samples. Someone was in the process of moving some very dangerous stuff around in the lab. Three of them remained sealed and locked and had a steady green light indicating their contents safely contained. The fourth lay opened and empty.

Panic seized me as I searched for the missing sample cartridge that should have been inside the container. After a few anxious minutes, I located it behind the glass of the lab's containment chamber. Similar in principle to the cylinders, its design provided a secure, isolated environment to manipulate and experiment on dangerous materials. Modern lab standards required that such a chamber's structure, windows and seals all have a security field net woven through them. When full power flowed, nothing could move between the molecules of the walls. It was overkill for most biological samples, but the technology was common in nanotech research.

I looked again at the amber LED that first caught my attention. The containment was running on emergency backup, but the light indicated a dangerously low charge. A normal virus shouldn't be able to move through a wall, let alone these ones, but whatever these guys worked on prompted the need for this level of security. They were anxious about something dangerous getting out. Based on what we found their fears were justified, and the failing power did not bode well for us.

"Schmaltz, where are you?"

"We're in engineering. Everything is a hell of a mess. Looks like some kind of explosion disabled the ship before it set down here. There are bodies everywhere."

"That's interesting, but we might have a bigger problem in medical. The reserve battery for the bio-containment chamber is almost exhausted. Is there another one down there?"

"I haven't see one yet. How much juice is left?"

"I dunno, maybe an hour or more. The indicator is amber and blinking."

"Mel, the place is a disaster. It may take us hours to find a pack if there is one."

"If you don't get some power to this lab, whatever killed the crew will be released and we'll be in the same shape as the people on this ship."

"How could the virus harm us?" Dunn interrupted the conversation between Schmaltz and me. "Nothing's been detected on the viral scanners."

"The bug may be dead, or only dormant in these conditions. According to the limited information you gave me, it can potentially survive for weeks in a vacuum. But there's a full sample cartridge open in the bio-containment chamber. If it gets airborne and on our suits, we won't be able to take them off without becoming exposed."

"Give me a minute. I have an idea," said Schmaltz.

I waited anxiously for what seemed like an hour, staring at

the blinking light; willing it to repeat; relieved every time it did.

"Mel, the main bus is intact. I can restart the power."

"Will that turn on the heat and the air flow?"

"Um, yeah."

"We can't do that. The containment chamber needs power, but we have to keep everything else aboard in a frozen vacuum. I don't want to risk activating any virus that might be dormant."

"Shit. I need another moment. Stand by." I heard the swish of the blood running through my ears and my mouth was dryer than a desert. The light continued to blink, but I could swear the frequency of the blinks slowed down since I first looked at it.

"The guys that built this ship were smart. The medical centre has a separate power line dedicated to the bio-containment unit. I can turn it on and leave the rest of the vessel freezing in the dark."

"Do it!"

"Already done Mel. Is it still blinking?"

My heart skipped a beat when I saw the amber LED was no longer on.

"It's gone out..." I could barely hear my own voice. Tears fogged up my vision. I was dead, thanks to a stupid battery.

"Can you find a green power indicator?"

My gaze frantically scanned the front of the containment control panel and was drawn to the steady glowing light on the other side of the access door.

"Yes, it's on!" I laughed with relief. I stared at it to assure myself that it showed no sign of going out.

"Doctor, is all secure?"

"Yes, Dunn, everything is good. We're safe."

"So what do you propose we do about the bodies? We need to restore power before the Terrans find us."

"The entire ship must be considered contaminated, especially anything touched by the blood of the victims. We have to determine if the cold killed the virus or just put it to sleep."

Careful thought was required before I gave any instructions. I didn't know how the pathogen had been released. From everything I could tell, it struck fast and hard, killing everyone within a few hours of exposure. I needed to get some tissue samples, preferably from the first and last to be exposed. I was pretty sure the poor fellow in the isolation unit was among the first.

"Hodgson, did you find anything on the bridge? Are there any bodies?"

"Yes, one."

"Where was he found?"

"He was wearing a pressure suite and strapped into the pilot's seat, but his visor was opened. I think the poor bastard committed suicide."

Somebody had to pilot the ship here. He might be the last victim.

"Bring the body to the medical bay. As far as the other remains go, take them outside."

"Will we contaminate ourselves by handling them?" Dunn seemed worried. It was good to know that something could frighten the man.

"I found no indications of a virus near anyone I've examined. The blood around them is frozen, just be careful not to get any of the ice crystals on your suits."

I honestly didn't know if what killed everyone was even transferable to us. I did know that we couldn't stay in these bulky spacesuits indefinitely. We would have to activate life support at some stage, either here or in the drop ship. I suppose a risk of contamination remained if we just left, returned to the shuttle and made a run from the Terrans with *Fortuna*, but I had no great desire to spend a safe life in a Terran detention facility, assuming they didn't blow us up instead. A chance existed that one of us had somehow gotten something on our boots or a part of our suits. If the viral agent was dormant, that single exposure would kill us more quickly than the Terran guns the minute we heated it up in our own ship.

Our best bet was for me to examine the tissue in the

isolation lab and determine the status of the virus. If dead, we could continue with Dunn's plan. Regardless, having the crew move corpses gave them something useful to do while I determined if we were going to live or die. No sense letting everyone worry until there was a reason.

"Do you want us to bury them?" asked Bogdan.

"I really don't think they care. Do as you think best."

CHAPTER SEVENTEEN

Felix Altius relaxed and permitted his mind to wander as he luxuriated in the nearly scalding waters of the *caldarium*. Spending time in Mundi's elaborate *balneum* was one of the few pleasures he took in the employment of his master.

On his return from the meeting with the Martians, Felix felt the need to wash the odour of their planet from his clothing and body. It seemed to permeate everything. Tomorrow he would order the entire yacht thoroughly fumigated to ensure it usable for his Dominus. Multiple ships remained at Regis Mundi's immediate disposal, many of them larger and far more opulent. He reasoned he could indulge in this one simple pleasure without any lingering guilt.

He occupied himself with the sensory input of the hot water caressing his skin and lost all perception of time as he became immersed in blissful nothing. The hypnotic sound of the water lapping the edge of the pool soothed him and allowed him to relax for the first time in weeks. The almost imperceptible pad of bare feet moving cautiously towards him on the warm floor tiles disturbed his hard-earned sense of calm. The familiar pattern of the offending footfalls told him who they belonged to. The intruder halted a respectful distance from him and remained still.

"Yes, Basilius?" Felix did not open his eyes. He always thought it an ironic name for a slave. The servant's greek name meaning "Emperor" exemplified his Dominus' unique humour when it came to naming his possessions.

"There is an urgent message for you, Sir."

Basilius was instructed on the short list of people permitted to interrupt. Felix exhaled noisily and rose from the steaming waters. The man held a towel and robe in hand, anticipating the response his announcement would provoke. Felix allowed his body slave to dry and dress him, then followed after the man to the small communications room secreted near the entrance to the baths.

Felix might have activated his implant to receive the message, but he loathed to use the technology, preferring to see the person he spoke with. He found the impact of an actual old style video communication better transmitted his annoyance at being interrupted.

The image resolved itself into the face of Kiri Mason. Her proactive efforts to keep him personally apprised of events as they occurred instead of burying them in formal reports, pleased him.

"Sir, there has been a development in the mission."

"I surmised as much." Felix didn't want to admonish her too severely. She would soon enough learn to be more succinct.

"One of your agents aboard the Terran cruiser, *Athena*, reported they are pursuing the *Fortuna*."

"They've identified it as their's?"

"The agent did not believe so. They flagged the vessel for investigation because it entered the search grid and had no active transponder."

"What were they even doing searching that area? Weren't we assured the Terran's directed their fleet to other coordinates?"

"We were, Sir. Our operative believes *Athena's* captain received intelligence directing him to the *Fortuna's* position."

Someone worked against them.

"Any word from Dunn?"

"His last communication confirmed the flight plan of *Victorem*, however, I believe he suspects something."

"Have the crew been replaced?"

"We are waiting until just before the scheduled launch. Do

you wish to change the order?"

"No, we will stick to the script. Let the events with the Terrans play out for a while more. If Dunn thinks his plans compromised, this may be a hint of what his new ones are to be. Stay in touch with the agent on *Athena*, and keep me informed of any further developments."

Kiri Mason acknowledged her orders with a nod and terminated the communication link. It pleased Felix she learned so quickly.

No proof existed the Terran's acted on the instigation of Dunn, but neither did any reason appear for him to believe they hadn't. He was familiar with Dunn's profile and he exhibited a history of employing elaborate plans to complete his missions. Using a double feint like this was in character.

He believed *Athena's* captain belonged to Dunn. If that were the case, desperate measures might be required aboard the Terran vessel. Such an action could only be sanctioned by Regis Mundi. Felix needed more than speculation. He would need to allow Dunn to make his intentions clearer. The deal with the Martians remained too important to let this continue very long.

He frowned, annoyed the benefits of his bath were so rapidly lost.

CHAPTER EIGHTEEN

With two frozen corpses now on the beds in the isolation unit, I started my makeshift forensic examination. The bulky space suit made the job terribly difficult, but I couldn't risk allowing Schmaltz to activate life support until I knew. He directed more power to the lab to let me use the molecular imaging microscope. I dared not ask him to turn on the lights, lest the temperature in the room get too high, so I had to work with the headlamps on my helmet. After securing tissue samples from the obvious sites of bleeding, I got them into the examination chamber and took a look at what killed the crew. What I saw scared the shit out of me.

This was no virus familiar to me. In every sample, I found the same thing, thousands of microscopic nanites, all inactive and totally inert. This was not a genetically engineered pathogen. It was a bio-engineered weapon. Nano-medicine was my specialty and I had never seen anything like this before.

After twenty minutes of discussion with Schmaltz, we figured out a way to create a small, isolated environment in the one of the lab's bio-manipulation chambers. I needed to test if the sample was dormant or dead. To my great relief, nothing happened. I ran several more specialized tests to make sure and repeated my experiments with other samples and with some of the crystallized blood found around the victims. The results remained consistent. The nano-virus was inactive, apparently programmed to remain active for a limited time and then self-destruct, like the perfect bio-weapon.

At least, that stood as my working theory. I considered the happy green light on the bio-containment chamber. A really keen scientist would next want to select a nano-virus sample and test how it progressed through live tissue. I didn't feel the need to be that informed at the moment.

I contacted the crew and told them they were safe with no chance of infection, but I kept the details of the nanites to myself. Garrick gave Schmaltz the order to turn on the life support and get the ship up to living conditions as soon as possible before beginning work on repairing the damage in engineering.

The lights abruptly came on in the medical lab. My eyes adjusted to the light levels and came to focus on Hodgson standing outside of the isolation chamber.

"Why weren't you helping the others?"

"I thought the presumed dead should bury the dead. I wanted to check in on you."

"Why?"

"Because if something had gone wrong, I didn't want you to die alone."

"Well, I wouldn't have..." I realized what the big goof was trying to tell me. Why do guys become sentimental and stupid when you sleep with them? He didn't realize if the virus had been only dormant, we all would have lived until we chose to remove our suits or just let the oxygen run out. Still, I thought his gesture sweet.

"Thanks for the thought, Dylan."

"You're welcome, Melanie."

Grateful the helmet hid my blushing, I changed to a safer topic.

"Can you please take these two outside with the others?" I indicated my patients on the tables.

While he wrestled with one of the corpses, I searched for a cleaning agent. There may not have been an active nanite population in the bodies or their fluids, but it was still a good idea to clean up the blood as much as possible before we got out of the suits. The next few hours were going to be tiring.

Garrick conscripted everyone not working in engineering to the task. The sooner we could remove the spacesuits, the better. Mine smelled overripe. By the time we cleaned up the few areas we intended to occupy, the temperature had risen to above freezing.

The door opened to Hodgson and Limn who struggled under the weight of the containment unit we had brought down in the drop ship.

"What am I supposed to do with that? The ship's field is running perfectly now."

"We didn't think it would do any good in the hangar with the shuttle. It might be useful for spare parts, or a backup," said Hodgson. "Being cautious can't hurt, can it?"

"Besides, I'm not carrying it anywhere else," added Limn, annoyed at my lack of appreciation.

I directed them to put it in a corner of the lab and returned to my task. What to do with the extra equipment proved the last thing I wished to spend time thinking about. Exhausted, I wanted to get to my cabin and take a shower.

CHAPTER NINETEEN

I entered engineering with three meal packs from the drop ship. The deck was strewn with cables and damaged components that were in the process of being replaced.

"Is anyone hungry?"

"Famished," replied Bogdan. He put down his tools and wiped off his hands as he came to collect one. Schmaltz was right behind him.

"Are you guys making any progress?"

"Yes, despite appearances, we are," he said while surveying the room. "We should be ready to launch in five hours."

"The Terrans are going to arrive in three."

"You're starting to sound like Dunn and the Captain," he said between mouthfuls.

He noticed the concern on my face and added, "Not to worry, Doctor. The *Fortuna* is due to leave orbit in twenty minutes. If everything goes according to Dunn's plan, that should buy us enough time to escape."

He wiped his mouth with his sleeve and transferred the cigar stub from his pocket to his teeth. "Is everything secure in medical? I don't want that virus doing an encore performance on us."

"It's not a...problem." I'd almost told him about the nanites in front of his assistant.

"Where's Hodgson?" I held up the last meal pack.

"He's installing some new buffers in the gravity controller. It turns out the man has some engineering skills. Not too bad at it, either," said Bogdan as he went back to the job I had interrupted.

"Seriously? Hodgson is an engineer too?"

"He knows his way around an engine room, for sure. He's been a huge help. I'm sure he deserves some lunch. He's over there." He pointed the way and returned to work.

Feeling somewhat like the farmer's wife taking food to the men in the field, I headed toward where he had indicated. I rounded the corner to see Hodgson, head and shoulders buried inside an access panel. I took a moment to admire his muscular ass before clearing my throat. He jumped and banged his head on the opening. He dropped to the floor, grimacing in pain while holding his injured noggin.

"Sorry, I didn't mean to startle you."

"I was a bit focused and wasn't expecting anyone."

"Are you all right? Let me take a look." There was blood running between his fingers from his wounded scalp.

"I'm okay."

"The hell you are. That's a nasty wound. I'm going to need to stitch you up."

"I've had worse."

"Doctor's orders, tough guy." I handed him the meal pack and reached out a hand to help him stand. "You can eat your lunch while I fix you. I'll have you back down here playing with your toys in no time."

He thought about it, then smiled and took my hand.

"Promise it won't hurt, Doc?"

"Nope, let's go."

By the time Dylan Hodgson sat on the examination table in the medical centre, the wound in his scalp no longer bled.

"I told you I'd be okay."

"This isn't normal." I frowned at him. "Spill everything, soldier. What's going on?" I suspected what he would say, but wanted to hear the explanation from him.

"Military enhancement. They injected me with tiny little..."

"I know what nanites are. When did this happen?" I cleaned the blood away to reveal a forming a scab.

"I received them when they assigned me to a combat unit."

"Well, it's an expensive procedure. I didn't realize the military used the technology so extensively."

"I suppose you think it's cheaper to replace soldiers instead?" He smiled.

"Why did you agree to come here to get stitched up?"

He grinned boyishly and shrugged his shoulders. "When a pretty lady offers to nurse me back to health, I learned a long time ago to not refuse."

"This happens a lot?" I went to the cabinet and took out a venipuncture kit.

"Uh, not really. What's that?"

"This is to take a blood sample. I want to examine your nanites if that's all right?"

"Why?"

"They are a special interest of mine. I study them. I'm an author of several papers on the topic."

"I believe you. I just prefer if you not do that. I signed a confidentiality agreement and all that." He jumped off the table. "Can I go now?"

"Sure, no problem. You don't appear to be suffering any ill effects from your bang on the head."

"Great. Thank's Doc. I need to get back down to finish up in engineering."

He waved goodbye cheerfully and hurried out the door. I watched the closed door after he left and tried to make sense of the last few minutes. His story about a confidentiality agreement seemed possible, but also sounded too convenient. He hadn't expected me to show any serious interest in his little buddies. What was he hiding? I then noticed I still held the gauze used to clean up his wound.

I smiled to myself as I took the bloody cloth to the microscope in the corner. My intentions violated some kind of patient confidentiality, but I wasn't hired for my ethical standards. I wanted to know Hodgson's big secret. Within ten minutes, I knew, and I was stunned.

I brought up on the screen a view of one of his nanites. Beside it, on a second monitor, I placed an image of a dead nano-virus. His nanite almost mirrored the shape of the virus. His bugs were an attempted engineered cure for the bio-weapon that killed the crew of Helios. On close examination, they weren't an exact match. They would slow down the virulence of the nano-virus, perhaps even render it harmless long enough for the bioweapon's lifetime to expire. One thing seemed certain. Hodgson possessed the closest thing to immunity of anyone. He obviously did not join this mission to cook meals for Dunn.

I looked at the bio-containment chamber, the green light glowing. I was tempted to extract a live nano-virus and test Hodgson's nanites effectiveness against them. I shook my head.

What the hell is the matter with you Destin?

Then I started to wonder; how would my own nanites do against the virus? I grabbed the venipuncture kit and within a minute held a sample of my own blood in a vial.

The image in the microscope soon reminded me of something I conveniently chose to forget. My system possessed two different populations, neither of them even close to the required parameters to put up a fight with the nano-killer. Somewhere in the back of my head, I came up with the vague notion that if the company went to such extreme measures to recruit me, perhaps they also manipulated the injection forced on me back on Luna. It would make sense for them to do so if they intended for me to risk exposure. I would have done so if I had been plotting the whole thing.

Maybe Rego didn't have the cure. Dunn owned no nanites in his system at all. Surely he would have been injected if one were available? All this suggested to me that Hodgson did not work for the corporation. He was a spy for someone else.

CHAPTER TWENTY

Erik Dunn entered his quarters and locked the door. He unlatched the helmet and pulled it off to the hiss of escaping air. Leaning against the door he inhaled deeply, glad to be rid of the pressure suit's confinement.

The room smelled musty and stale and he detected an odd chemical odour. He decided it must be the precautionary cleansing agent the doctor ordered pumped through the environmental system. He shook his head at her naivety. If she only perceived what she was up against she would realize the stupidity of her order. Just as well that she didn't understand. If she did, it would be more difficult for him to accomplish what he intended.

He chuckled at her impertinent attempt to force a better deal for herself. She had absolutely no clue what she'd become involved in. Charlie Wong had been right about her, though. She was intelligent and resourceful. She would need to be watched.

Now, though, more pressing matters demanded his attention. The idiot Terran captain showed up far too soon. Apparently he doubted Dunn's word and set out to confirm the course of the *Fortuna* for himself, putting everything in jeopardy by allowing himself to be spotted. To further complicate everything, Mundi's spies infested every ship in the fleet. Dunn needed to find out what Mundi suspected.

He retrieved his personal bag from the closet and removed a

small box from a secret compartment. It cost him considerably to customize a quantum radio transmitter into such a compact package, but his need for near instantaneous confidential communications necessitated the expense. Unavoidably, the miniaturization lengthened the time required for it to establish the linkage with its counterpart. Dunn decided he could enjoy a shower while that took place.

By the time he returned to it, the transmitter indicated an established a link. He sat on the side of the bed wrapped in a towel and entered the contact protocol. Following a short wait, he heard the raspy voice of a woman, obviously roused from sleep.

"Erik? Is everything all right?"

"Sorry to wake you. There's been a development and I need your help."

"What's happened?" Kiri sounded wide awake now.

"We're being tracked by a Terran military cruiser."

"What? There aren't supposed to be any in your sector for another three days."

He smiled at her apparent surprise.

She continued, "If the Terran's spotted you, how do you intend to proceed? Do you want me to launch the *Victorem* early to meet with you?"

"No, proceed as planned. I'll think of something to distract them."

"Mundi has spies on board all the Terran ships. I'll try to find out what I can."

"I'll contact you again once I come up with a plan to shake the Terrans," he said.

"Be careful, Erik." She sounded genuinely concerned for his well-being. There was more to her than her looks.

Dunn signed off and stared at the wall.

Kiri had strong potential, but her inexperienced slip up doomed her. She couldn't know the extent of Mundi's network unless told by someone like Felix Altius.

Damn! Such a waste.

He made an adjustment to the small box and established a

second communication link. The ability to pair the Q-radio to more than one other receiver is what really cost him the credits.

A deep male voice responded to the hail.

"I have a mission for you," said Dunn.

"Yes?"

"I want to leave a message for someone. Once the *Victorem* launches, retire Kiri Mason."

"Understood."

The link-up ended.

Dunn wondered who first approached whom? Altius probably sought her out. She was impressionable, and Felix Altius could be extremely persuasive. A pity she wouldn't survive to collect the rich fee he undoubtedly bribed her with.

Not yet bedding Kiri was his biggest regret about her. He should have done so right away after hiring her, but her sweet face tempted him with the foolish romantic notion that it would be better for her if he waited and built her trust.

Trust is a two edged blade. Dunn trusted nobody. Why he made that mistake with Kiri, he didn't know. Maybe he was getting old and sloppy. Perhaps now was the perfect time for him to retire.

The point was moot, anyway. Mundi would not let him live, even if he didn't plan betrayal. The very fact that Mundi co-opted one of his agents demonstrated his precarious position.

He smiled. It was good to have no options. It prevented wavering from the chosen path.

Now he needed to consider how to handle his other situation. The loyalty of almost every other person on board he owned. The doctor and the engineer were acquired by less conventional means and certainly not motivated or inclined to work on his behalf. Schmaltz he could do nothing about at the moment. His skills were needed for a while, yet. As for Melanie Destin, it would be best to minimize her interaction with the crew.

Now convinced of his plan of action, he unpacked his bag and looked for a change of clothing.

The Ares Weapon

CHAPTER TWENTY-ONE

I re-ran the facts but came to the same conclusion. Hodgson was a spy. Only two questions concerned me now: who did he spy for, and what should I do? I locked myself in the med bay's water closet. I needed time to think without interruption.

Dozens would kill to possess the nano-virus. Rego Corporation demonstrated that quite clearly. We only found the *Helios* because someone sabotaged it, murdered the crew and abandoned it here. Somehow, Dunn miraculously knew where to look, so a genius level IQ wasn't needed to determine who was behind everything. Something went terribly wrong. Perhaps the release was intentional and hadn't gone as planned?

Think, Destin! Think! This ship is Terran, so the virus must be as well. Hodgson is former Terran forces. Is he working for them to recover their missing bio-weapon? How he managed to dupe his boss into recruiting him for the mission by declaring himself up front as ex-Terran military smelled of some level of genius.

What could I do? Informing Dunn was the first obvious dumb answer. I didn't like where the trail led. Hodgson would die, and despite the fact he possibly worked against us, I had become fond of him. I had done a lot of questionable things in my life, but killing was not one of them. Exposing him would make me as culpable in his death as Dunn.

If Dunn conspired with Hodgson and I told him what I

know, he would murder me, a prospect I liked even less. So, telling him anything was obviously not a good idea.

They must have some kind of a plan to take the viral agent and escape without our immediate objections. I hoped their plans didn't involve releasing it amongst the rest of us though Hodgson's anti-nanites indicated that a strong possibility. Of course, that line of thinking suggested he didn't work with Dunn.

My head started to hurt.

A viral release remained possible and Dunn, if involved, must hold a means to deal with the situation. Hodgson's presence in engineering was the answer. His voluntary helpfulness gave him access to any of the systems. What had he been so focused on when I surprised him? I needed to talk to Schmaltz.

I heard the door to medical open and somebody call for me.

"Give me a moment!" I flushed the toilet and washed my hands to complete the charade, then exited to find Dunn waiting for me.

"What can I do for you?"

"I want to inspect the integrity of the isolation containment field."

I'll bet you do. "Of course, it's over here."

I led him to the chamber and he glanced at the monitors still displaying my nanites. He stopped to examine them without any change of expression. My stomach tied itself in knots. I had to assume he was familiar enough with nanotechnology to grasp what he saw. If he suspected I understood the nature of the nano-virus, things might become bad for me.

"Is this the virus?"

I relaxed a bit. He was either ignorant or leading me on.

"No, those nanites are from my system. I hoped they might offer some kind of resistance to what killed the crew."

"And do they?"

"I can't tell. The samples are too degraded to determine their exact structure."

"Oh, that's a pity. It would have been comforting to know

there might be a way to protect us from another accidental outbreak."

"Yeah, that was my hope. We'll just need to maintain the highest level of security in this room and make sure the power isn't interrupted."

"My thoughts exactly. As of this moment, I am giving you sole access to this facility. Nobody is to enter. You will be sleeping and taking your meals in here."

A jolt of adrenaline shot through me and my hands shook involuntarily.

"Do I have visitation rights?"

Dunn chuckled. "Not to worry. The situation will only be for a few days until we reach our destination. Besides, you'll be able to guard the prize so I don't cheat you and run off with it."

The predatory grin spread across his face. I responded with my best 'fuck you' smile. He left the medical centre without another word and I could only stand there and watch him leave, helpless to do anything else.

The klaxon sounded once and Garrick's voice boomed over the speaker.

"All crew, report to launch stations. Lift off in five minutes."

The Terrans would be waiting for us unless they took the bait and chased after *Fortuna*. I wished I knew who Dunn played for in all this. I hoped he still worked for Rego as that gave us the best chance of escape and not being shot at if his plan succeeded.

I was not surprised to find the door locked from the outside. Panic welled up in me. I did not like being confined. I had endured enough of that shit as a kid. I looked desperately around the room for something to distract me.

If part of the scheme entailed a viral release then I would be the first to die unless I came up with a way to prevent that. The easiest way for Hodgson to engineer things was to cause the containment field fail. If that happened, the nanites would move through the spaces between the molecules of the wall and escape. It took some time to happen, usually on the order of an hour for facilities built to laboratory specs. I required a way to ensure the power couldn't be interrupted.

I scanned the room and spotted the isolation chamber Hodgson and Limn wrestled in only a few hours before.

"Hello, there!"

I rushed over and placed my hands on top, wanting to give the bulky box a big hug. It contained an independent battery source that might be usable as a power backup for the ship's system. I wanted to dance around the room. Maybe I wouldn't die a horrible death.

It took me a long time to figure out how to remove it from the portable unit. Not having the right tools, I modified a surgical laser to cut the casing, a major accomplishment in itself but once done, the rest of the operation was easy.

Within two hours I was finished. With Schmaltz's help, I could have installed an automatic power transfer switch. As things stood, I had to keep an eye on that fucking green light and flip to the battery when it went out. The situation would be nerve-wracking, but this solution would keep me, and everyone else, alive, at least until Hodgson figured out the virus wasn't released. He only needed to unlock the door, smack me around and turn off my creation. I'd only bought myself a little time.

My eyes fell to the monitor that distracted Dunn. There sat an image of my useless nanites. But were they totally useless? On closer examination I found a strange looking, second nanite. It was a hybrid of mine and the ones I'd had forced on me on Luna. Somehow, when the two populations encountered each other in my bloodstream, they went about creating something new. I thought about the biophysics of the whole process, then turned to consider the chamber holding the nano-virus.

A very dangerous, desperate, hail Mary idea formed in my churning little brain. What if they could do it all over again? Why not try to push their evolution into something that might save my life, if nobody else?

I was out of my mind. Why else would I even be consider

using my nanites, along with the sampled ones from Hodgson to bio-engineer my own version of a vaccination. To do that, I would need to extract an active sample of the nano-virus. I was definitely crazy.

CHAPTER TWENTY-TWO

Though the engineering behind the containment field technology existed for years, I was still nervous. While I handled the most deadly bio-weapon ever invented with the robotic manipulator arms, visions danced through my head of the tiny little machines crawling through the gloves and into my body.

With a sample extracted from the chamber, I began my experiment to try modifying my nanites to fight off the nano-virus.

The truth about medical school for me was that I found it boring and considered quitting before I took my first class in nano-medicine. Charlie might have called me a brilliant doctor, but my passion resided in these little buggers. Nanites fascinated me and I made them the focus of my studies, taking extra classes and pulling off insane hours to graduate with a double doctorate in medicine and nano-medical technology. I guess I was good at both, but I loved the nano-research. I was prepared to do post-doctoral work in the subject when my life turned to shit and I left everything.

After a few failed experiments, I glanced at the chronometer to see six hours now passed. No wonder my stomach protested. When Dunn told me I'd have to take my meals in here, I assumed they would bring them to me. I called him on the comm.

"Hey, Warden, do I get fed in this dump?"

"Feeling peckish, Doctor? I'll have something brought down to you."

"No chance for me to earn a day pass for exercise?" I knew what the answer would be.

"Hodgson will be down shortly."

Hodgson! I couldn't risk letting him see what I might be up to. I scrambled to clean up the experimental chamber and make the place appear unused. As I turned off the monitors displaying the microscopic images, the door to medical opened and he entered, pushing a trolly.

"Are you bored out of your mind yet? Dunn tells me you are babysitting the virus." His broad, genuine smile displayed white, slightly misaligned teeth.

"Yes, we can't afford for a repeat of what happened to the previous tenants, can we? Since we haven't blown up, I'm assuming Dunn's plan is working? Any sign of the Terrans?"

"Looks like they fell for the bait and are chasing our old ship in the opposite direction. We'll be out of their detection range soon if they even bother to look back."

"Let's hope that's the case. I don't really want to spend the rest of my days in a Terran work prison."

"That would not be good." He uncovered the tray to reveal a beautiful looking steak dinner, with fresh vegetables.

"Where did we get the meat?"

"It's soy. The food system on this ship is better than most. It actually tastes like the genuine article."

"I don't remember the taste of steak. I've only eaten it once when we splurged at graduation from med school. My stomach ached for two days after."

"Yeah, real meat will do that to you. This should be okay, though."

After asking if I needed anything else, he left me to my dinner, giving no sign to suggest this would be my last meal.

I returned to my work and pressed on for the next twelve hours, every attempt to modify a change in my own nanites a failure. In truth, I didn't realistically expect to succeed. Random hybridization was rare and dependent on too many factors. Though the populations inside of me accomplished the miraculous once, there was never any guarantee that I would be able to force a second adaptation.

Nano-tech had been around for almost three centuries, but nobody had figured out how to invent a general purpose nanite. My own were as close as possible, but they were just programmed to identify and isolate a small number of common viruses that I would be expected to encounter as a doctor. The ones the Morality Police injected me with were specifically designed to fight sexually transmitted microbes. Hodgson's had clearly been developed with the single purpose of defending his system against the nano-virus. Though they all attacked different invaders, all remained fixed in the scope of what they could accomplish, and I had pushed them as far as I could without success.

But all was not lost to me. I still could try to replicate Hodgson's nanites and inject yet a third population into me. The lab was equipped with some rudimentary equipment that would allow me to do so, but it would take time. With any luck, their design might be good enough to keep me alive if exposed. I wasn't sure I had a statistically large enough sample from Hodgson to build a working version with enough of the correct structure to be useful. Still, it was the only chance I had for when the inevitable happened. I only hoped enough time remained for me to pull things off.

I awoke to a hand insistently shaking my shoulder. I'd fallen asleep at the desk and took a few seconds to groggily recall where I was.

Dylan Hodgson stood over me, amused.

"Napping on the job?"

"Late night. Why are you here?"

"You didn't answer when we pinged you, so Garrick sent me down here."

"I'm touched by his concern."

"Don't be. Everyone is being summoned to the bridge for a briefing. Turns out that the Terran's didn't take our bait. They are coming for us at full burn."

We gathered in the crew compartment for the meeting. Dunn arrived last and immediately began the briefing. "We have to make a decision."

"What decision is that, exactly? Seems to me like our options are limited to death or capture at this point." I said.

"The option of escape remains, Doctor. It is the only one I am willing to consider. I will destroy this ship before I allow it to fall into the hands of the Terrans."

As bad as the news was, I was relieved to finally learn where Dunn's loyalties lay. I reviewed the grim faces of the others. Nobody seemed prepared to argue with him, so I kept my mouth shut too.

Garrick took up the briefing. "We've put some distance between us for the moment with a boost in thrust from the engines, thanks to your efforts, gentlemen," he indicated Schmaltz and Bogdan. "However, it is not a question of if *Athena* catches up to us, only when. We've doubled back and are now on acceleration burn en route to Venus."

I volunteered the query, "Why?"

"They will, naturally, expect us to use the gravitational assist from our approach to the planet for a high speed heading to Luna. Once inside Luna's jurisdiction, they know they cannot touch us without violating the peace treaty."

"This is a Terran ship, isn't it? Won't we be in treaty violation?"

Dunn interjected. "This is a research vessel, not military. It was constructed by Rego in their facility and leased to the Terran science council. It possesses a Lunar registration. Once we enter orbit and request sanctuary, the Terrans can do nothing."

Garrick interjected, "We've run all the scenarios and we cannot outrun them, even with a gravity boost from Venus. They simply have more thrust. They intend to cut us off long before we reach safety."

"Then what's the point?" I asked.

"We aren't going to Luna, at least, not right away," said Dunn. His smugness annoyed me. "We will use the gravitational boost to take us towards the sun. With a close pass to Venus, we will pick up speed and should easily be able to lose *Athena*."

"How close a pass?" A lump developed in my throat.

"Close," said Garrick. His voice dripped with condescension.

"Why can't they just do the same and follow us?" asked Bogdan. His voice shook and his eyes were twin moons on his face.

Garrick glared at him. I was thankful somebody else asked stupid questions too. "Because they already made their course correction to intercept us, assuming our destination is Luna. The Terrans tipped their hand. By the time they realize our plan, it will take too long for them to change their own course to pursue us directly. We'll be long gone."

"Yeah, but flying into the sun? Isn't that, well, dangerous?" I am not a space jockey and didn't really care how dumb I sounded.

"A good question, Doctor," said Garrick. It was the nicest thing he had ever said to my face since I came aboard. "Under the circumstances this plan wouldn't work, but we hold an advantage over any other ship, including *Athena* because this vessel is designed to fly much closer to our star than anyone else. We will accelerate on an oblique trajectory to enter orbit within the cover of the chromosphere, well beyond *Athena's* ability follow. So, as you see, we have an escape plan, but it is far from risk-free."

Finished his lecture, Garrick allowed Shigeko to continue.

"While *Athena* won't be able to catch us, she can still make an emergency course correction once she sees what we are up to. The maneuver will put us into her firing solution after we slingshot out from behind Venus. It is a narrow window, only forty-three seconds, but we will be vulnerable."

I looked around at the heads nodding like they were agreeing on a restaurant for dinner.

"Am I the only one with a concern about this?"

"You may be as concerned as you wish, Doctor. You don't get a vote. This is merely an informative meeting so that you can all prepare. Another ship has been dispatched by our employers. They intend to intercept us as we enter solar orbit, allowing us to transfer over and escape." Dunn's posture made it clear that he would brook no further discussion.

As much as it galled me, he had come up with a reasonable plan. How he had arranged for a second vessel wasn't an issue anyone wanted to inquire about. The idea, as crazy as it sounded, was our only shot at surviving this.

CHAPTER TWENTY-THREE

With no further questions, the meeting broke up and we proceeded to our stations to prepare the ship for the gravity boost. Hodgson walked with me towards medical.

"You were pretty quiet in there," I said.

"I'm not what you would call a tactician."

"Hmm. Just a jarhead who follows orders, huh?"

"Something like that."

"I think you, Mister Hodgson, are a man of many hidden talents. How did someone as clever as you come to work for a guy like Dunn?"

"Right place and time, I suppose."

I stopped and gazed up at his handsome face.

"But what are you to him? At first, I thought you might be his paid muscle. Then you turn out to be a chef and an assistant engineer. Bogdan told me you know almost as much as he does. So what is your story?"

He smiled and resumed walking, forcing me to catch up. I needed to try a different approach.

"How long did you serve in the military?"

"Fifteen years. Why the sudden interest in my background?"

"I'm bored! I've got nothing to do on this ride except strap in and scream. Besides, you are a mystery to me and I like to solve mysteries. It's the diagnostician in me, I guess."

"There's not much mysterious about me. I joined up in the last few years of the Lunar war. Never experienced combat.

I'm good at cooking, the Admiral found out and hired me. When my term ended I shipped out to find other employment. I met Dunn through some of the Admiral's contacts and the rest is history."

"So how does a Terran ex-soldier end up working for an enemy corporation?"

"Last I checked, the war has been over for seven years. We're all living peacefully and Dunn had work for me. Money is money."

"You found it that easy?"

"Like I said, I never saw combat. I imagine my perspective might be a little more biased if I had."

We reached the medical centre but I didn't want to go inside, mostly because I enjoyed Hodgson's company.

"So, Doctor, are you going to tell me about yourself?"

"Oh, my story now? You wouldn't want to hear that."

He leaned against the door, blocking my path.

"I think I would."

"Not much to tell. Born on Terra. Mom was a military companion, so I've no idea of who my dad was. Lousy home life. Got into a lot of trouble until somebody took an interest in me and sponsored my education and entry into med school. After the war ended I signed on as a doc on one of the cargo ships until I got recruited by Dunn."

He grinned and said, "That wasn't so hard. Now I feel like we have the start of a real relationship."

My jaw clamped shut and I ground my teeth for a second before I caught myself and returned his smile.

"I should get inside and finish up some things."

"Sure." He stepped aside and opened the door.

"Join me after we make it through the gauntlet? We can celebrate our survival."

"Why not?"

"Great! See you on the other side, then, Doctor."

He smiled broadly and strolled down the corridor towards engineering. I stood in the doorway and regarded him for a moment. What did I know about Hodgson, anyway? Besides being a decent lay, the only other things I knew were he cooked, could fix things and he worked for Dunn. Maybe he normally did Dunn's dirty work. Would Dunn eventually send him to kill me when it became time?

Sixteen hours later on the bridge, most of us sat strapped in and watched the milky sphere of Venus grow rapidly in the monitors. Dunn was nowhere to be seen. I would have asked about him, but I didn't want to care and, frankly, I had more pressing concerns on my mind.

I had been witness to a couple of gravity assist maneuvers, but never one this challenging. We headed straight for Venus, planning a sharp turn around it. The idea was to add the acceleration of our approach along with the planet's momentum to speed us up and outrun *Athena*.

Or something like that. I hated physics. To the best of my understanding, we needed to get close to the planet to pull it off. Insanely close in my humble opinion which Garrick made clear, nobody was interested in hearing.

I occupied myself by digging my fingers into the arm of my chair and tried to keep from hyperventilating. It wouldn't do to have the ship's physician freak out before all the fun started. I consoled myself with the knowledge if things didn't work out as planned, we would all get a brief opportunity to scream and I could fill the air with my useless I-told-you-so's as we burned up in the atmosphere. I thought I may as well make my last words creative, so I spent some time composing a particularly acidic vindictive to hurl at Dunn, in the event he ever decided to grace us with his presence. As I finished that thought, he arrived and wordlessly took his seat behind the Captain.

"More important things to attend to, Mister Dunn?" I asked.

He gave me his predatory smile and replied, "Everything I do is important, Doctor."

Not in the humour to spar with him, I shut up before I voiced my real thoughts.

Even though we flirted with death in this maneuver, everything on the bridge remained calm and routine. There was no violent shaking of the ship as we approached the planet or any indication suggesting the danger in what we attempted. I closed my eyes to distract myself by imagining my hands around Charlie Wong's throat and what I intended to do to him if I ever encountered that son-of-a-bitch again. I hoped my ghost would be able to haunt him at the very least.

Athena apparently figured out what we were up to several hours before and made the trajectory adjustment Limn predicted. I originally thought forty-five seconds not an awful lot of time for them to shoot at us. When we were first told the plan, I imagined some scruffy jarhead lining us up in his sights, pulling the trigger and missing as we flipped our middle fingers in his direction and zipped away.

The truth was far less dramatic, *Athena* having released her missiles after making her course correction. It was a last, desperate effort on their part to destroy us while we remained in range. Since they could not know how close we would approach or what kind of engine boost we would use, they took their best guess and laid down a spread of missiles to hedge their bets.

"The last of their payload has been released, Captain," announced Limn, far too calm for somebody being shot at.

"Engaging course correction," responded Garrick.

The ship vibrated slightly as the engines fired, altering our velocity by just enough to theoretically avoid the firing solution.

"Exactly how many missiles did they shoot at us?" I asked.

"Two hundred and forty-seven," said Limn. "They employed a statistical distribution to account for any changes..."

"Thanks. I'm sorry I asked."

I thought the entire manner of our possible deaths in that missile spread unjustifiably anticlimactic. I had always imagined dying in a dramatic fashion. Though the prospect of being incinerated shortly did qualify, my rational self argued the navigation was expertly plotted and there existed little chance my fears would be realized.

That was the funny thing about fear. It didn't need to be

based on fact or reason. It was primal; the body's way of warning you not to try something stupid.

But as I came to understand on this day, a war in space was nothing more than an algorithm; an exercise in applied statistics. No romantic concept of two ships spinning around each other in a dogfight. No dramatic weaving or running along side and boarding like the days of sailing vessels on the Terran seas. In space, war became cold calculation and nothing else. You shot at your opponent and never saw them blown to little bits because, by the time it happened, you would be long gone. It was too impersonal for my tastes. I sat back in my seat and closed my eyes to resume my imagined murder of Charlie.

I felt a warm hand grasp mine and opened my eyes to Hodgson leaning across the aisle.

"We'll be fine," he whispered. His eyes showed legitimate concern for me, and I wondered how I ever considered him to be Dunn's willing stooge.

I gave him an insincere smile to make sure he understood I didn't believe him and resumed rehearsing my especially creative curse for Dunn.

CHAPTER TWENTY-FOUR

Like many things in my life, the fears I held for our fiery demise in the Venusian atmosphere were unjustified. Garrick and Limn executed the required maneuvers calmly and expertly. If I had kept my eyes closed and not compulsively checked the monitor for our progress, I never would have known what was happening. With the planet receding in our rear facing camera, I relaxed my grip on my chair arm.

"Fifty-three minutes to missile spread," said Limn.

How she remained so calm under the circumstances fascinated me. She was a trained professional who performed her job almost by rote. We all were selected for our expertise, and, despite the methods of recruitment, Charlie had assembled an exceptional team.

Dunn sat behind the Captain lost in his own thoughts. I wondered how many deaths he had been responsible for in his career and how many others would die before someone put him down. My life, as chaotic and contradictory as it seemed, was entirely predictable to the likes of him who made a business of exploiting other people's weakness. He seemed to know what I would do, even in situations where I didn't. I dearly wanted to surprise him, but I appreciated to do so would mean for me to cross lines which shouldn't be.

I observed the others in the cabin and wondered what he had on them; what was his power over them allowing him to sit so easily in all this, assured none of us would slit his throat? He left little doubt he would not hesitate to order any of our deaths.

I thought of Dylan Hodgson and the mystery he posed. I'd misjudged his allegiances once, already. Was he more closely associated with Dunn than he let on? Would he kill for Dunn, or did he work for someone else? One thing was certain, the nanites in his system were deliberately engineered to combat the nano-virus or one much like it. Hodgson's presence on this mission was no accident, but his role remained a mystery. I just hoped it didn't involve me or anyone else dying.

Before I realized the passage of time, my musings were interrupted by another announcement from Shigeko Limn. We would soon be encountering the first missile cluster. I took a deep breath and exhaled, glancing at Hodgson.

"Okay," I said, failing to hide my anxiety. "Only two hundred and forty-seven booms and we are in the clear, right? I can count that high." I smiled tensely at him.

"Actually, there will be more than that."

"What? But Shigeko said..."

"Yes, they launched that many missiles, but they are just a primary delivery system. Each missile includes nine cluster missiles and every one of those contains five actual warheads."

I did the math in my head. "Over eleven thousand!"

"Yes. Distributed over an area designed to maximize the likelihood of a hit...or two."

I couldn't keep the panic out of my voice. "So, that means?"

"You should keep yourself strapped in. One or two will be close."

I swallowed hard. "How close do they have to be to...you know?"

"If they are using standard munitions, anything within a kilometre will probably cause us damage." He looked at me with regret in his eyes, "Sorry."

"And if they're not?"

He shook his head but said nothing.

"I thought as much." Suddenly, forty-five seconds seemed like an eternity.

"Entering the firing solution now," said the calm voice of Limn.

Nothing happened.

"Ten-seconds."

A moment later we were bounced about as the shrapnel from an exploding warhead rattled off our reinforced hull. My hand convulsively gripped the arm of my chair.

"Twenty-seconds."

Everyone seemed to hold their breath, willing the deadly warheads to miss us. A more violent shaking caused me to cry out. Hodgson's hand reassuringly covered mine.

"Thirty-seconds."

What sounded like gravel spraying our exterior chattered over our heads and I looked up expecting to see stars and experience my lungs exploding as the atmosphere was sucked out of the cabin.

"Forty-seconds."

Only five-seconds left. I started to believe we would survive the gauntlet of destruction *Athena* laid out before us.

The ship shook violently and the lights went out on the bridge. An emergency alarm went off and the hands of Garrick and Limn flashed across the bright red and green buttons blinking at them in the darkness. A rapid exchange of commands and responses went between the two of them. For the first time since everything began, the calmness had left Limn's voice.

"We are clear of the firing solution," she announced.

"Damage report," shouted Garrick, his hands still flying over the control panel.

"We took a hit along the port engine casing. Power is out. Gravity is out. We are on ancillary power. No loss of pressure," responded Schmaltz.

"Navigation and sensor array down. Life support failing. No response on any critical system. We need somebody down in engineering," said Limn.

"On it!" yelled Schmaltz as both he and Bogdan unstrapped themselves and floated to the exit. As I watched them leave, I remembered the blinking green light in medical. I released myself and drifted towards the door.

"Please remain seated," Garrick ordered. "We're awaiting a complete assessment from engineering."

"Does medical have power?" I asked impatiently.

"We have no power anywhere at the moment Doctor."

"I need to go down there." I resumed my motion to the door and didn't pay any attention to what he yelled after me.

With the power off, nothing prevented the nano-virus from breaching its confinement except for my little engineering kludge with the backup battery. If I couldn't activate it, we would be as dead as the previous crew.

I never faired well in weightless conditions and with the additional disorientation of the darkness, I fought to keep from puking up my last meal. In my rush to escape Garrick's protests, I neglected to find and take something to light my way and so my progress was slower than I planned.

When I reached medical, I opened the access panel and activated the manual override controls to the door. Finding the emergency kit, I recovered the torch and shone the ghostly white beam around the room.

The green LED on the containment chamber was not on, as I feared. Nudging my weightless self towards it, I banged clumsily into the wall, finding difficulty judging my speed in the darkness. Within a few moments, I located and attempted to activate the switch I'd built.

Nothing happened. I desperately flipped it off and on again, at least, a dozen times, with the same result. No backup power. Somewhere along the line, I fucked up. The blood pounded in my ears as I checked the time.

Almost twenty minutes had passed since the power went out. At best, the virus wouldn't breach the dense chamber walls for another forty minutes, but they would be breached. If I couldn't restore power, we were all going to be dead.

I remembered my synthesis process and pushed myself towards that part of the lab. Retrieving the replicated nanites from the unit, I held the container up to the torchlight to reveal the milky fluid supporting the few million of them I managed to build. There was enough for one dose with no guarantee of any match for the nano-virus. But this vial contained the only chance for its recipient. I intended to be that person.

As I prepared the hypospray, images of the dead bodies we found aboard this ship only a few days before flashed into my mind. I placed the injector on my forearm and I hesitated. By doing this I doomed everyone else, with the possible exception of Hodgson, to a horribly painful death. A small voice in the back of my head I normally paid little attention to reminded me of my Hippocratic oath and all the other accompanying bullshit. Altruism was a luxury I couldn't afford. No fair way existed to select who would receive the injection, and I would not leave the decision up to Dunn who would choose himself. If the others knew anything about this possible vaccine, they would all murder each other and me in an attempt to claim the dose for themselves. I wanted to live.

I injected the compound into my arm. The conflicting emotions of relief and guilt battled inside of me. Perhaps I just saved myself; possibly I'd accomplished nothing. I stared at the empty injector and a great shroud of emptiness covered me. My self-serving act certainly hadn't helped anyone else aboard. With a growing sense of remorse, I came to the realization I had to somehow tell the crew about the impending release and, at least, give them a fighting opportunity for survival. If we all put on our pressure suits and boarded the drop ship we stood a realistic chance of escaping with our lives. The walls of the containment unit would keep the nano-virus at bay for a short time.

The comm panel, like everything else, didn't function. My chronometer showed only ten minutes before the first of the nano-viruses breached the chamber seals. Once they entered the general ventilation system, there would be no stopping them. Only one needed to enter a human host and begin to rapidly replicate. There was not enough time to save them all. Schmaltz and Bogdan were in engineering which would take me five minutes to run to and convince them of the danger. Then I would have to inform those on the bridge, including Dunn. I couldn't possibly warn everyone in time. Schmaltz was my friend. That should trump every other consideration.

Memories, unbidden, came flooding back to me. I tried to forget the events of that day, but they would no longer stay behind the wall I built to contain them.

A year and a half after graduation the terror attack changed everything. Every emergency room in the city overflowed with the injured and dying and resources were stretched beyond anything disaster planners ever imagined possible. I'd been called in after just getting off a long night shift and was running on adrenaline.

In a situation like that, people cease to be individuals and become statistical outcomes. I found myself making critical care decisions based on stupid things like likelihood of survival. Professional detachment became the only tool even close to useful in the chaos, an instrument of self-defence.

Only after the situation came under control and things slowed down I realized one of the attack sites was near my own apartment building. Two days later, after a lot of anxiety and searching, I learned what happened to Carlos. He'd been on his way to my place to prepare our dinner, just like always when I finished a string of night shifts. I located him, or what was left of him, unclaimed, in a makeshift morgue. He was an unrecognizable mess and they only identified him at my insistence from a DNA profile on file. Some doctor made the call his wounds were too severe to treat and allowed him to die alone on a gurney in the hallway of the hospital. It was the same kind of decision I made for other victims countless times during the crisis.

After that, I decided professional detachment was a disease of the system and I wanted no part of it. I would not let it determine the fate of people like a lottery. If I couldn't help friends first, then what the hell was the point of being a doctor?

I drifted my way through the medical centre door and into the dark corridor. I pushed hard off the edge of the door to propel myself towards engineering. As I did so, everything became flooded with blinding light. I cried out involuntarily and covered my face, unaware the gravity field had also been restored. A second later I was sprawled on the floor. I remained face down and took inventory of my injuries. My scraped chin, along with both elbows and knees, all suddenly became forgotten as I remembered the bio-sample chamber.

I ran back to medical and peered inside. There across the room happily blinked the green power light on the panel of the bio-containment unit. I checked my chronometer to note it had been out for eighteen minutes. Whatever nano-viruses made their way into the walls were incinerated when the containment field reactivated. They probably weakened the integrity of the seals, but nothing could be done about that. We'd bought ourselves a stay of execution only.

I heard running behind me and turned to see Dunn.

"Is everything okay?"

"Everything came back on with moments to spare."

He eyed the backup containment unit in the corner which contained the three undisturbed virus tubes.

"If we lose power again, we'll be forced to abandon the ship. We won't have the time to move anything from here without being contaminated. I don't want to risk losing what we've gone to all this trouble to recover. I'm ordering Hodgson to put it back aboard our dropship."

I started to tell him about what I used it for, but he interrupted me. "I'm well aware of your little backup plan, Doctor. How well did things work?"

"Umm. I'm afraid it didn't."

Dunn did not appear surprised. "Then the unit is wasting its purpose in here. Mister Skorupa will repair whatever damage you've done and store it aboard the drop ship. If the power fails again, we will abandon ship." He looked around the isolation chamber. "I would feel more comfortable if you would do another viral scan. Just to make sure nothing got out."

"Of course." I wanted to tell him he would already know if

a release happened.

After he left, I inspected my backup connection. While I am not an engineer, neither am I incompetent. I had trouble imagining how I screwed up. I checked the actual battery and found it functioning properly, and the switch seemed to work as well as when I first installed it.

Dunn's knowing about my modifications bothered me, though. I held no doubts he was capable of sabotaging my efforts, but I could not imagine why he would, as doing so placed his life in the same danger as the rest of us.

Deciding I couldn't solve the mystery, I collected the viral detector and began my detailed scan about the room. I would need a couple of hours to complete the entire ship to his satisfaction which suited me. I'd go crazy sitting on the bridge with nothing to do.

I absently rubbed my arm where I impetuously injected myself only a few minutes earlier. I now possessed a third nanite population floating around in my bloodstream. I felt fine; none of the symptoms experienced at the hands of the MP. In the calm following the drama, I worried I may have done something irreversibly stupid.

CHAPTER TWENTY-FIVE

Regis Mundi sat grim-faced at his elaborate desk. It was the only piece of furniture in his palace not of roman design. He rescued the baroque monstrosity early in his career and remained fond of it for many years as it gathered dust in a Terran storage locker. He dreamed of liberating and putting it to use for so long he was willing to forget its anachronistic quality. He hated any sort of waste.

On the desk lay a pad containing the report he had been awaiting. Annoyed Felix Altius was not here to present to him directly, he understood even his exceptionally talented lieutenant remained limited to being in only one place at a time.

The dour man who stood before him swallowed hard.

"I'm aware you're here, Marcus," Mundi did not look up. The disturbing content of the report occupied him. "How did this happen? We pay these people well, do we not? Was he not one of your most trusted agents?"

"I had no reason to doubt his loyalty, Dominus."

"And yet, you have been betrayed." He flung the offending pad skittering across the polished surface. Marcus stood at attention, only his eyes moving to note its crash to the marble floor. He returned his eyes to Mundi who scowled at him.

"Start at the beginning with what you know."

Marcus swallowed hard and took a deep, cleansing breath. "The last reports we received indicated the Terran captain was in pursuit of the *Helios*..."

"I knew that, fool! I want to know how the idiot came to fire upon our ship!"

"Our agent is a low ranking bridge officer, Dominus. He is in no position to interfere with the Captain's orders."

"The person you refer to is NOT our agent. He is a watchdog set in place to keep an eye on the Captain, who is our agent, at least until the moment he decided to act without our permission and attack our vessel."

"Yes, Dominus." Sweat beaded on Marcus' forehead.

"Continue."

"We believe the captain did not fire with the intent of hitting the *Helios*."

Mundi sat forward in his chair and glared at Marcus. "How do we know this?"

"Our...watchdog took the initiative of reviewing the firing solution. It was designed to miss. Our conclusion is the Captain is, somehow, in league with Dunn and Dunn intends to sell the item to the Terrans."

"That is the first intelligent thing I've heard you say. You are dismissed."

Mundi's eyes stalked the nervous man exiting the office. He remained undecided whether to allow Marcus to continue in his service. He would have to defer the matter to Felix, who handled such matters less emotionally.

Now he pondered the avoided question. Should he cut his losses and start over?

Against Felix's council, he granted Agent 324 permission to proceed with the recovery mission. Felix thought it less risky to simply point the Martians to the location of their virus and let them deal with the jurisdictional issues. As pointed out, they were the fools who originally lost it.

But Regis had been desperate to regain the good will squandered so long ago. Return of the virus to its rightful owners would have put them into his debt and allowed him to approach the Triumvirate as an equal, instead of grovelling before them for the crumbs of commerce they offered as an insult. He risked much to gain much, but now he stood to become a fool for being outwitted by his own man.

Agent 324, or Dunn as he now called himself, had exceeded his reputation for byzantine scheming within plans. He was most certainly aware of Felix's interception of his recovery vessel. The death of the new agent, the woman whose name he forgot, proved that.

Dunn made arrangements to sell the prize to the Terrans. That would never be permitted. Failure to deliver was one thing, but allowing the weapon to fall into Terran hands was something the Triumvirate would never forgive him for.

Mundi opened a drawer in the desk and accessed a secret compartment. He pressed the concealed button and the desk's top hummed and cracked open to reveal a quantum communicator. The unwieldy machine was the prototype, and he maintained it as an amusing enhancement to his antique desk. The usefulness of a device permitting instantaneous communication with its counterpart, theoretically located anywhere in the universe contrasted dramatically with the anachronistic piece of furniture it lay hidden within. Such contrasts amused him.

Struggling to recall how to operate the radio, he took a few minutes to adjust the finicky settings to begin the process of linking it to the one in the possession of Felix Altius.

Felix's distinct voice emerged from the speaker. "Agricola, this is Omega Prime. I await your instructions."

Regis Mundi opted to maintain the prototype because it only communicated in audio. He hated the risk of revealing his identity by visual communication and did not trust the assurances of his scientists the signal from the quantum radio would never be intercepted.

"Omega Prime, this is Agricola," Mundi giggled to himself like a small child. He'd invented the code names himself and had eagerly awaited the opportunity to use them. "Our gardener friend has invited himself to the bacchanal." He covered his mouth and sniggered at his clever turn of phrase, confident Felix correctly interpreted his meaning.

"That is unfortunate, but not unexpected. They will, of course, be arriving late."

Mundi thought carefully. He had the option of ending the party completely by destroying the *Helios*. Then while his Martian friends would not get their prize, and he would lose face, at least, the Terrans would not get the virus. But he wasn't ready to call an end to things if there remained a chance Felix could salvage the situation.

"There is a concern the host of the event may want to spend his time with the gardeners instead of fulfilling his obligations. Should that occur, the gardener and the host must be released."

The silence of a long pause filled the air while Felix interpreted Mundi's meaning and composed his own coded response. When the delay extended into the second minute, Mundi began to fear he had been too cryptic. He wanted Felix to destroy the Terran ship and Dunn if he attempted to go to them.

Felix's voice jumped from the speaker.

"The gardener is falling behind. I will watch for his late arrival and prevent him from attending if necessary."

As always, Felix thought things through with a clear head. It only made sense to wait until the Terrans actually posed a threat. Felix seemed to think they would not arrive in time to interfere with his recovery of the virus from Dunn. He was happy to defer to his lieutenant's experience.

"Very well, Omega Prime. I leave you to check the invitations."

"I will keep you apprised. Omega Prime, out."

He regarded the marvellous device before him with satisfaction. He trusted Felix, above all others, to do the right thing. Of course destroying a Terran military vessel was a poor, last resort. Even if Felix made the incident look like an accident, which lay within his capabilities, the very fact Mundi exerted influence in a search ending with the loss of a warship would not play well under any circumstance. The complications from such an action might cripple his business enterprises for decades to come. Felix was right to suggest less drastic measures to begin with.

Satisfied the situation under control, he concealed the radio and rose from his desk. Soon, the treacherous Erik Dunn would be dealt with and all his operatives involved in this mission would breathe their last. Mundi thought it a shame, the need to kill so many. He hated waste.

CHAPTER TWENTY-SIX

Navigating the dark corridors while weightless, while not terribly challenging, had taken them far too long.

Bogdan, who reached engineering before him, accessed the emergency panel by the door.

"Wait! Don't open that door."

"What? Why not?"

Schmaltz floated up next to him and gently pulled his hand away from the controls. "Because if there is a hull breach and you override the safety lock, we'll be sucking vacuum."

"Sorry, Boss."

Schmaltz didn't respond, too engrossed with the readout beside the door.

"The indicator says the pressure is normal inside, but the temperature is slightly elevated."

He turned to his assistant. "Which means?" he cocked an eyebrow as he asked.

"Is this really the time for another teaching moment? What if something critical is damaged or burning?"

"Good question. Think fast, kid. Why aren't we opening the door yet with higher temperatures inside?"

Bogdan slapped his forehead with his palm. "Because something might be on fire."

"And if I open the door, we may be overcome with toxic gas or incinerated by a back draft." He pointed his torch to the service locker. "Go put on emergency gear."

The two engineers needed a little time to don the bulky suits and breathing apparatus. They had trained and drilled for so many times that each of them could have done so in his sleep, but weightlessness made the exercise more challenging than practiced during drills.

Once suited up, they floated before the doors and Bogdan accessed the panel.

"Wait."

"Now what, Boss?"

Schmaltz took held his bare palm to the door for several seconds. He noted Bogdan's furrowed brow. "Another teaching moment, Kid. In an emergency, instruments can fail. I'm feeling how hot it is. An old trick my grand-dad taught me. He worked as a firefighter on Terra."

He put his glove back on and pushed to float away from the door. "It feels normal. I don't think there is a fire in there. Open 'er up."

The blackness swallowed their torchlight as they probed for a clue of what lay beyond the opened door.

"Nothing burning and definitely no hull breach," said Bogdan. "Why is it so hot in here?"

Schmaltz pulled off the mask and hood. "The ventilation fans are down. See what condition the reactor is in."

After the younger man left, Schmaltz played his light over the control console, searching for any kind of damage or scorch marks to indicate a power surge. He noticed nothing on the casing.

Bogdan's voice chimed in his earpiece, "The reactor's on and purring like a kitten. Why isn't the ship getting any juice?"

Schmaltz didn't answer but got to work on the access panel. He shone the light around inside, stopping on something that didn't belong. "Hello, what are you?"

He pushed his upper body into the tight opening to obtain a better view of the foreign equipment. His heart skipped a beat. A device that he didn't recognize was spliced into the main control bus. From what he could guess, it blocked anything flowing to the distribution cluster. Several feeds came out of the unit and led directly to the gravity, light and heat controls as well as those for environmental. A separate connection fed power to the medical facilities. All the lights on the device blinked red except for the green one above the output to medical.

"Bogdan, check if the dedicated line we set up to the med bay is hot." If it wasn't, then nothing kept the isolation field around the virus active.

"It's flowing, Boss. No worries."

He released his held breath and tried to compose himself.

Bogdan returned and said, "That's weird. The reactor is on and power is running to medical, but nowhere else as far as I can tell. You see anything going on in there?"

Schmaltz pulled his head out of the access and explained what he found.

"Who would do something like that?"

"Somebody who wanted to make sure we thought we'd been hit, but didn't want to take any chances with the virus. Who last worked on this?"

"Umm, I think it might have been Hodgson, but I can't be sure. You think maybe he's a spy?"

Schmaltz thought about that prospect for a moment, remembering the warning he gave Mel before they'd left Luna. Somebody was playing with them, but figuring out who would be a challenge, given the sophisticated nature of the device. Hodgson was the most likely suspect at the moment.

"Don't say a word about this to anyone, Kid."

"Not the Captain?"

"Especially not him. Give me some time to figure things out. There's no sense upsetting people until we have proof of who did this."

"Umm, okay, if you say so."

"Our first priority is getting this thing off and putting everything back to normal."

Within twenty minutes, Schmaltz had detached the casing from the unwelcome object and gotten a better idea of how it worked. Ten minutes later, he had it removed.

"The control panel should be live now. Reactivate all downed systems."

With gravity and lights back on, he pulled himself out of the access way and sat on the floor to look at the foreign device. An elegant design, obviously built to purpose by people who knew their way around a ship's power grid, he had never seen anything like it before.

His thoughts were interrupted by a footstep behind him and he realized Bogdan had returned. The kid probably waited for instructions. He lifted his head to speak, but a strong hand covered his mouth. A cool metal object touched his throat and panic rose up at the realization it was a knife.

He slammed his weight backward in an attempt to knock the other man off his feet and avoid the blade, but his assailant kept his balance. Schmaltz fought to turn, desperate to learn the identity of his attacker, but a strong arm held his head immobile.

The sharp edge pushed down and slid sideways, trailing a cold sting followed by excruciating pain. He tried to inhale but blood filled his lungs and he flailed in desperation. Bloody hands releasing their hold on him.

Norbert Schmaltz slumped to the floor. His vision darkened and all he could hear was his slowing pulse in his ears and the desperate gurgling sounds from his open wound. His legs and hands grew numb and then the pain was gone and he drifted as if falling asleep. He wished he could kiss his wife Sarah one last time.

CHAPTER TWENTY-SEVEN

Bogdan's voice and the hammer of his running feet echoed off the corridor walls.

"Doctor! Doctor! Come quick!" He halted in front of me panting heavily, hands covered in blood.

"Oh, my God! What's happened to you?"

He blinked, confused by my question, then followed my gaze to his bloody hands. He held them up, seemingly bewildered and wiped at his cheek, leaving a crimson smear in its wake.

He snapped back to the present. "I'm fine. The Boss has been stabbed. Please hurry!"

He grabbed my arm and pulled me back in the direction of engineering. I retrieved my hand from his and ran after him. We passed Hodgson who watched us go by with shock on his face at the sight of Bogdan. His footfall fell in behind us. I was grateful he didn't waste our time with questions.

Schmaltz lay on his side in a large pool of blood. My training kicked in and I rushed to him, feeling for a pulse and looking for the source of bleeding. My probing hand found the ugly gash across his throat and I knew without any further examination that he had bled out long before my arrival.

I turned him to his back and gazed helplessly upon his pale face, his final agony etched across it. His sightless eyes stared accusingly at me, admonishing me for not coming sooner.

My professional demeanour evaporated in an explosion of grief. I pulled his face into my chest and cradled him while I rocked back and forth. My tears fell to the floor and mixed with his congealing blood.

Who could do this to you? He made friends everywhere he went; never enemies. If ever a disagreement arose between crew mates Schmaltz always diffused the situation, coaxing both parties to reconcile over a friendly drink. He possessed the gentlest of souls and became the most faithful of friends. I would never have lasted as long as I had on *Requiem* without his kind, teasing manner. Any bad mood I had, he cajoled me out of, like the big brother I always wanted. He took care of me, and I loved him for it.

His poor wife, Sarah! Despite all the temptations to stray on a long space journey, Schmaltz never once betrayed her trust in him. He never betrayed anyone.

"Who did this to you?" I muttered into his ear.

"I don't know. I found him like this," said Bogdan, sobbing.

Hodgson released me from the task of probing the young engineer further. I buried my face back into Schmaltz's chest and silently wept while I listened to their exchange.

"How did you find him?"

"I...I asked him something and when he didn't answer I went to speak with him..."

"How were you communicating?" Hodgson gave him no time between questions.

"What?"

"Were you on comms, or linked or talking like we are now?"

"Um, um, on the comm, I think."

"And you got no indication of anything wrong?"

"No, the connection just died. We've been getting interference lately..."

"Where were you?"

"Around the corner. I was checking the power readouts for medical." Annoyance appeared in Bogdan's answers.

"What is that? About ten meters? And when you discovered him he was already dead?"

"Uhh...yeah, I think." I could hear Bogdan losing his composure, grief and anger rising in his voice.

"You think?" Hodgson let his incredulity sink in before he continued, "You were ten meters away? He stopped answering and you took how long before you came looking for him?"

"I...I...don't remember," answered a sobbing Bogdan. "All I know is I found him like that. So much blood everywhere. I rushed to him and tried to turn him. But there was so much blood. I ran to get the doctor. Oh God." His words turned into a wail followed by loud and uncontrolled weeping.

I put my hand gently on Hodgson's boot. "Leave him for a while. He's in no condition."

Hodgson nodded to me and left to investigate another part of engineering, leaving the two of us to our grief. The door opened and footsteps approached. Dunn's voice echoed, "Jesus Christ! What's happened here?"

I looked up to see him staring gape-mouthed at the scene. Something was different about him, but I couldn't place it and didn't care to try. I focussed on his face and studied him. If anyone could commit murder on this ship it was, by his own admission, him. Dunn squatted to examine Schmaltz but I hugged him protectively closer to me. He took my warning and pulled back, redirecting his gaze to the rest of the grizzly scene.

"I take it he found the body?" He indicated the almost catatonic Bogdan who stood far to the side of us. I nodded.

Dunn turned at the sound of Hodgson's return. "You've checked the entire facility?"

"I didn't find any other signs of a struggle. It looks like his attacker surprised him from behind with a knife," said Hodgson.

Dunn regarded Schmaltz once more. "Someone familiar with killing. A single, deep stroke. I don't think we'll discover any hesitation marks on his neck."

Angry that Dunn would think me so stupid as to not suspect him, I shouted at him, "That will be up to me to judge!"

He held up his hands in mock surrender. "Naturally, Doctor, I merely speculate."

"Go speculate somewhere else."

"As you wish." He walked to the door but stopped when I

called out to him.

"Wait. Where have you been since I last saw you? You're wearing a clean shirt." I had finally recalled what was different about him.

"I went to my quarters and changed. I ran into something and tore the other one. Is there a problem with that?"

I glared at him, then turned to Hodgson, who, as far as I was concerned, now directed the investigation. He took my meaning and addressed Dunn. "If I might be able to examine that shirt, Sir?"

Dunn looked from Hodgson to me, amusement on his face. "You want to eliminate me as a suspect, I suppose? Make sure no blood is on the shirt. Of course. Follow me." He walked toward the door.

Hodgson spoke softly to me. "I'll contact Shigeko and have her bring a gurney down here and help you take him to medical."

"Are you coming, Mister Hodgson? You don't want me to disturb the evidence, do you?"

He gave me an apologetic look. "I have to go."

I nodded, not trusting myself to say anything. He followed Dunn out of engineering.

That son-of-a-bitch was far too smug with himself. If he killed poor Schmaltz, he was smart enough not to leave incriminating evidence lying around. Hodgson was being conned but had no choice at the moment.

And Bogdan, the kid was a basket case unless he was a very good actor. I would need to examine him for any defensive wounds Schmaltz may have inflicted on him.

That left Hodgson. Though I found him in the hallway, I had yet to learn where he'd been during the disruption. I'd left him on the bridge when I rushed to medical. If he's the one who murdered Schmaltz, he, like Dunn, acted very cool about it.

My head spun. I needed some time to think things through. I hugged Schmaltz closer to me and kissed his forehead.

Don't worry, my friend. I'll find whoever did this to you and make them pay.

CHAPTER TWENTY-EIGHT

"Please, come in." Erik Dunn made no effort to hide his self-satisfied smile as he invited Dylan Hodgson into his quarters.

The two men stood just inside the doorway to the spacious room. Hodgson showed no emotion and waited for Dunn to address him further.

"I'm gratified that you're taking your role in all this so seriously. You are wise to maintain appearances."

"Yes, Sir."

"Yes, Sir. No, Sir. You don't really say much, do you? That's one of the things I like about you. And yet..." Dunn let the criticism hang. When Hodgson didn't rise to the bait, he continued.

"I suppose, for completeness in this little drama, you should produce some kind of evidence, just to keep our little doct-whore off balance." He grinned at his joke, but Hodgson's face remained unreadable.

"Oh, come on. That was funny."

"I wouldn't know, Sir."

"You're trying to tell me that you don't possess a sense of humour?"

"I don't think you're paying me to have one, Sir."

Dunn sighed and shook his head. He rummaged through his dirty laundry pile and produced a torn shirt. After examination, he decided he could part with it and tossed the garment to Hodgson.

"You were more fun before she came on board. You aren't getting sweet on her, are you?"

"No, Sir, she's just an assignment."

"Right." Dunn sounded unconvinced. He studied his man, not sure he liked the changes in Hodgson's demeanour over the past few weeks. She'd definitely affected him. He was surprised someone so insignificant produced such a profound and complicating influence on an otherwise useful associate.

"You know, any man could fall for her feminine wiles. She is an attractive woman and a satisfying lover. Of course, I'm not telling you anything new, am I?"

Hodgson swallowed hard but maintained his silence and stony face while his eyes followed Dunn about the room.

"Oh, you HAVE fallen for her. Don't be a fool. Yes, feel free to enjoy her while you can, but don't get attached. It's harder to put down a pet you've become fond of."

"Are you speaking from experience, Sir?"

Dunn did not answer the uncharacteristic question. The fact Hodgson was attracted to the doctor like a stupid schoolboy was obvious. For all his attributes as a soldier, Hodgson displayed a discomforting sentimentality.

"You're not going to have a problem doing what is required, are you?"

Hodgson turned his head and his gaze bored into Dunn. "No, Sir."

Dunn watched him examine the torn shirt and doubt began to creep into his mind. He had vetted him carefully, as he did all his agents, but spies and traitors occasionally slipped in. When discovered, Dunn had no compunction about dealing with them. He had been more sure about Hodgson than most. Perhaps that should have been a flag. Still, he gave no reason to believe in his disloyalty—yet.

Dunn resolved to keep a closer eye on the man, especially as the critical juncture of this mission approached. He would like to be able to retain one good agent through this, but was prepared to eliminate everyone if required.

"You'd better get on with the rest of your 'investigation'."

"Yes, Sir." Hodgson turned on his heel and marched straight-backed out of the door, his military training on full display.

Dunn sat on the edge of the unmade bed. All the consideration over Hodgson's loyalty left a sour taste in his own mouth. Of all the sins that another might perpetrate on him, he considered betrayal to be the least forgivable. Perhaps, he mused, that was why his intended actions bothered him to the degree they did.

Dunn's plans to betray Regis Mundi did not develop in a sudden flash of inspiration. They started as a germ of a concept, years before when an opportunity arose on a mission. He'd quashed the thought as fast as it sprang into being, or believed so until the notion resurfaced again on another assignment. After four or five visits to the door of his imagination, he gave serious consideration to something he, up until that time, considered unthinkable.

The concept grew in his mind like a noxious weed. He would root it out and it would re-grow, stronger and more widespread in his imaginings, seeming to feed off his resistance. He thought he would deal with the demon directly. He gave the notion of betrayal a thorough exploration and made a business case for it as an academic exercise. He hoped that by exposing the weed to the light of reason would prove its foolishness and he might finally rid himself of it. The effort failed miserably.

Instead, he saw a legitimate argument existed for the betrayal of his patron under the right circumstances. Horrified at discovering a way to justify the sin he always considered mortal, he tried to bury the idea as deeply as possible and refused to give it any more active thought. But once released, there was no putting the jinn back, and Dunn soon found himself actively examining every opportunity for betrayal's profitability.

Now he stood on the shore of the Rubicon of his conscience. Time remained for him to abort everything and loyally complete the assignment, but the opportunity was fast passing. Too many things were in motion to easily go back. Plans within plans and contingencies for plans were his trademark and he had outdone himself this time. This mission demonstrated some of his most intricately conceived work. It would be a shame to abandon the project because of scruples. With an effort, he might still do so. Once this ship entered solar orbit, however, his decision must be made.

He rose from the bed and retrieved his bag with the secret compartment. He removed the remote control unit for their original vessel, the *Fortuna*. The engineer, Schmaltz, had been talented and impressed him with the sophistication of the programming put into the device. A great pity he needed to be killed, and perhaps the youngster had acted too rashly. Still, nothing was to be done about it now. He was grateful for the elimination of one variable from the equation with the death of Schmaltz. Better for his own man to be in charge of what happened in engineering.

His hand hesitated over the interface as he considered the consequences. If he activated the pre-programmed sequence, he would set into play unstoppable events. He knew his own people on *Victorem* had been replaced by Mundi's. It would be difficult to justify keeping the ship a secret from his patron, but he was confident he would still salvage their relationship if he kept the planned rendezvous.

Of course, there would still be the idiot Captain of the *Athena* to deal with. Buying him off did not prove any challenge. The man didn't even know how to properly negotiate and had settled for the opportunity to recover the abandoned *Helios* and a sample of the virus. Eliminating him to assure his silence would be simple.

Or, he could follow through with his plan and instruct the *Fortuna* to intercept the *Helios*. A heavily armed warship would be a definite asset if he chose to betray Mundi. Then the only decision remaining would be how many, if any, of this crew he would take with him.

His finger traced the hard outer edge of the thin control unit. No matter which way he looked at the situation, the

Fortuna might be the most valuable piece on the board. He turned on the device and entered the command.

His decision made, he now needed to ensure that there were no witnesses to his departure.

CHAPTER TWENTY-NINE

We gently laid Schmalz on an examining table in medical.

"Do you want me to stay with you for a bit?" asked Shigeko.

"No, thanks. I think I just prefer to be alone."

Before she got to the door I called after her. "What happened on the bridge after I left?"

"Garrick got pretty mad at you for ignoring him. Dunn offered to retrieve you and followed."

I frowned. "What about Hodgson?"

"He left right after the gravity came on. Garrick sent him to find out why you and Dunn weren't answering."

I thanked her. I was glad for her answers but gladder for her departure. I didn't trust her more than the rest of them. The only two people I knew anything about were Schmaltz and myself. Everyone else could be in this with Dunn. Any of them might be Schmaltz's murderer and I was most likely the next on their list.

My whole body shivered and my stomach insisted it turn over and empty itself. I needed a distraction, so decided to perform the medical examination on Schmaltz. Probably not the smartest thing for me, but I wanted to do something for him. A good stiff drink would have helped, but that wouldn't be wise, even if I managed to locate any booze aboard Garrick's ship.

I threw a sheet over Schmaltz's face and forced myself to take deep, slow breaths. My pulse raced and a thousand confusing thoughts fought at once for my attention. I experienced similar emotions when I looked after my first patient on the day of the terror attack, the day that claimed Carlos.

The victim was a kid, barely four years old, his hips and legs crushed by falling debris. I only found the courage to work on him by pushing my emotion into the backseat. I desperately wanted that to happen again. I closed my eyes and placed myself back in the chaos of that emergency room. I tried to imagine the bloody metallic odours and nauseating stench of charred flesh and listened hard for the screams of dying and injured people. Strangely, once the images formed in my mind, I became calm enough to begin my examination of Schmaltz.

I cleaned and examined the wound to his neck. That bastard Dunn was correct. A solitary, deep laceration cut into the trachea and severed the carotid and jugular. The killer required a lot of strength and skill to subdue a man of Schmaltz's size while dealing this killing blow with a single stroke, eliminating Shigeko from the list of suspects.

No other marks or wounds appeared on the body. The murder had been fast and professional, but there would have been a huge amount of blood. The murderer would not avoid getting covered. Bogdan was the only person with blood on him, but that would also result from trying to help Schmaltz, as he claimed.

Physically, the young man didn't impress. Taller than Schmaltz by ten centimetres, he possessed a thin, wiry build. Possibly, with training, he might be able to pull it off. He certainly appeared to be in shock, but perhaps he was a good actor.

Dunn, of course, remained the prime suspect. His change of clothes gave me the biggest reason to convict him. Even if Hodgson found a clean, torn shirt in his quarters, there's nothing to say that Dunn didn't plant it as part of an alibi, though I didn't understand why he needed one. If the crew worked for him, he could act with impunity and everyone would go along with him, so maybe he acted alone. A possibility remained Dunn told the truth, but I would never want to accept that.

Garrick was big and strong enough to murder, but Shigeko told me he stayed with her the entire time.

What about Hodgson? Where did he go after the power outage? I'd left him on the bridge and hadn't seen him again until he followed Bogdan and me to engineering. He had no blood on him, but possibly he slipped away and changed before Bogdan found the body.

My brain spun. I covered up Schmaltz again. The door to medical opened and Hodgson entered, grim. He placed a long double edged knife on the counter and stepped back without saying anything. I regarded the weapon from a safe distance, not wishing to touch it. The handle, hilt and blade were coated with dried blood.

"Where did you find it?"

"In engineering."

I looked at him quizzically, and he quickly added, "Bogdan was with me when I found it."

"And now your fingerprints are all over it." I frowned at him.

He shook his head and held up the rag he'd brought the knife in. "Mel, I don't know how to lift fingerprints, do you?"

My shoulders slumped. Then I straightened up again and asked, "What about Dunn's shirt?"

"He still thinks I'm his man. He provided a clean, torn shirt."

"But you think he's guilty?" It was more of a plea than a question.

Hodgson nodded. He changed the topic. "How are you doing?"

"I'm a wreck. Why did he need to kill Schmaltz?"

"The boy could have been the killer. We have no proof that it was Dunn directly..."

"Yes, it was! You fucking well know that. He may not have cut Schmaltz's throat, but it happened on his orders." I glared at him, ready to tear him apart. "Are you Dunn's man? Where the hell were you when all this came down?"

"Me? Nowhere near engineering."

"Stop evading."

"After the gravity and lights came on, I left to locate Dunn."

"Not me?"

"What?"

"Garrick didn't tell you to learn why I didn't answer his calls? Shigeko told me. So why didn't you do it? Why didn't you come look for me? Is it because you were helping Dunn kill my friend?"

I backed up to the counter and reached behind me, making sure the knife behind my back remained within my reach. Hodgson watched every movement of mine.

"I didn't go looking for you. That is true."

"So you went to find Dunn and helped him, then?"

"No, I didn't find him either. I went to his quarters and he wasn't there."

"Why did you go there?"

"I needed to search them."

"What the fuck are you talking about?"

He stepped towards me. I picked up the bloody knife and pointed it at him. He raised his hands in surrender and retreated. "Please try to calm yourself, Mel. I'm with you in this."

"The hell you are. You're working for him."

"I don't work for Dunn. I work for Mars."

CHAPTER THIRTY

"Bullshit." I threatened Hodgson with the knife I pretended I knew how to use but lost my resolve at his unexpected revelation.

"I swear I'm telling the truth."

"Prove it." The larger portion of me didn't want to believe anything I heard, but that part was shrinking rapidly.

He raised his eyebrow at me. "Prove you're a doctor."

"I'm the one holding the knife, asshole." I again waved the blade around like an ignorant child.

"You're going to hurt yourself if you don't calm down. Put it down and let me explain. If you don't like what I say, I'll let you cut my throat." He glanced at Schmaltz's body on the examining table.

The sight of Schmaltz overwhelmed me and my tears exploded from me like a volcanic eruption. I dropped my would be weapon and fell to my knees with my hands over my face, sobbing like the pain of my loss was going to kill me.

Strong, gentle hands took me by the shoulders and helped me to a seat. Hodgson brought me a glass of water, then pulled up the other chair to sit knee to knee with me and patiently waited for my grief to subside.

"That was an asshole thing to say to me." I sniffled.

"I'm sorry, I just couldn't disarm you without hurting you." He offered me the knife, handle first. "Hang on to this if you don't trust me. Just, please, listen to me?"

I waved it away. He was bigger, stronger and more skilled than I. He could easily overcome me and end my life with minimal effort.

"I am an agent for the Martian Governing Council." He indicated the isolation chamber at the other side of the room. "I have been on the trail of that nano-virus since it was stolen from our research facility two years ago."

"Who took it?"

"We don't know. It dropped off the grid until last year when intelligence surfaced indicating Terra had acquired a special ship to study it. This one."

"Okay, that could be an explanation for your own nanites."

Hodgson smiled. "Yes, as you've determined, mine are not exact antigens because the original virus and all the specs vanished along with the all the backup data. Our scientists only had incomplete notes available to try again."

"They came close, from what I could tell."

"Yeah, but there is no prize for second place. It's a doomsday weapon, Mel, and I need to recover or destroy it before it falls into the wrong hands."

"Why did Mars build a doomsday weapon? Who did they plan to use it against?"

"Terra."

I stared at him, stunned into silence. What he proposed was monumentally absurd.

"More bullshit," I said.

"I know it's not something easy to believe, but it is true. There is an influential faction which believes our terraforming efforts are doomed to fail, or at least not succeed for several thousand years. That version of things is significantly different from the bill of goods sold to the general populace who believe Mars will be the second Eden in another few generations."

"Is that true? Will terraforming take thousands of years?"

"I'm not a scientist. All I know is if the belief becomes widespread, Martian society will collapse."

"Why?"

"A small elite lives in the orbiting cities protected from

radiation and living in Terran normal gravity. The rest of the populace, 35 million, are in underground habitats. Neither environment is designed to support a population growth of more than five generations. The original idea was for Mars to sustain human life within a couple of centuries and we would live on the transformed planet long before our infrastructure failed."

"So why not build more habitats and space stations?"

"The Terran embargo is the biggest reason. Since they lost control of Luna, they've been more hardline in their relations with Mars. All trade in graviton tech is now restricted, as well as the sophisticated medical treatments available to long-term Lunar residents which prevent the genetic drift we're experiencing. If we're to survive as a society, let alone a species, we desperately need those technologies since we can't produce them ourselves."

"How does the bio-weapon figure in all this?"

"The old government believed our only hope was to abandon the terraforming effort and return to Terra en masse."

"With a Terran population of 500 billion people there'd be nowhere to put them." As I said this, the penny dropped and I understood. "It comes down to you or them?"

He nodded. "Martians would become the refugee trash of the solar system. With nowhere to put us on Terra, we would be confined to Mars. Our home would become a planet sized concentration camp. The old regime determined that to save our own people, a place needed to be made. The nano-virus would kill most of the humans on Terra, making room for a mass migration of Martians."

"You mean an invasion."

"Semantics, I suppose. The plan is monstrous no matter how you couch it. The people who commissioned the virus were deposed, but while in power, they put into play plans for a first strike against Terra."

"What would end the embargo? Governments change. Surely if not the current Terran regime, a future one might be amenable to negotiation on humanitarian grounds?"

"The stakes are high for the Terrans as well. Their growing population needs increasing access to the mineral resources controlled by Mars in the asteroid belt. A terraformed fourth planet is an ideal place for the excess children of Earth in a few thousand years, relieving the overpopulation problem. Terra wants to control Mars. Martians want autonomy."

"So everything comes down to a pissing contest? Unbelievable!" I regarded Hodgson, who had dispassionately recited all the facts like a professor describing an amoeba. "Where do you stand in all this?"

"There is still a chance the millennialists are wrong. Regardless, I'll be long dead by the time either scenario is proved true. I think I agree with you and a solution can be worked out between the two worlds. That's only going to happen if this doomsday weapon is removed from the table."

"And you share this view with your current leaders?"

"Politicians are...fluid. Publicly, the knowledge of the terraforming controversy is restricted to a few members of the elite, for the obvious reason its revelation would have on the populace."

"You mean the people might not look too kindly on them?"

He smiled. "Something like that."

"So, to maintain civil order, you infiltrated Dunn's organization to gain access to this mission?"

"Not just civil order, but our survival. If Terra ever discovers the nature of this weapon, I shudder to think what their military response will be."

"What is Dunn's roll in all of this?"

"Our network flagged him as a key player and I wormed my way into his inner circle. His assignment was to recover the nano-virus for Rego Corporation, which in itself would not have been a bad scenario. Regis Mundi is desperate to ingratiate himself with certain parties on Mars. He intends to return the lost sample and get back into favour with them."

"Then why not simply let Dunn complete his mission?"

"Yes, well, as you might guess, Erik Dunn is an ambitious

man. He is also not above betraying his patron for a large enough prize. He plans to steal the nano-virus for himself, presumably to sell to the highest bidder."

"So you just buy it from him. Duh?"

Hodgson regarded me like I was the class dunce. "He doesn't want money. He wants power, and possessing this virus would make him the most powerful person in the system. He would deal it to multiple parties. There is nothing better for business than conflict, and he would find a way to profit, even from a war of armageddon. He is ruthless, resourceful, with no conscience and would happily serve as the first horseman of the apocalypse for what he would gain. He killed your friend and is behind the deaths of countless others. What happens to him is not my assignment and I'm supposed to be able to keep a distance from my feelings, but he makes my soul sick and I mean to see him dead before this mission is completed."

"Get in line behind me. I'm presuming you have a plan?"

"I had one. Now I'm improvising, but I think Dunn is too."

"Can you tell me or is it above my pay grade?"

He grinned at me. "Dunn's original mandate was simple. Retrieve the nano-virus and return to Luna in the *Fortuna*. However, I found out he commissioned a second ship to rendezvous with. He planned to kill this crew and take the virus, leaving Mundi with a stolen Terran vessel to explain. We infiltrated the secondary craft intending to intercept this one and recover the nano-weapon."

"But something went wrong, I'm guessing."

"I lost contact with my people on *Victorem*, the other ship. I think Mundi learned Dunn's plans and replaced the crew with his own people. Worse, I think Dunn knows and is scrambling for another escape plan. I believe he's using the Terrans to that end."

"If that is the case, why did they fire missiles at us?"

"If a Terran warship was really shooting to hit us, they would have done so. There was no damage in engineering from the barrage. We were never struck."

"A smokescreen? Why?"

"First, I believe Dunn plans to double-cross his own people on this vessel; Garrick, Limn, myself. I think the boy is his as well, especially after the death of your friend. Dunn needed an excuse to move the sealed samples in medical to the drop ship, as a precaution, without arousing undue suspicion among his people."

"Well, his little plan almost killed us all. If the power hadn't come back on, the released virus in the chamber would have flooded the air system."

"I'm afraid he was counting on that belief. The reality is, the power to medical was never interrupted."

"How would you know?"

"Remember the day I bumped my head? You surprised me while I was installing a specialized shunt. It was designed to interrupt all power to most systems, but still maintain an active, undetected flow to any chosen location, in this case, medical and the isolation field."

"Why would you install something like that?"

"All part of my original plan. When the *Victorem* got within docking range, I would have deactivated gravity and general life support so my people could board and take control without releasing the virus.

"Someone in engineering, probably Bogdan, discovered my device and Dunn activated it when the Terrans shot around us, giving the impression we'd been hit and the power to medical failed."

"And Schmaltz found it by accident and was killed?"

"I believe so. I'm sorry for my part in his death. I never intended any of you to die in this operation."

"A good-hearted spy? Forgive me if I don't trust your sincerity."

Hodgson had no reply for me.

I asked him, "So, what is Dunn's new plan?"

"That is what I was trying to discover by searching his quarters. I was looking for some type of communications device or another clue, but I couldn't find anything. My best guess is he's going to make an escape in the drop ship, but he'll need to act before we get too close to orbit around the sun. Garrick's current flight plan puts us in closer than *Athena* can match, but the shuttle can't survive in that kind of heat and radiation."

"Do you think he's made a deal with the Terran Captain? Perhaps he plans on jumping ship and getting picked up by them. It would explain why they didn't hit us."

"It would. But it would also mean he runs a good chance of losing control of the virus to the Terrans. I don't think he would do that."

"Why are you telling me all this, Hodgson? What makes you think I won't betray you to Dunn and risk he'll let me go?"

He glanced at Schmaltz, then turned back to me. "I think we both realize how that would turn out. I read your file and I know how you ended up here. He manipulated you and it is pretty clear to me, if not you, he intends to dispose of you when your usefulness is done."

Hodgson was right, of course. I had no illusions Dunn would not kill me. I saw it in his eyes when I thought I'd outsmarted him at the start of all this. He never had any intention of letting me live long enough to collect.

"How can I help?"

"Keep your eyes and ears open. Learn what you can. Maybe you can play the kid. I caught him in some inconsistencies in his story. He's Dunn's man, and while I think he was your friend's killer, I don't think he's an experienced one and it's eating at him. Maybe he'll let something slip if you work him the right way."

"If there's one thing I'm good at it's working a man. I'll find out what I can."

He squeezed my hand to reassure me, then walked towards the exit.

"I have some more things to check. Be careful. Trust no one."

I smiled at him before I replied, "I don't trust anyone. I don't trust you either, just to be upfront about it. But your's is the best deal I've been offered."

He nodded, a sad look on his face.
"Fair enough."

CHAPTER THIRTY-ONE

I did not want to spend my time in the medical centre so I returned to my cabin I had seen little of recently. The sheets were still a rumpled mess from my romp between them with Hodgson.

I made up the bed and decided to indulge in a hot shower. With all the stress of the previous few days accumulated, I couldn't stand my own smell for one minute longer.

I emerged to the sound of my door chime. Wrapped in a towel, I answered the door and immediately regretted my casual attire. Bogdan Skorupa stood at the door. He turned two shades of red and averted his eyes from my dripping self.

"No sisters?" I indicated for him to sit on my bed since I had no chair.

He perched himself awkwardly on the side and inspected everything around him. "No, I am an only child."

"Well, there's nothing to be embarrassed about. I'm completely covered. You'll see more on the beach. Try looking at my eyes if the towel makes you nervous."

He continued to distract himself by playing with my hairbrush on the bedside table. I toyed with the idea of telling him who last occupied that side of the bed.

"Bogdan, why are you here?"

He stared at me, confusion all over his face."You left me a message."

"And I told you it was urgent. Sorry, I forgot."

"I can come back later..."

"No, it's okay. I won't take long. I just have a question for you."

He fidgeted nervously while trying to maintain eye contact. I wondered what he imagined I might ask. "Bogdan, what was Schmaltz doing just before his death?"

He swallowed and studied the floor. Dark spots began to form in his armpits. "Checking the feeds."

"Did he discover anything unusual? Anything someone didn't want him to?"

"What are you talking about?" He squirmed and wrung his hands absently.

"What did he find?"

"I...I'm not sure. He never got a chance to tell me. He asked me to confirm the flow to medical and...he got killed. At first, I thought he touched an exposed contact, but...I saw all the blood." The pitch of his voice rose higher with every word. I worried he might piss himself.

"So, as far as you could tell, what shut off the power?"

"A surge, I think."

"Did it happen when *Athena's* missiles struck us?"

Clearly not the question he anticipated, he frowned first. "It blew out when we were shot at, but not because we were hit. The *Athena* never touched us. There was no structural damage or anything."

"What happened?"

"Some kind of power pulse. I don't know much else. The Boss fixed the problem."

"Who had access to that panel?"

"Well, the last was Mister Schmaltz..." His voice cracked and his eyes teared up. He looked away while he tried to compose himself, faced me again and continued. "The only other person who ever accessed it was Hodgson."

His eyes widened with an epiphany. "Do you think he had something to do with the sabotage?"

"What sabotage?"

"I...I meant murder."

This kid was no professional killer. If I could spook him he was more of a liability to Dunn than an asset. But he lied, and I needed to know why.

"Did you examine the panel Schmaltz worked on?"

"Umm...no." *A lie.*

A crushing weight squeezed my chest. I realized at this moment I'd wanted to suspect Hodgson of being anything other than what he claimed. The accumulating evidence forced me to accept a different conclusion. Bogdan's involvement in Schmaltz's death became ridiculously obvious. I required all my self-control to not reach out and scratch the little shit's eyes out.

He was not smart enough to be acting on his own. Dunn worked him and most likely set him up to take the fall for the murder to distract us from his real goal. With the virus now aboard the drop ship, Dunn would make his final play soon. I hoped Bogdan didn't serve any further use for him. In any case, he couldn't be trusted.

We sat silently for a moment. He fidgeted and avoided eye contact. Under other circumstances, his behaviour would have been endearing.

"Did you move the portable containment unit to the drop ship yet?" I asked.

He exhaled and visibly relaxed, apparently glad for the change of topic. "Yes, I finished this afternoon."

"That didn't take very long," I said.

"We tied it into the shuttle's grid as an additional layer of power continuity," said Bogdan. "Its design didn't provide for it, but your modifications gave me the idea."

"So my kludge was okay?"

"I couldn't have come up with a better way to do it."

"Why didn't it work?"

"It worked fine."

I began to doubt myself. *Did I flip the switch?* Possibly in the panic of the moment, I might have only thought I did. It would be a first. I was good in a crisis. Maybe my own life being on the line made the difference.

The mystery of my malfunctioning modifications also presented another confirmation of Hodgson's theory. If Dunn somehow messed with the portable unit to make everything look like the backup power failed, fewer arguments would occur on my part when he ordered it moved to the shuttle.

"Bogdan."

"Yes, Doctor?"

"Do you want to watch me get dressed?"

"Yes...I mean no, ma'am...I mean...What?"

"I want to get dressed now. You should go."

"Oh! I... Yes, of course. Sorry, I should go."

"Good idea." I accompanied him to the door as he backed towards it.

"It was a pleasure to see you, Doctor." He blushed. "No, not you. Not a pleasure. No. That's not what I mean..."

I gently pressed on his chest until he stepped into the hallway. "Thank you. You were most helpful."

I watched Bogdan's back as he hurried to engineering. Catching movement out of the corner of my eye, I turned to the sight of Hodgson staring gape-mouthed at the scene in front of my door. I smiled at him, slipped off the towel and went back inside my quarters.

CHAPTER THIRTY-TWO

Freshly showered and dressed, I went to the mess hall before we were all called to the bridge for our orbital approach. Shigeko and Dunn sat together, eating but not conversing. I ordered a hot tray from the dispenser and took a table across the room, not wanting to interrupt their riveting conversation.

Hodgson entered and got himself a cup of coffee. He nodded to the others, then came to sit with me. Recovered from his dumbfounded look in the hallway, he winked. "So. Bogdan, huh?".

"I had a leak in my shower."

"I understand." He took a sip from his steaming mug and watched me over its edge. The twinkle remained in his eye.

"Are you not cooking for your boss anymore?" I nodded towards Dunn, who now exited the room with Limn.

"What? No, just a one-off thing. He found out about my little adventure in the Admiral's service and decided he wanted to impress you."

"You are a man of many hidden talents, Mister Hodgson."

"So I'm told." He glanced around the room, ensuring we were alone. "Dunn is planning his move to happen soon. He and Garrick have been conspiring on the bridge."

"What do they have planned? We're almost in solar orbit. He hasn't much time"

He shrugged. "With him, the plan is probably as elaborate as you can imagine. Do yourself a favour and ensure your pressure suit is always handy and prepped. If the power fails again, medical won't be overlooked. The likely protocol will be an emergency depressurization to try to evacuate the bugs."

I nodded. "The virus can't survive in a vacuum. But a purge would never get rid of the ones still transiting the wall of the isolation chamber."

"Make sure about your pressure suit, Mel. It's important."

"You act like they aren't going to give us any warning."

"They haven't told anyone. I don't think they were planning on doing so either."

"Do you think Shigeko knows? Bogdan?"

"I'm not sure about Limn. I don't trust her. Bogdan said he wasn't told anything about such a protocol, but he's a shitty liar. I asked him after he...fixed your shower." He smirked, despite the seriousness of the topic.

"How does he plan to do it?"

"It would be from engineering. I need to sneak in there and look for what he can do."

"Won't he use your device again?"

"It won't accomplish what he needs. I think he'll opt for explosives and create a catastrophic systems failure."

"Where would he get those?"

"This is a big ship, Mel, and he's a resourceful guy. I'm sure he made some provision for them before we left Luna."

"Bogdan will be watching you."

"I'll think of something to keep him occupied." He reached across the table and took my hand in his. "If it comes down to the virus being released, vacuum or not, *Victorem* will destroy this ship. They can't risk any chance of Terra obtaining even a small sample of it."

My hands were freezing and I savoured the warmth of his on top of mine. "Why are you trusting me with this? Aren't you breaking a dozen spy rules or something?"

"Just because I don't want to marry you doesn't mean I want to see any harm come to you, Mel."

"You don't want to marry me after I gave you my body? I'm crushed. I must be losing my edge."

"I'm being serious. What I'm trying to say is I owe it to you."

"What do you owe me? I have treated you pretty poorly since I met you. Though, admittedly, up until a short time ago I thought you were Dunn's hitman."

He smiled and squeezed my hand. "I accessed your file."

"If you had access to Dunn's file about me..." I blushed. I didn't actively share my colourful past with people, but I deny it if somebody knew. Discussing it with Hodgson, however, was proving uncomfortable.

"Charlie Wong had info on you which he never passed on to Dunn."

"Charlie? How...?"

"I'm a spy, remember? I went through the records of everyone connected with this op. Your name kept coming up, but not much of what Dunn was given went further back than a year. The more extensive data Wong held on you came from Rego Corp, and they only gave him part of what they have."

"The corporation keeps a file on me?" My mouth was parched. I knew Dunn and Charlie set me up and were likely behind all the shenanigans on Luna, but I thought that was the extent of what might be in any file. What he now revealed was downright creepy.

"What kind of information do these files contain?" I could barely hear my own voice.

"It was pretty complete. From what I could tell, they've been tracking you since you were born."

"The fucking corporation has tracked me for my entire life? Why? What did it say?" In all the years I sold my body for money, I never once felt as violated as I did in that moment.

"It contains the name of your mother, where you lived, when you left home, your criminal activities, your juvenile record. There are school reports, IQ tests, aptitude assessments, psych profiles, med records..." He noticed my discomfort and stopped though his expression told me there was more.

I sat frozen in my chair and my heart pounded wildly. My

life had just been ripped open and my entire sordid history laid out for Hodgson to pick through. I tried to swallow the lump in my throat and croaked, "What else?"

"You're sure about this?" he asked.

I nodded and he grabbed my hand and squeezed it before he continued.

"It names your benefactor."

"Walter Bickell," I recalled the kind face of the wealthy, much older client who took an interest in me. He pulled some strings, allowing me to write and pass the entrance exams to medical school. He paid for everything I needed and sponsored me until I graduated. We met once a year when he would join me for coffee and check up on me. After graduation, I never heard from him again and he never left me a way to contact him.

"Yes, but his real name is Talus Varr."

"What?" The man I always considered to be my 'fairy godmother' turned out to be a fraud? I would not have believed it except for the other revelations. "Does the file say anything about where he is now?"

"No, it only named him and listed the funds he passed on to you."

The tears ran down my cheeks as I stared at the wall. I glanced down to see my nails digging into Hodgson's hand. I let go to see I'd drawn blood. "Oh, I'm so sorry..."

"Don't worry about it." Hodgson seemed to know doing nothing was the best thing for me. He sat quietly, held my hand and gave me the time to process everything. His face showed pain and regret though I didn't blame him for anything.

"Is there more?" I wiped my eyes, sure I could produce no more tears.

He hesitated. "Yes."

"Is it bad too?"

He nodded. "Worse."

I thought I had ridden out the worst part of what Hodgson might tell me, but the anticipation of news more disturbing than what I'd already learned panicked me. I had trouble catching my breath. I've never been punched in the stomach, but I'm sure it would come close to what I experienced. I took a moment to compose myself, then asked him to tell me.

"The file documents Carlos Montoya and is pretty complete; birth, education, military service..."

"What are you talking about? Carlos never served in the military."

"I'm afraid he did. He served in a Terran black ops group. How Rego got this information is beyond me, but I cross-referenced the data with my own sources and confirmed it. He was active, right up to his disappearance."

"He died. I identified his body and they confirmed the DNA profile."

Hodgson shook his head as I spoke.

"He DIED! He was killed in a terror attack just before the war ended. I saw his body, dammit!"

"You saw a mangled body with an associated DNA profile matching the one in his file."

Suddenly I remembered what Dunn requested of me on the day he came aboard the ship. He wanted me to place his DNA profile into the real Erik Dunn's medical record. Dunn couldn't be the first person to try the trick.

"You mean to say somebody gave Carlos' DNA profile to the corpse I identified?"

"Yes."

"Where did he go?" I looked at Hodgson and new tears poured from my eyes. "Was his name even Carlos?" I sobbed into his shoulder. I was an empty shell. I owned nothing about my life. It had been manipulated since the day of my birth and I had no understanding of why. Who the hell was I to garner such interest?

He softly spoke into my ear as he hugged me, "The file doesn't contain any more information about him after that. I'm so sorry."

After a long time, I ran out of tears but continued to cling to Hodgson. He was literally the only real person left in my life, and he was a spy with as many secrets as I apparently had.

"Thank you for telling me."

"You deserved to know."

I released him from my grasp and looked in his eyes. "I don't really have my own life, do I?"

"You always had a life, Mel. Now you've finally been given the opportunity to claim it for yourself."

"I suppose you're right. Maybe I can start by helping us get out of this mess. There are some people who owe me an explanation when all this is over."

CHAPTER THIRTY-THREE

Erik Dunn contemplated the small, open container before him. Inside sat, six deceptively harmless looking, wafer-thin disks, each the size of one of the ancient Roman coins in Regis Mundi's private collection. Collectively they were capable of destroying half the ship. They only needed the attachment of the receiver modules which would accept the detonation command. Those six, palm-sized units lay neatly aligned on the desk beside the unassuming container.

Smuggling the explosives aboard did not prove difficult. Finding a suitable place to hide them was more challenging. The growing strength of magnetic field as they approached the Sun also created a bigger problem than he accounted for. He needed a shielded location to prevent the wafers' molecular structure from acquiring a preferred alignment, otherwise, the wafers would be rendered useless. The only sufficiently protected part of the vessel was the medical centre.

Before he departed the mess, Hodgson and Destin began what looked to become an intimate conversation, providing him with the perfect opportunity. He'd hidden the container inside what he thought would be a little-used corner of the facility prior to the doctor's arrival aboard ship. Fortunately, the box and its contents remained undisturbed.

Her busy nature in medical concerned him and he worried she might stumble across it. He certainly didn't foresee her attempt to use the portable isolation chamber's power as an auxiliary backup. Her brilliant thinking almost disrupted his plans. If he hadn't spotted and sabotaged her modifications before the staged hit from Athena, things would be more complicated than at present.

Of all the people on the ship, Dunn trusted Melanie Destin the least when he really needed to be able to trust her implicitly. The situation was his own fault. Against his better judgement, he assumed the identity of her client, Jake Matthiews, thinking it would be fun seeing the final consummation of his efforts to recruit her. He originally hoped she would have appreciated the cleverness of his plan and admire him as a fellow confidence artist; a kindred spirit. He came to regret his lapse more than once during the current mission. She demonstrated herself different from the person her file painted her to be, an issue he would take up with Charlie Wong at some point in the future. His misjudgment of Melanie Destin's response to him was his worst mistake in years. He hoped to put it permanently behind him in a few short hours.

The unforeseen elimination of the chief engineer would prove to be beneficial now. Bogdan could deploy the explosives in the most effective locations throughout engineering, ensuring the precise damage he required to assist his escape. The timing would need to be exact and he would have little room for error, but he had operated under more difficult circumstances on previous assignments. The worst part remained the nature of the prize. One misstep in handling the virus and he would die along with everyone else. Having the doctor fully allied with him would have reduced that risk and ensured her survival.

Dunn thought long and hard about who, if anyone, he would take with him aboard the drop ship. Garrick, at one time, occupied the top of the list, having proven himself in the past as a skilled and innovative commander. His disappointing performance on this particular assignment changed his fortunes. Of course, this was Dunn's first opportunity to observe the Captain directly. His prior impressions relied on post-operational reports written by others.

Perhaps starting over would be good for him. His own network demonstrated itself as flawed and needing to be rebuilt. The disappointing betrayal by Kiri Mason brought that home to him more than any of the other, far too numerous surprises of this mission.

He never considered including Limn. She was Garrick's choice for a first officer and his fate sealed hers.

Bogdan presented an intriguing case. He had been included on the recommendation of Charlie Wong, who also brought him Destin and Schmaltz. With the unexpected deaths of the original doctor and chief engineer, finding the ideal candidates proved a near impossibility. Dunn had been skeptical, but open to Wong's idea to recruit them under deceptive conditions. He made a strong case, especially, for the doctor's eventual compliance, and argued his own man, Skorupa, could keep the engineer in check. Wong would have much to explain before his death.

Still, the young man demonstrated a degree of original thinking and personal strength, if not good judgement, in the killing of Schmaltz. Bogdan Skorupa's convincing act of shock and innocence in the whole matter impressed him. With some training, the boy might become a useful asset.

The only remaining problem became Hodgson. He was sure the man worked for another party. He was a good enough agent and never gave Dunn any cause to suspect him. The fact he had gone as deep as he had suggested sponsorship by someone with extensive resources. There were only a handful of corporations capable of supporting an operator like him; fewer governments. He had vetted the man himself, which disappointed him the most.

In assessing his role in all this, his own performance disturbed him. He'd misjudged so many people on this mission, and in potentially fatal ways which never happened before. Perhaps it was time to get out of this business and do something else. His failings would eventually come to Mundi's attention.

In betraying his patron, their relationship would become clarified. They would be enemies and Dunn could be assured Mundi would intend to kill him. If he had remained loyal, his slipping performance would continue to seed doubt in the old man. The only question remaining to resolve would not be if, but when he would be ordered terminated.

He picked up the first wafer and inserted it into a receiver. It was only a matter of a few hours now before this would all be behind him. Yes, a fresh start was in order, thought Dunn.

CHAPTER THIRTY-FOUR

"We have an hour before we're all called to the bridge. What is the plan?" I asked Hodgson in a hushed tone. I had been looking all over the ship for him and was beyond being annoyed. Our proximity to the Sun had scrambled the long range effectiveness of everyone's cortical implant as well as the ship's comm system, making normal communications impossible. I spent thirty minutes in a frustrating search to finally locate him near the storage bays.

A fringe culture arises in every society which wants to reject technology and live a mythically simpler life, with rainbow farting unicorns and the like. While risky surgical removal of their CI was the extreme and permanent expression of this delusion, most of the card carrying members of the Luddite Brigade, as I call them, opted for voluntary deactivation of their cortical implants. Personally, I thought them crazy to cut themselves off from society in such a drastic protest. I, like everyone else, relied on my CI and the loss of it to me now, when everything was going to shit, was frustrating, annoying and frightening.

"I searched every critical area except engineering." He held up a small black device I assumed was some kind of explosive detector. "I need you to lure the kid out of there so I can search. I only need twenty minutes, tops."

"What if you don't find anything?"

"We're at Dunn's mercy because I can't imagine what he

might come up with."

"Isn't there still a chance he's not going to pull anything? Perhaps he is using the Sun to escape the Terrans and we'll all end up safe, sound and rich on Luna in a few weeks? What then?"

Hodgson scowled at the device in his hand. "That's not going to happen, Mel."

"But you're not sure, are you?"

He spoke sharply to me. "If you're asking whether he's confided his plan in me, the answer is no. But I understand people. I know him. He will pull something and it will take place before we make solar orbit."

"You're betting heavily on this, Hodgson. Are you sure you're not acting emotionally? Making this personal?"

"My professional experience is guiding me. There is no time for this debate. I could use your help, but can make do without it. Are you in or out?"

"Of course, I'm in. Don't misunderstand me, I'm not defending Dunn."

"Where is this coming from?"

That was a question I had started to ask myself. Why was I so reluctant to accept Hodgson's analysis?

"I suppose I'm worried about what to do if you don't find anything. Finding nothing means he has a plan he's kept under wraps and we'll all die, horribly. I think a part of me wants to hold out hope there is still a chance everything with this mission is legitimate, we've misjudged him terribly and we'll all survive."

Hodgson's frown softened and he nodded. "I understand your fears. Trust me when I say I have looked at this every way. Dunn's history is to leave bodies in his wake and he's gone all in on this one. This is his only option."

"Okay, sorry for being a pussy about all this. I'll keep Bogdan out of your way, but you should keep an ear open because the CI's aren't working."

"I can do my job, Mel. Make sure you do yours, please?"

"Hey, distracting men is my schtick." I smiled with more

confidence than I felt.

"So, out of curiosity, how do you intend to get him out of engineering?"

"Oh, I thought I might ask him to check my shower again." I winked.

"Be careful. He seems like an innocent boy, but I'm positive he butchered Schmaltz. You'll be in more danger than you can imagine if he suspects something is up."

At the mention of my dead friend a wave of anger rose up in my guts. I wanted Dunn to be the killer. I didn't want to think of Bogdan as capable of murder and pulling off the act of shock he had. But Hodgson was right. All the evidence pointed to the young engineer and Dunn working together. If he thought I suspected him, he could easily end my life too.

"Give me ten minutes, before you send him to me in medical. Tell him I need his help."

Ten short minutes later I sat facing the door and fought down my anxiety as I waited for Bogdan's arrival. In the pocket of my jacket I had a prepared hypospray with enough sedative to put a horse under. It was my last line of defence if I had gotten things wrong about him.

Bogdan wouldn't be the first psycho I'd been locked up in a room with. In my time I've faced my share of loosely hinged people. As a young girl I quickly learned how to turn a discussion to safe topics and keep them there. At some cost I discovered the need to watch for the signs of the crazy train arriving at the station and how to avoid meeting it.

Dealing with Bogdan would be unique for me. Unlike my previous experiences I couldn't really offer to fuck the boy to keep him placated. It's not that I wasn't capable or even willing to use that strategy. Experience told me sex would not be an option today. There was something unusual about Bogdan and I had a sense for different. My life often depended on it. Maybe he didn't care for girls though I could almost always tell. Perhaps he was a virgin or raised in a suppressed religious home environment. More than likely it was because he viewed me as a mentor of sorts like he had Schmaltz. Regardless of the reason, I believed if I were to come on to him it would unhinge him faster than anything else I might do or say.

I intended to employ a woman's oldest weapon and engage him in a conversation about himself. I knew Bogdan, above all else, lacked confidence and wanted reassurance. With most men it involved praising their looks or the impressive nature of their package. I was pretty sure he craved approval from someone he trusted and admired. I was the closest thing to a sister he had on this ship so I needed to be that for him for twenty minutes.

The door slid open and revealed the tall, anxious young man standing beyond. "You want my help with something, Doc?"

"Yes, but it can wait. Come in, please. I'd like to talk with you first."

He looked uncertainly down the corridor before he stepped in and let the door close behind him. He fidgeted and glanced around the room, like a feral dog expecting a trap.

"Everything is all right, Bogdan. I'm the only one here. I wanted to ask you how are you doing?" Both of my hands were thrust into my jacket pockets and I nervously fingered the hypospray.

"I'm...okay, I guess." He watched the floor, then lifted his head to see if he'd given me the right answer.

I smiled reassuringly at him and invited him to sit in the chair across from me. He hesitated for a moment, then shuffled to it and sat down. He perched near the edge of the chair with a stooped posture. His knees were squeezed tightly together and he buried his hands between them.

"What happened in engineering was pretty traumatic. Any feelings you experience are normal and sometimes, it's good to share them with somebody. I'm here to listen if you like."

"Okay." He stared at a point in front of him on the carpet.

"Do you want to talk, Bogdan?"

"I...I dunno, maybe. I don't know what to say."

"How do you feel?"

"I...I... my head is a bag full of fighting cats. I'm confused.

I'm fine one minute and then I cry the next. I can't eat and I can't sleep. I shake like a leaf every time I go to engineering."

"Those feelings are perfectly normal. I experience some of them too."

"How long will they torture me? I don't think I can live with my guilt!"

Oh God! I can't deal with a fucking confession. "Everyone takes a different amount of time to process this kind of thing. But you will get through it. I can offer you some tips which might help you cope."

"Like what? The feelings just come and I can't stop them. I think I'm going crazy."

YOU think you're crazy? "One thing I do when that happens is to not fight it. Let the feelings come and wash over you, like an ocean wave. Have you ever seen the oceans on Terra, Bogdan?"

He nodded. "My family used to take me to the seashore when I was little."

"Good, so you know how the waves flow up on the shore and drop away? Your emotions will do that too. Don't give them any power. Just allow them to happen, acknowledge them but don't react to them. They will pass and you will learn they have no control over you. Do you think you can do that, Bogdan?"

"It sort of makes sense. I'll give it a try."

He was the most relaxed I had seen him since he entered medical. We sat in silence and during the quiet I realized I'd dodged a bullet and needed to collect myself before I said something stupid which might set him off.

"Why haven't you asked me yet?"

My heart leaped to my throat. "Asked you what?"

"You didn't ask me who I thought did it." His eyes bored into mine.

I tried to swallow and my hand inched towards the pocket with the hypospray. "Who do you think did it?"

"You think I did it, don't you?" His tone was more urgent.

Yes, you psycho son-of-a-bitch, I think you did it and I want to stick you with this hypo and send you to hell.

"There's no way you could have been the one to do anything like that, Bogdan."

"Why couldn't I? I'm not scrawny anymore. I work out and I'm a lot stronger than I look. Why do you think I couldn't have done it?"

Oh shit! Here comes the crazy train.

I produced what I hoped the most sincere fake smile of my life. "Anyone can see how strong and capable you are. I didn't mean you couldn't do it. I meant I didn't think you would do it. You're too nice of a person." The words almost caught in my throat, and I prayed they were the right ones because they had cost me so much to say to him.

He relaxed. "I couldn't bear if you thought I was the killer. I don't know what I would do."

I have a pretty good idea. I accessed my chronometer. Hodgson's twenty minutes were done.

Before I could reply to him the door buzzer sounded.

"Enter, please," I said, a little too loudly.

The door slid open to reveal Hodgson.

"Everything is ready for Solar orbit. The Captain wants us all on the bridge. He sent me to collect you."

I relaxed and noticed I had been clutching the hypospray through my jacket. I released my grip and stood.

"We had better go." I didn't care if the relief in my voice was obvious.

I looked at Bogdan and said, "We can talk again, later, if you like."

I really hoped he wouldn't want to take me up on my offer.

CHAPTER THIRTY-FIVE

Talus Varr arrived at the garden almost an hour after Regis Mundy was informed of his arrival. He didn't expect his uninvited visitor came to give him good news, so he instructed the escort to bring him by the longest possible route.

Talus, a fit man for his age, seemed only slightly out of breath and did not try to hide the annoyance written clearly on his face. Mundi remained seated on the stone bench and continued to feed his pigeons which gathered about him and stupidly jostled for the bread crumbs he offered them.

"So this is how you treat your guests, then?"

Mundi did not look up. "Guests are invited. You arrived unannounced. I am not presuming you bear any news I want to hear." He tossed the last of the offering to the pigeons and brushed his hands together.

"You would be correct. The agreement your man Felix forged for you is terminated."

"You no longer wish to prevent the Terrans from obtaining your weapon?"

"We don't require your services."

"Oh?"

"Our own agent is about to secure it for us and the deal with you isn't necessary."

"I see." Mundi fought to keep his temper.

"However, in light of your relationship with some of the Triumvirate, it has been agreed that you will be compensated for all reasonably incurred expenses. We recognize that your initial efforts to locate the virus have been of assistance."

"You are most generous." Mundi ground his teeth around the words.

"We will also grant you a small charter for mining transport. Perhaps, with time, you will prove yourself worthy of a Martian citizenship and can expand your business ventures from this foothold."

"Once again, your generosity overwhelms me."

The two men stared toxically at each other for a long moment. Mundi nodded his head to the armed guard standing at attention a respectful distance behind his visitor. Without a word, Varr turned and left with the escort.

When he was certain they were gone and could no longer hear, he leapt to his feet and startled the pigeons into panicked flight. He waved his arms in mockery of them and screamed incoherently at the top of his lungs.

They inserted their own agent into Dunn's group. The man's betrayals compounded themselves at every turn. He couldn't really blame the Triumvirate for using their own resources. He would have done the same. But the fool, Dunn somehow permitted his organization to be penetrated, and that was unforgivable.

With the virus about to be acquired by their own man, he'd lost the last leverage available to him for regaining his former position on Mars. His long dreams of a triumphant return were now fading nightmares, and it was all the fault of Erik Dunn.

This changed everything. He would not permit Dunn any chance of escape. Nor would he allow the Triumvirate an opportunity to retrieve their bio-weapon. It was time to reset the game board. It was time to destroy the nano-virus and everybody involved in this project.

CHAPTER THIRTY-SIX

The ship approached orbit without incident. The specially constructed *Helios* could withstand solar prominences and any other close proximity dangers from the sun. It wouldn't be able to maintain this distance indefinitely, but we were well within the safety margins for our tight swing around to the other side. Once out of visual contact with the pursuing Terran ship, the plan called for a course correction to double back towards Luna under their noses. The Terrans seemed to guess our intentions because they maintained constant acceleration in an effort to catch us before we vanished around the edge of the star.

The mood on the bridge was understandably tense. Garrick and Limn intently focused all their attention on executing the orbit. Dunn appeared nervous, repeatedly examining the monitors displaying all the shipboard functions.

I glanced at Hodgson, seated beside me. He surreptitiously removed the palm-sized receiver from his pocket and revealed it to me. He nodded towards Dunn to suggest he was its owner. I heard a sharp intake of breath behind me and turned to discover Bogdan also saw what Hodgson showed me. The colour drained from his face and sheen of nervous sweat formed across his forehead.

I leant back and whispered to him over my shoulder, "Calm down. Everything will be all right."

He became more agitated and nervously glanced around in

expectation of some imminent doom.

"I need to check the inertial transfer coils. They were acting up and I don't want them to fail," he blurted. He jumped up and rushed off the bridge, ignoring Garrick's order to remain seated.

Dunn leaned forward and patted the Captain on the shoulder. "Don't worry. I'll get him."

Garrick nodded his assent. Dunn unbuckled his restraints and pursued Bogdan through the doorway.

Hodgson and I exchanged looks. Before I said anything, he too unstrapped himself and followed the parade.

Garrick shouted himself hoarse in his unsuccessful effort to call him back to his seat. His attention was called back to something at the helm and the bridge fell awkwardly silent, except for the hushed discussion between captain and copilot.

Anxiety filled my mind as I impotently sat like an obedient crewman; the only one on the ship from the look of things. Scenarios of Dunn cutting the power to the lab rushed through my imagination. I envisioned Hodgson and Bogdan both lying in pools of their own blood, shot by Dunn.

I mentally reviewed how to put on the pressure suit I stored nearby after Hodgson's warning. I had been dismayed to find mine the last one remaining in the locker, and I started to believe the scenario Hodgson painted for me.

Gone for over five minutes, no word had come from any of the three who'd left. I couldn't abide waiting another second for disaster to strike. I unbuckled myself and sprang towards the doorway.

"Doctor! Remain in your seat! That is an order!"

I froze in my tracks, held in place, not by his command, but by his tone and a lifetime of conditioning. I stared at Garrick and disgust for him rose in my gut. He may be my commanding officer, true, but he'd shown me nothing but contempt since my arrival.

For most of my life I'd endured derisive comments and accepted treatment as second-hand garbage, much of it at the hands of scum a lot worse than Garrick. But for some reason, today, I knew I deserved the respect he denied me. Yes, I used to be a whore. I couldn't change that. I was also once a prominent physician and researcher. Neither of those stations in life had any bearing on my value as a human being. I understood Garrick wasn't contemptuous of my whoring past. He reviled my personhood, which made all the difference. It spoke more of him than me, and in that moment, I believed Cinderella could stay at the ball because she was worthy in her own right, not because of the fleeting boon of the fairy godmother. Before I mustered the words to tell him where to stick it, the helm warning panel lit up.

"Report!" he shouted.

"Another ship has shown up on our long-distance scanners," said Limn.

"Where?" He forgot all about me and resumed his place at the pilot station.

"They are just clearing the solar horizon now."

"Identity?" Uncertainty shook Garrick's voice.

"We are not receiving a transponder signal. It's getting scrambled this close to the chromosphere."

"What is their heading?"

Shigeko Limn's hands flew across the controls. "They appear to be changing trajectory."

Both Garrick and I watched as she computed the new ship's course and position. Sweat beaded on Garrick's brow. I looked uselessly out the front window, its adaptive graphene molecules having adjusted it to dim the blinding glare outside.

"What is the delay, Limn? What are they doing?"

"Give me a moment, Sir. The sun is interfering with the readings."

The solar interference seemed to be affecting most of our systems.

"Captain. The solar activity might be disrupting the confinement grid around the virus. I should go and check it," I said.

Engrossed in Limn's efforts to track the movements of the mystery vessel, he didn't seem to hear me. I decided to exploit the opportunity to leave. I also wanted to find Hodgson and warn him about the other ship.

"Got it!" said Limn. "It has changed its course since we've sighted it. They are now on an intercept trajectory with us."

"How long?"

"They have accelerated. We will pass in six hours and eighteen minutes. Oh, and I now have a clearer ping on their transponder. It is encoded. They are Rego Corporation. Military class. The *Victorem*."

The Captain relaxed at the news. "Excellent."

"Is it the ship we are expecting?" I asked.

Garrick started at my question, reminded about my presence. He scowled at me and addressed Limn. "Prepare to send them a coded hail. I'll supply you with the message when you're ready."

He then got a far-away look in his eye. I suspected he tried to flag Dunn using his CI. He frowned and leaned over the console to activate the comm. "Mister Dunn, please contact the bridge."

After several tense seconds, he repeated himself twice more with no reply returned.

"Mister Hodgson, contact the bridge." Annoyance tinged his voice.

With no response, he made the same request of Bogdan with identical results.

"Solar activity must be affecting those systems as well," said Limn. "I'm ready to transmit the message, Sir."

"We need Mister Dunn," he said as he rose from his chair. "I'll get him. Tell the *Victorem* to stand by."

He'd reached the door when she made a panicked announcement, "They have locked on us with a tracking beam."

"What?" Garrick returned and examined the readouts for himself.

"They must think we're Terran. Explain to them we are Rego Corporation. Send my personal ID code."

Corporations all employed military class vessels to secure

their own interests against piracy, corporately sanctioned and otherwise. I was concerned *Victorem* did not seem to be aware who we were.

"No response. Beam still active."

"The solar activity must be scrambling all our communications. Send an old style encoded laser signal with our Rego transponder ID."

"That was the first thing I tried," she replied, frustration in her voice.

Garrick stared at the console, out of ideas.

"Sir, they are close enough now to give me a visual on the long scope," said Limn.

She studied the image for several long seconds before she looked at us, shock written across her features.

"Their missile ports are open."

CHAPTER THIRTY-SEVEN

Victorem orbited Sol exactly where and when the original crew had been instructed. Felix Altius watched *Helios* rise above the solar horizon on the scope. They entered an orbit opposite of *Victorem's* and at an extreme velocity, allowing them to skim the chromosphere much closer than the pursuing Terran vessel. With *Helios'* specially shielded hull, they were certainly nearer to the sun than *Victorem* had the capability to match. That set of facts alone was all the confirmation he needed that Dunn had no intention of meeting with this ship and had made other plans, likely to use their superior orbital velocity to outrun the Terrans and make their final escape.

What had he offered his crew to entice their complicity? Did they actually believe they would be able to betray the Corpus Rego and live, retelling the tale into their old age? Of course, he may have betrayed them and, if he hadn't yet killed them, intended to leave them for the Terran Captain to deal with.

"Sir, we've sighted another ship."

Felix searched his memory for the young officer's name. "What is its vector, Bates?"

After the briefest of pauses, he replied, "It appears to be on an intercept course with *Helios*."

"Time to closest approach?"

Another pause. "Five hours and forty-seven minutes."

"What is the ID of the other vessel?"

Another voice on the bridge, Chen's, responded, "No ID

beacon, sir."

Annoyed, Felix returned to the scope. He enhanced the image as much as possible. It appeared to be Terran military. Definitely armoured, and well armed. That would complicate matters. Had Dunn made arrangements with the Terrans after all?

"Feed the imaging into the computer. Get me a match."

Felix leaned over Bates' shoulder and whispered, "I want you to compute a firing solution on the *Helios*. What is our launch window to hit them before they are close enough to rendezvous with the second vessel? We need to be able to fire and then escape should the other ship respond. Assume their armaments are comparable to ours."

Bates nodded without looking up and began to work on the task.

Firing on them would be the last resort. His mission was to recover the nano-virus. There would be no deal with the Martians without it. But if any chance existed Dunn might escape with it, he would become the biggest threat Regis Mundi would ever face. He could sell it to Terra or Luna, or even make an alternate arrangement with Mars and cut his Dominus out completely. Any scenario Felix could imagine gave the traitor far too much power.

Bates interrupted his musings. "Sir, I have a firing solution. Our window opens up in twenty-one minutes and will remain open for eleven minutes."

Felix stared absently ahead, his mind focused on the tactical situation. They couldn't change course and follow Dunn, even if he slowed and moved to a higher orbit for his rendezvous with the mystery ship. By the time *Victorem* responded, he would be long gone in either one of them. There were too many variables.

"Sir," announced Chen, "I have a ninety percent positive likelihood for the other craft being the *Fortuna*."

That was the first development in all this which made any sense to Felix. Dunn intended to meet with his original ship. At least, there wasn't a second Terran warship to deal with.

There remained the complication of the pursuing *Athena*. Even though Victorem still had the sun between themselves and the Terrans, eventually they would sight each other and an entirely new set of problems would arise. Unmarked, *Victorem* traveled without a conventional ID beacon. The warship would be compelled to challenge and engage.

He didn't really know what the outcome of a shooting contest between them would be. While the corporation's military ships were designed to be formidable, they were meant to deter pirates, not Terran battlecruisers. Felix was not concerned for his life, or those of his crew. He always knew he would die in the service of his Dominus. What bothered him to distraction were the consequences for Regis Mundi. The fallout of such an encounter would damage Mundi's interests on Terra for decades to come.

"Sir, *Helios* is attempting to contact us," said Chen. "The signal contains the ID trace for Captain Clive Garrick."

"Garrick? Not Dunn?"

"No, Sir, should I respond?"

Before he could answer, Felix's cortical implant pinged, informing him of a pending hail on the Q-radio, coded with Regis Mundi's ID code. Things must be dire if his master wished to communicate with him a second time. Leaving the young officer waiting, Felix marched to the shielded communications booth at the back of the bridge and sealed himself inside.

He activated the Q-radio and waited while it established the quantum link with the corresponding machine in his Dominus' private office. The screen initiated to reveal only the sigil of the Corpus Rego. Mundi's obsession with privacy extended to all forms of communication. Even though the nearly instantaneous transmission link between the respective quantum receivers was unhackable, Mundi would not risk being personally connected to any communique in this project.

Felix pushed down his anxiety. "Omega Prime ready to receive."

"Omega Prime, this is Agricola. Mission changed. Ares will

not be attending the bacchanal. The guests are too unruly. Rescind their invitations. We will attempt another gathering at a later date. Agricola, out."

Felix turned off the receiver and sat back in the chair to contemplate the coded message. Something drastic must have happened in his absence from Mundi. For some reason, the deal with Mars would not go through as negotiated. They would try another day, and all that remained was to put things to bed.

He exited the booth and moved to the centre of the bridge, all eyes attentive to him, awaiting his orders.

"Mister Bates, at the earliest opportunity, lock weapons on both ships and launch missiles."

CHAPTER THIRTY-EIGHT

"What do you mean?" The question came from Garrick.

"They've targeted us and opened their missile doors," repeated Limn.

"Repeat the hail. Send Dunn's ID flag."

She did as ordered and returned her attention to the long range scope. "Oh my god!" She stared into the instrument like she couldn't believe what her eyes told her.

"What is happening Shigeko?"

She lifted her gaze from the scanner, defeat written across her face. "They launched their missiles."

"They did what?" Garrick leapt from his seat and pushed Limn away from the scope. "Why would they do this?"

"Well, they clearly don't like you or Dunn," I said. He continued to stare at the image as if he hoped to verify he'd made some kind of mistake.

"Garrick! Are you not going to do something?" I shouted.

"What?" He stared at me, confused. He snapped back to himself. "Yes. Limn, give me options. Time to impact."

Shocked into action, Shigeko sat down and her hands played across the console. We waited for what felt like far too long. Even though the quantum computer crunched numbers faster than I could imagine, the answer took a lot longer than I had the patience for.

"Got it. We've got four hours, six minutes."

I almost laughed. "We have plenty of time to move out of

the way, don't we?"

She shook her head. "Even at our present orbital velocity, we can't outrun those missiles. If we change course, they'll track us. They've got a lock."

"Then we have to abandon this ship, don't we? The drop ship is still in the hangar."

"Too small," he said.

"What the hell do you mean?"

"The shuttle isn't shielded like this one. We would die from the radiation before we got a hundred metres."

Both Garrick and Limn were pale and exhibited the defeated appearance of someone who accepted their fate, choosing to go quietly without any discussion, bargaining or futile screaming and sniffling.

"Well, there must be something we can do?"

He shook his head and slumped into his seat. I glared at him and shifted my gaze to Shigeko. Tears welled up in her eyes and she turned away from me. Was I stupid? I didn't want to accept my fate the same way they did. I needed to know there was a way out of this.

I'm not sure what I expected to see, but I moved to the navigation control cluster and scanned the various readouts and controls, looking for something, anything, that could give me hope. My eyes fell on the navigational schematic.

"What is that?" I pointed at a blip on the screen.

Shigeko glanced at the console and dropped back into her chair, frowning. "The Rego ship that fired on us."

"And these little flashing blips? Are they the missiles?" I waved my hand at a cluster that was slowly resolving itself into individual markers; one for each missile, I presumed.

She nodded without looking up. "Yes, those are the missiles. You can stay there and watch them approach if you don't believe me."

"You're not being helpful, Shigeko." I didn't look up from the display. My eye had caught sight of another feature.

"What is this blip, over here?" I pointed again and regarded her. She refused to acknowledge me, preferring to lose herself in her despair.

"Limn! Is this another ship?"

My query prompted Garrick out of his stupor and he rose to look at what I indicated with my finger. He examined the image for several seconds, seeming to be confused by what he saw.

"It is another vessel." He punched in a few commands and the screen zoomed in on the new player in the game. He gazed at me, slack jawed for a moment before he realized who I was. His mouth snapped shut and he straightened his posture.

"That is the *Fortuna*."

"Our old ship? What's she doing out here?"

He ignored me and directed his attention to another instrument cluster. "She's on an intercept vector."

"I thought it was on auto-pilot or something?" I asked.

"She is," he said. "Apparently Dunn programmed her to rendezvous with us."

"How long until it reaches us?"

"Five hours, thirteen minutes," he said without looking up.

"Great," I said, "just far enough away to get a good view of us being blown to atoms."

Garrick made no response. He stood at the console, staring at some spot in the distance, his shoulders slouched. He seemed to be running on empty for ideas, but I wasn't nearly finished. I learned a long time ago that you don't save lives without a little out of the box thinking.

"Can we go to it? Can we cut the time down if we change course?" I asked. "Think, man! How the hell did you make Captain?"

He looked at me and I could finally see lights come on behind his eyes. He returned his attention to the navigation console and ran some calculations. "If *Fortuna* stays on the same trajectory, we can meet her in three hours and forty minutes."

His arms fell to his sides and he turned to face me. "We'll just get two ships destroyed." There was none of the usual condescension in his voice, only resignation.

He was right, of course. We didn't have time to dock with the *Fortuna*, let alone get aboard and escape in it. Even I knew that.

The bridge was as silent as a mausoleum while the three of us came to grips with the inevitable. How could we be so close to an escape and not be able to use it? I wondered if karma was always going to fuck me. Well, not for much longer, it appeared.

What the hell was *Fortuna* doing out here? Schmaltz sent it away as a decoy and gave control to Dunn. What was he up to? The only silver lining, well, schadenfreude really, was that if he had been trying to screw us and escape, he had failed. That Rego ship had to know that he was aboard and they still fired on us. He must have pissed off some powerful people.

I slumped into my chair and recalled how all this had begun. Dunn manipulated me, and probably a lot of others to lure me on this mission. He'd killed the real Erik Dunn and Jake Matthiews as part of his scheme. He or that son-of-a-bitch Charlie had screwed up Schmaltz's situation to coerce him here as well. Poor Schmaltz. I knew, if I lived, I would miss him for the rest of my life.

I remembered something he told me when I first came aboard.

"Isn't the *Fortuna* armed?" I said to nobody in particular.

Garrick replied, "Yes." He sat up and stared at me. "How did you know that?"

"And the ship is under remote control from this one, isn't it? Why can't we tell it to shoot down those missiles?"

I had the attention of both of them now. Garrick turned to the controls while Limn hovered over his shoulder. After a few minutes of trying several different keystrokes, he slammed his fists on the console. "Dunn locked the interface. He's the only one that can make that command."

"Well, then, we have to bring him back to the bridge." I started for the doorway. Taking nothing to chance, I turned and addressed him in my best doctor voice, "In the meantime, we need to alter our course and move towards *Fortuna*. It's an armoured military vessel. Maybe at the very least, we can hide behind it."

Garrick actually smiled at me. I left to find Dunn.

CHAPTER THIRTY-NINE

I made my way first to Medical and discovered the door was locked. I entered to find the facility empty and undisturbed. The green light on the containment power unit blinked steadily. Relieved that the virus remained untampered with, I resumed my search of the ship for the three men.

The section door before engineering was open and raised voices carried from beyond the doorway. I crept towards the opening, hoping not to make a sound and crouched out of view to listen. In the corridor, out of sight, two men argued.

"I told you already, Mister Dunn, the explosives were gone. I didn't take them, Hodgson did."

"And I don't believe you, Skorupa. Why are you wearing your pressure suit?"

I leaned forward to risk a peek at the scene. Bogdan sweated profusely and Dunn glowered at him. They stood in front of the aft airlock and the younger man was half dressed in a pressure suit, the gloves and boots on the floor waiting to be attached. Dunn held the helmet, having taken it from him.

"I was afraid you were going to release the virus and depressurize the ship. I wanted to be ready."

"And how could I do that if you removed the charges? You know what I think Skorupa? I think YOU planned on setting them off yourself. I think you got frightened at the last second and rushed down here to remove them. Then you decided you would evacuate the atmosphere anyway without risking the virus being released. But I found you and now all you can do is sputter and lie to my face!"

"No, Mister Dunn, that's not what I..."

"I thought I invested enough to trust you. I should have known that was a mistake."

"You can trust me! I did like you asked. Just like you hired me to do. I'm loyal. I told you everything the Doctor asked. Everything Hodgson did. I'm worth everything you've paid me."

"You took those charges and betrayed me."

Bogdan's renewed round of protests were cut off when Dunn swung the helmet around and struck him on head with it. The young man fell heavily. I rose up to intervene, but lost my courage and crouched back behind the edge of the doorframe.

Dunn advanced to the stunned engineer, brandishing his improvised club. He stood over Bogdan who held up his arm and begged for his life. Wordlessly, Dunn rained down blows repeatedly on him. Arcs of blood painted the wall of the corridor as he savagely beat the man senseless. He dropped his weapon and dragged his bloodied victim to the nearby airlock. He activated the inner door and while it opened, returned to pick up the semi-conscious form. He pulled Bogdan over the rim of the hatchway and dumped him inside. As the door closed, Dunn noticed the bloody discarded helmet and tossed it in as well.

I couldn't let him send Bogdan out the other side. Without thinking, I picked up a wrench that lay beside the door. It was sticky with something, but I didn't want to afford the time to examine it. Dunn accessed the controls, his back to me. Realizing this would be my only chance, I sprang out from the opening and rushed at him, my primitive weapon raised above my head. That was the extent of my plan, and it proved as effective as it was sophisticated.

He heard me and moved forward to block my downward swing with his forearm. He expertly caught my wrist and twisted sharply, sending agonizing pain into my shoulder. The wrench clattered noisily at my feet. Dunn backhanded me across the jaw and sent me sprawling to the deck. With a self-satisfied grin, he returned his attention to the control panel.

The warning buzzer sounded and the red light flashed as the air pressure within the airlock dropped. Dunn lunged towards me and grabbed me by my hair, pulling until I stood. He pushed me to the door and directed my gaze through the glass to the unconscious figure of Bogdan Skorupa, lying on the floor. He smiled sickly at me, then leaned to the side and hit a button. The outer hatch blew out and in a rush of the remaining air inside, Bogdan's body was blown out into the icy void of space.

The sight of the empty airlock and the tumbling, rapidly receding body should have prompted some kind of emotion, but I experienced nothing. The scene unfolded in silence, like a video with the sound turned off. I thought I should weep or cry out in outrage but my mind was in a fog and only numbness engulfed my body. Dunn yanked on my hair once more and turned me to face him, painfully jerking me back to my deadly reality.

"You won't go so easily, Doctor. I have a much more fitting end for you. We have to collect a few things first for me to tie up some loose ends."

He pulled me down the hallway in the direction of the hangar.

CHAPTER FORTY

As I struggled against him I caught sight of someone lying on the floor near the bulkhead doorway I hid behind. Dunn noticed my distraction. With a cruel smile, he pulled me towards the unconscious form.

Dylan Hodgson lay against the wall, his face a bloody beaten mass. I couldn't tell if he lived or not, and Dunn would not allow me to get close to him.

"Your boyfriend was sniffing around down here for me. Fortunately, I'm resourceful."

My mind flashed back to the sticky wrench I tried to strike him with. It now registered to me that the wrench was covered in blood. Dunn must have somehow gotten the drop on Hodgson and beaten him senseless with it.

"What are you going to do to him?"

"To him? I would think you'd be more concerned about yourself, Doctor. Don't worry. He'll be dead soon enough."

"Listen to me Dunn. The ship we were supposed to meet has fired on us. You need to..."

He dragged me by my injured wrist, twisting it cruelly to force me along. He wasn't a big man, but he was surprisingly muscular, and regardless of that, he was still bigger than me. I learned long ago how cruel men liked to throw their weight advantage around.

I've only ever been severely beaten once. A client wanted me to perform a particularly distasteful act which I refused a little more firmly than he appreciated. While I healed from that assault, the man eventually paid a bigger price in a dark alley a few weeks later. My handlers, while not gentle and caring folks, didn't like their merchandise damaged, and took a dim view of anyone who disregarded that rule.

While many years and a lot of distance are between me and my pimps, this was the first time I ever appreciated their methods of retribution. There would be nobody to avenge me this time. The irony of the inverse relationship between my improved social status and my present personal safety did not escape me.

The door to the hangar opened and he shoved me through. He followed me inside and frog-marched me to the drop ship. I held no delusions of him taking me with him. He most likely was going to beat me senseless, and leave me to the vacuum when he departed. I wanted to fight him; turn on him and go ape shit crazy, biting and scratching at his eyes. I knew I wouldn't defeat him, but I thought the price of my death should be something he would remember. He never gave me the opportunity, always pushing and pulling me off balance; grabbing me by my injured wrist, by my hair, or by the back of my neck. Dunn understood how to control others, and I, with my slight build, proved no match for his experience. I wondered how many women he had murdered.

He spun me around, and struck me, sending me sprawling to the deck. He pulled the pistol from his waistband and levelled it at me. I decided to make him look me in the eyes when he killed me, so I glared at him, defied him silently to do his worst. He stood, gun pointed at me, his gaze never wavering. He formed the same predatory smile he had shown me before.

"No, I have something far more entertaining in mind than this." He put the firearm back, bent forward and seized my wrist again. I tried to take a swing at him with my other arm, but he slapped me across the face and squeezed the wrist until the pain brought me under his control.

Dunn forced me into the shuttle and pushed me into a passenger seat. He knelt beside the portable containment unit and peered through the glass at the three silver cylinders within. He opened it and removed one. The green power button flashed brightly to reassure us its contents safely controlled and not about to escape and swarm our fragile bodies.

"Have you never been curious how this works, Doctor?"

"I know what it does."

"No, you know the mechanics. I refer to how a person's body reacts. How fast does it respond? How painful is it? You see, that's the kind of thing I am fascinated by. The limits of the human body to pain and torture. Call it professional curiosity, if you will."

He studied me, the cylinder casually balanced in his left hand, like an item he considered purchasing at a kiosk.

"Aren't you in the least bit curious in how the last crew died? What were their first symptoms? I would think the doctor in you would be most interested in knowing that."

I didn't reply. I couldn't tell where he intended to go with this and didn't want to give him the satisfaction of any kind response.

"Let's find out, shall we?" He put on a jacket draped across a chair and zippered the silver cylinder into the pocket. Satisfied that it was secure, he once more pulled me to my feet.

"Dunn, didn't you hear me? We are under attack. Use your control of the *Fortuna* and shoot those missiles down before it's too late."

He ignored my words and forced me ahead of him. My mind raced with scenarios of what he planned for the contents of the cylinder. He couldn't open it without exposing himself, so the number of ways he could perform his little experiment remained limited. We made our way towards the front of the ship.

The door to the bridge was closed. Through the portal in the door I saw Garrick and Limn both busy at the helm and navigation consoles, their backs turned toward us. Dunn shoved me to the opposite side of the hallway and pulled his pistol out to level at me.

"I need you to remain there for a moment."

I looked down the corridor for some kind of escape route. He observed me and shook his head.

"Please, Doctor. Don't make me shoot you yet. Stay still."

I had no doubt about the man's sincerity, so I sat on the floor. With the gun levelled at me, he used his other hand to open the access panel to the door to reveal the inner workings of the door control. He did something to the components and stepped back with a satisfied look on his face.

"What have you done?"

"Just making sure our subjects don't get away."

Keeping the pistol pointed at me, he moved to another panel along the wall and opened the environmental access port. He searched for the line that fed air to the bridge. He pulled out the tube that allowed a rescue crew to provide emergency oxygen to an isolated section of the ship. Dunn removed the cylinder from his pocket and unthreaded the end. He connected it to the air supply line. I realized it was engineered for such a purpose and wondered what sick bastard came up with the design.

With a smile, he looked at me and turned on the comm. "Captain, this is Dunn."

"Mister Dunn, I'm glad you're all right. When the others left and I hadn't heard from you, I became concerned. We have a situation and..."

"And yet you made no effort to stop any of them from following me."

"What? *Victorem* has fired on us. We need to access the *Fortuna* to..."

"Yes, yes, Garrick. I was disappointed you didn't bother to check up on me. I would think you might be concerned with something happening to me; to our deal."

"Are you insane?"

"I was attacked, Captain, by both Hodgson and the Doctor. It was everything I could do to fend them off and make my way back to the bridge." Dunn grinned at me, amused by the sick fabrication he sold to Garrick.

"Do you require assistance now?"

"No, no, I'm quite fine now. I'm merely disappointed in your lack of support in the entire affair. It leads me to think that you two conspired with the others."

"I assure you Mister Dunn, there was no conspiracy. At least, none I was aware of. I am as loyal to you as I always have been. We both are."

"Well, thank you for the reassuring words, Captain. I feel better now. Loyalty is so hard to buy these days. There is only one thing I require of you and Miss Limn now."

"Yes, Sir. What can we do for you?"

Dunn released the comm button and stepped over to the emergency air supply. He turned the dial and emptied the contents of the viral cylinder into the sealed off bridge.

CHAPTER FORTY-ONE

Dunn forced me to my feet and made me witness everything unfold on the bridge through the port in the closed access door. Dark crimson blood ran from Garrick's nose into his moustache. He absently wiped at it and continued talking to Dunn, who was no longer listening and had turned off the comm. I helplessly gazed through the window as realization dawned on him. He stared at his bloody hands and his eyes grew wide in terror. Then, he reacted in a way I never in a million years would have predicted. He wept like a four-year-old child. His shoulders quaked as sobs convulsed him.

Dunn shook his head in disgust. "Pathetic."

Soon blood streamed from both of the Captain's nostrils and his eyes as evidence of the unbelievable pace of the nano-virus overwhelming his system. Garrick doubled over in pain, clutching at his abdomen. He staggered a couple of steps, then dropped to his knees and vomited a bloody mixture of his stomach's contents.

Shigeko Limn overcame her shock and rose from her chair to begin pounding on the door, begging anyone to let her out and away from the dying man.

Tears ran down my cheeks as I watched the weakened skin on her hands split from their impacts with the door and leave bloody smears across the glass of the portal. Her high-pitched scream of terror mixed with the sound of Garrick's cries.

"Enough, Dunn!" I glared at him.

He smiled at me in his way. "What would you have me do, Melanie?"

I shook my head, my own vision fogged in tears.

"End it! I beg you, please!"

"Really, Doctor, you disappoint me. I expected the scientist in you to want to follow the experiment through to its conclusion."

"End it, you sadistic pig! In the name of decency!" My voice cracked with the shriek of my demand.

Dunn shook his head in disappointment and returned his attention to the slaughter.

I refused to observe, at first. But eventually, I believed someone needed to bear witness to Dunn's callous disregard and forced myself to watch every moment of their final agonies. The last of Limn's sobs died faintly and the bridge became silent. Dunn contemplated the results.

"I don't believe we learned anything new at all. I mean, I'm only a layman, but I at least expected some kind of difference between them. Didn't you?"

"You're a monster." I was hoarse from my screaming.

"Well, yes. Perhaps I am," he said with all sincerity and in that moment, I realized nothing I said would affect this man.

He seized my wounded arm and squeezed until I cried out in pain.

"Let's see how our next experiment goes, shall we?" He pulled me roughly to my feet and shoved me down the corridor.

"What are you trying to prove, Dunn? You've got the nano-virus. Why not just abandon us here and be on your way?"

"Doctor, you surprise me. I would think that you, of all people, would appreciate I wouldn't depart with any loose threads hanging if I could avoid it. You want me to leave you for that fool, the Terran Captain? You think he'll spare your life when, in fact, he will do just the opposite."

I regarded him narrowly. "What are you talking about?"

"He thinks he has made an arrangement with me. When he finds this ship abandoned and the bio-weapon missing, he will be most put out. I'm doing you all a favour by killing you before he gets his hands on you."

"What deal? You're working for the Terrans?"

Dunn laughed heartily, thoroughly enjoying my confusion.

"I knew that the chances of us making it past their firing solution were slim to none, so I took the liberty of contacting the commander of the *Athena* and offered him an opportunity."

"Why are you doing this? The nano-virus is dangerous. What possible reasons can you have for betraying your employers and pissing off the Terrans? They'll hunt you down."

"They might. By the time they discover I am still alive, it will be too late. They are all only thinking short term. My employer is looking at the virus as political capital. Terra only perceives its potential as a weapon. I don't care if armies slaughter each other, or even if they kill off significant portions of planetary populations. I only need them to leave enough survivors who want to pay for a cure."

"This was all about profiteering?"

"I would think that with your business activities you would understand opportunistic profit. War is coming Doctor. War is always about profiteering."

"But you don't have any kind of antidote, Dunn."

"Sadly, that little gambit didn't work out as planned. You, my dear, were always a wild card experiment. When I arranged for you to be injected with a second nanite population on Luna, it was my hope that your system would react to the traces that were included. I had some clues as to the nature of the nano-virus and had my people design an adaptive prototype to act against it. Of course, there was no live virus to test it on, until now."

We had stopped in front of medical and he keyed the access code and shoved me inside. He directed me towards the isolation chamber with the pistol.

"So I've been nothing more than your guinea pig?"

"The engineers want to learn how their little pet fares against the actual virus. Observing your response to it will give them data for the next stage of research."

He pushed me into the chamber and locked the door behind me.

CHAPTER FORTY-TWO

Dunn watched me through the glass of the isolation chamber like I was a zoo animal. I stood in the centre of the room, clutching my injured arm and stared at him. I did not want to give the bastard the satisfaction of an emotional outburst. He shrugged his shoulders and moved to the containment chamber.

My heart drummed and I couldn't stop the cold sweat from beading on my forehead and soaking my armpits. My body might betray my fear, but I would not show him with my eyes and I would never entertain him by begging for mercy.

He paused over the control panel, considering something. Then that evil smile I hated so much appeared. He wagged his finger at me.

"I almost forgot something. Please be patient, Doctor. I'll be right back." He strode brusquely across the lab and exited the medical centre, leaving me alone with my fears.

Instinctively I searched for something that I could use to force the lock. My eyes fell on the bio-containment chamber on the other side of the window. Behind the clear, thick, polymer pane lay the metal tube containing the instruments of my death. Billions of them, patiently waiting for human tissue to feed their unstoppable appetite. The transparent walls of this isolation room were all that stood between my agony and Dunn's sadistic entertainment.

My imagination fixed on the seals holding the windows in

place. Beneath one, hidden from outside view but in plain sight to me was the toolkit I'd used to modify the portable containment unit.

I dashed across the room and tore open the case, spilling the tools on the desk. I seized a screwdriver and plied it against the connector seal in the glass. I frantically worked the tool back and forth, digging it into the hardened material. A tiny section popped off, followed by several more chunks.

I laughed out loud that my theory proved correct. The original power loss that marooned *Helios* exposed the entire ship to the virus. The nanites weakened the normally steel hard seals. Bits of it flaked away like hardened rubber under my determined efforts until I succeeded in poking a small hole through.

I worked away at it trying to make the breach as large as possible, keeping an anxious eye on the door for Dunn's return. Suddenly it slid open and I immediately pulled away from my work and moved back into the middle of the chamber.

Hodgson staggered into the medical centre. His face was so severely swollen his eyes were barely visible and I could sense his frustration. He limped and his arms were bound behind his back. Dunn followed him with a more than self-satisfied look on his face and kicked him in the backs of his legs to force him to his knees.

"Why don't you step inside, Dunn? I'll give you a farewell blowjob," I said.

He laughed. "I'm tempted, Melanie. Really. You were exceptional that night. Worth every credit I paid for you."

He moved to the abandoned control and activated the manipulator. He picked up the metal cylinder and awkwardly unscrewed it with the robotic arms, removed the sample cartridge and broke its seal. Seeming to savour the moment, he opened the inside access window and exposed the isolation chamber to the virus.

Dunn stood behind Hodgson, never taking his eyes off me. Anticipation painted his face as he awaited the first signs of my inevitable response to the nano-virus.

I don't know what I expected. My skin crawled, but I knew that was from my anxiety and not from any infection. Based on what I observed of Garrick and Limn, I supposed the initial symptom would be irritation of the eyes and nasal passages, but I felt perfectly normal. By the time I had been exposed to the contagion for more than three times as long as the others, he started to appear worried. I decided to try something.

"Is something wrong? Why are you pulling my chain? Release the fucking virus and finish this."

He attempted to smile, but it faded from his face as fast as the doubt grew. A frown creased his brow as he returned to the manipulator's arm. He picked up the viral container and re-examined it through the window.

"What have you done? Did you swap containers out?" he asked.

I said nothing. I needed him to spend as much time close to the hole I'd opened as possible. I prayed that whatever kept the virus in check inside of me would last long enough for my plan to work. I wanted to see the shock on his face when he realized what I had done to him.

My nose began to run and I hesitantly reached up to wipe it, revealing only clear mucous on the back of my hand.

"Are you sure you opened it, Dunn? Maybe you should bring it inside here yourself?"

"You obviously have developed some resistance, after all." He didn't sound convinced, still searching the container for some sign that he botched his moment.

A bloody metallic tang appeared in the back of my mouth. The mucous running from my nostril was faintly pink. The nano-virus was making headway. I hoped it was working as determinedly at the opening I poked in the seal.

Dunn blinked his eyes like he had something in them. He rubbed them and then staggered back in horror when his hand came away covered in blood.

"No!"

He brushed at his now bloody running nose and flapped his hands uselessly around in front of him in panic.

"No, no, no! This isn't possible."

He glared at me and screamed, "What have you done?"

"I'm pretty sure I just killed you." It was good to say those words.

"You bitch!" He flew into a rage, flailing his arms and knocking anything loose from the counter and around the lab. He pounded on the window with his fists, leaving the same kind of smeared, bloody trails that Shigeko Limn did on the bridge door. Shocked by the sight of the blood on the glass, he examined his bleeding hands.

"I'm not going to let the bugs have time to kill you!" He removed the pistol from his waistband and advanced towards the locked door. Revenge his only thought, he pulled the door open, no longer concerned about releasing the virus. Neither had he any concern for Dylan Hodgson.

Hodgson leapt to his feet and collided into Dunn's back. The momentum sent the two of them sprawling to the floor beside me. Dunn's pistol flew from his hand across the room. He lay winded and disoriented. Hodgson, hands bound behind him, struggled to stand.

I kicked Dunn in the head pitching him on his back, a spray of blood arching from his mouth. I grabbed Hodgson by the shoulders and shoved him out of the room with more strength than I ever realized I possessed. I secured the door behind me, leaving Dunn alone inside.

Blood dripping from his eye sockets, he blindly groped in search of this pistol. By some miracle, he found it and stood, waving it about the chamber. Though he couldn't see, he emptied the entire clip randomly about the room, each bullet disintegrating against the impenetrable glass.

"You're dead! I've killed you both!" he gurgled as he dropped to his knees, bloody sockets where his eyes should have been.

I wanted to say something dramatic and final; to make the last words he ever heard a taunting reminder of his defeat. Instead, I hugged Dylan Hodgson and buried my face in his shoulder, not caring to watch Dunn's last agonizing moments.

CHAPTER FORTY-THREE

"He's right, you know," said Hodgson as I cut the plastic ties around his wrists. "We're both dead, along with anyone else who ever comes aboard this ship."

I held his face and examined it. His eyes were bloodshot and his face, swollen and bloody, though most of that the result of the beating.

"Your face is a mess. I can't tell if... How are you feeling?"

"Like shit. My nanites will fight the weapon as long as they can, but they can't win. I don't understand why you're not more affected, though."

I stared in the mirror. My face was a bit puffy, and I noted light bruises along my jaw. I opened my mouth to see my gums starting to bleed, but that was the extent of the damage. I had been exposed for longer than anyone. I turned to say something to Hodgson and noticed blood trickling from his nose. I grabbed his hands and compared his fingernails to my own. His were bleeding around the cuticles while mine appeared relatively normal. He was losing the battle.

I lunged across the lab to the supply cabinet and found a syringe. After a couple of tries, I located a vein in my arm and extracted a blood sample. Hodgson coughed and a spray of bloody sputum covered his chin. I had no time to check. No time to test. He would be dead by the time I confirmed my theory.

I pulled up his sleeve and searched for a spot not bruised or bleeding. Locating a usable vein, I jammed the needle in and injected my blood into him in desperation. I just wanted to get my nanite population into the fight.

He faded quickly, his own nanites overrun by the invading phage. I sniffed back the tears and guided him to the nearest bed. I could do nothing but try to make him comfortable.

I absently wiped at my dripping nose with the back of my hand. The fluid was clear. While Hodgson lay dying before me, my own freakish stew of nanites somehow continued holding off the advance. If only I'd gotten them into him sooner, he might have had a chance, if one even existed. I had no way to know how long I would last before succumbing as well. At the very least, we would enjoy a few more minutes together.

I stood next to him and held his hand. His breathing rattled from his fluid filled lungs. He had already lasted ten times longer than Dunn. His soldiers had put up a good fight. I patted his hand and looked at his face, but he was unconscious. I sighed, relieved he would not experience any pain.

I sat with him for an hour, listening to every laboured breath, dreading each one taken would not be followed by another.

At some point, unnoticed by me, his breaths became regular, and no longer gurgled. I released his hand and fetched a stethoscope to confirm my hope. Some fluid remained in his lungs, but not as much as before. His own nanites were now at work repairing his damaged body. I did a quick examination of his eyes, nose, mouth and fingers. All were clotted with dried blood but showed no active bleeding. My desperate bid actually worked.

I rested my head on his chest and listened to his regular breath and the strong steady beat of his heart. There is something primordial about a heartbeat. I'm at peace when I hear one. Maybe my subconscious remembers being in the womb. Who knows? If we survived this, we could survive anything and perhaps in Hodgson I found someone to invest some of my soul in.

Then a wave of terror washed over me, unbidden. Images

of missiles rocketing towards us boiled up in my mind and I knew with Dunn dead, we would not be able to contact *Fortuna* and were about to be robbed of any time we had remaining.

Resigned to my fate, I buried my face in Hodgson's chest. I spent time cataloguing every distinct smell of his I could; his soap, his cologne, his sweat, his blood. It started as a mixed bouquet and lingered until my grieving brain pulled every odour out and owned it individually. I've no idea how long I dwelt in my own little surrender ritual, but I was coaxed from my trance by a gentle hand caressing my hair. I lifted my head to the sight of Dylan Hodgson's bloodshot eyes staring back at me.

"Hi." His voice was a heavy box being pulled along a concrete floor.

I blinked the remaining tears from my sore eyes and appreciated him with a part of my heart that hadn't been open for many years.

"You're alive." I didn't care how stupidly obvious that sounded. I just needed to say it to convince myself I wasn't dreaming.

"I don't feel alive, but I suppose the fact everything I own hurts means I am." He tried to smile, but just came off looking goofy, and despite our recent horrors, I burst out laughing.

I didn't want to break the spell. I didn't want to curse his relief with the burdensome knowledge of how little time remained for us. I lay my head back on his chest and closed my eyes, drinking in his steady heartbeat. One that strong didn't deserve to be cheated out of a long life.

I accessed my implant to determine how much time was left. I clung tighter to him and fought back the tears, desperate for the peace his beating heart had given me earlier. Now it only marked time like a clock ticking down our final minutes.

It wasn't fair he should survive the virus only to have his heartbeat snuffed out shortly after. His heart should be permitted to beat until it wore itself out many long years from now. I was frantic for him to live and my brain searched for a solution, no matter how impossible.

"You wouldn't happen to know how Dunn controlled the *Fortuna*, would you?"

I mentally kicked myself the moment I said it and determined I would come up with an excuse for the stupid question.

"Yes, why?"

My head shot up and I straightened, staring into his eyes for even the smallest hint he might be bullshitting me. My gaze was met by his bewilderment at my nonsensical query.

"Because-Dunn's-dead-and-we-need-it-to-keep-from-being-blown-up-in-less-than-thirty-minutes."

"Wait. What? Slow down."

I pulled him to his feet and explained our situation. He listened to me while bent with vertigo. He nodded and stood straighter. "I saw the control unit in his quarters when I searched them."

I dragged him out of the medical centre. It took him a few steps before he extracted his arm from my grip. He leant against a bulkhead and steadied himself while he waved me off.

"I'm good."

He powered himself forward and weaved down the hallway, not looking to see if I would follow.

I took a last lingering look at the bloody mass that used to be Erik Dunn and then, satisfied he could do us no more harm, followed Hodgson.

CHAPTER FORTY-FOUR

I checked my chronometer. Twenty-two minutes remained before the missiles were going to blow us into a cloud of debris orbiting the sun. By the time I caught up with him, Hodgson had broken into Dunn's quarters. He went straight to the bureau and pulled open the top drawer.

"Shit!"

He began hurling clothing over his shoulder.

"What?"

"It isn't here!" He yanked the next one out and emptied the contents on the floor.

Not waiting to be told the obvious, I scanned the room for any clue to where the remote control device might be. I opened the closet and threw everything into the middle of the room. I banged on the wall looking for any kind of hidden panel.

We had to find it. There was no way I was going to let that son-of-a-bitch reach back and kill us from the grave.

In an orgy of destruction, we violated every drawer and overturned every container and piece of furniture.

I found a knife and cut the mattress and pillows.

Fifteen-minutes.

Hodgson tore the grating off the air duct and boosted me up to dig around inside.

Twelve-minutes.

He pulled the chair into the centre of the room to stand on and began ripping apart the light fixtures. When he yanked the panels from the ceiling I watched and wondered why Dunn would have hidden the fucking thing so well? Wouldn't he need to access the damned thing quickly?

I took another quick scan around the room and then went to search the water closet. There, sitting beside the toilet on the floor lay the control panel. The asshole last used it while he took a shit.

"Found it!" I yelled.

Hodgson almost ran into me at the doorway. He grabbed the device out of my hands and powered it up, his military experience must have emboldened him to press buttons with confidence that I would have never felt.

"I can't establish a signal lock. Something is interfering."

"The Sun! It's been jamming up communications. Limn used some kind of old style laser signalling device to cut through the interference."

I hardly finished my sentence before Hodgson sprinted out of the door and down the corridor towards the bridge.

Out of breath, I caught up with him as he struggled with the door. I explained to him what happened and he located the access switch to release the lock. With no reason to fear the virus, we opened it and rushed in.

Hodgson only paused for a second to take in the bloody mess that used to be Garrick. He pushed his corpse from the communications console and plugged Dunn's device into the interface.

Five-minutes.

I hoped we wouldn't take too long to get *Fortuna's* weapons systems online. I looked over at the barely recognizable remains of Shigeko, lying in foetal position in the corner. A wave of sorrow hit, but in that moment, I couldn't tell if I grieved for her or for us.

"Fuck!" Hodgson slammed his fists on the desk, in almost the same way as Garrick. He stared at me with disbelief on his face.

"I need a passcode."

I rushed to the console to see large numbers flashing in a

countdown on the remote device.

...7...6...5...4...

Dunn taunted me from the grave.

...3...2...1...0

A blinding flash that outshone the sun bloomed outside the window. A white light enveloped the bridge as the *Fortuna* self destructed in the fire of a dozen exploding warheads.

I checked my chronometer.

Three-minutes.

Victorem's missiles were still on the way. *Fortuna* provided a preview of our own end.

CHAPTER FORTY-FIVE

Hodgson slumped in the command chair and I sat on the floor and hugged my knees to my chest next to Shigeko. Numbness rapidly spread through me. I couldn't think of who I ever screwed over for this kind of karma. Possibly I was being punished for hating my mother. You're supposed to love your mother. Everybody knew that.

The universe laughed at me for daring to think I deserved redemption. Born a worthless pile of shit, it took me this long to truly accept it. I'd once worn the glass slippers and kissed the prince, but I would never reside in the palace. That fairy tale belonged to somebody else. In the last three minutes of my pathetic existence, I finally understood and it stung.

All my life I believed I needed to buy respect; to pay for the right to eat or even live. First with my body, then later with my brain, life didn't give without taking. There was a price to stay alive and I was out of credits. The Grim Reaper was coming in a couple of minutes to repossess my soul, and he was the one honest guy who wasn't buying anything I was selling. Even if he could be bought, I had nothing left.

Or didn't I? An idea started to form. A crazy, last ditch, hail Mary. Perhaps I didn't need to try bribing the Reaper. Maybe one person remained who would be interested in what I could sell him.

Two-minutes.

I recalled how Shigeko sent the message to the *Victorem* and pressed the same sequence on the comm panel. Hodgson gave me a puzzled look. I took his hand in mine and sat in the chair next to him.

"Hey there. You guys shooting at us." I spoke into the mic without trying to hide my nerves.

"Listen, I don't even know if I turned this thing on properly. If I'm not just talking to myself, I have something you might want to hear.

"My name is Doctor Melanie Destin. I'm the one your boys tricked into coming to work for you. Sorry for being so honest, but the way I see it I don't have the time or desire to tell you anything but the truth.

"So here it is. You are about to blow up a ship full of dead people.

"You need to understand your man Dunn sold you out. He planned to steal the virus for himself and leave you with nothing to show for all your effort, but I suppose you already figured that out, since you shot a bunch of missiles at us.

"Anyway, the reason he and everyone else onboard is dead is because the nano-virus got released and killed them all, including Dunn.

"Now, you may be wondering if everyone is supposed to be dead, how am I talking to you? The answer, though difficult to believe, is simple; I'm still alive because I have the anti-virus for this thing running through my veins.

"Now, I know this nano-weapon was valuable enough to you to kill for. How much are the virus AND its antigen worth to you? If you let those missiles blow us up in the next," I checked my chronometer, "thirty-seconds, you'll never find out. It's all up to you, boys."

I left the channel open and moved to sit on Hodgson's lap. I kissed him on the lips and he returned it. Not a passionate, I-wanna-fuck-your-brains-out kiss, but a simple one that said, 'I love you.'

The window was suddenly filled with a succession of bright flashing lights as the *Victorem's* missiles self-destructed. I decided to imagine them as fireworks and kissed Hodgson again.

The Ares Weapon

CHAPTER FORTY-SIX

An hour and a bit later, Hodgson and I stood in our pressure suits in front of the closed hangar entrance.

"Are you ready for this?" he asked while fitting a harness over my space suit.

"No."

"I didn't think so." He handed me one to put on him. We hooked them by short tethers to the emergency hand holds along the corridor walls.

"Are you sure about this, Mel?"

"We've been over this. The hangar is the only place on the ship that hasn't been exposed."

"Yeah, but a rapid depressurization is pretty drastic. A lot can go wrong."

"We've been contaminated with a virus, shot at by two different ships and you almost died. I don't think this belongs on the list of things that can ruin our day."

He chuckled.

"Besides, it's the only way I can think of that will vent most of the airborne nanites into space," I said.

"Most?"

I smiled at him, but I didn't think he could see my face through the visor. "Just turn off the gravity, big guy."

Hodgson accessed the control panel on the arm of his suit. He'd rigged a remote link with the ship's engineering and environmental functions. At the press of a button, the field released its hold of us and I floated off the floor. I felt a slight pull as the tether held me in place.

He then set off the explosive release bolts on the exterior hatchway closest to our location on the ship. I heard a faint pop, followed by the rumble of air rushing past my helmet. My whole body jerked a few centimetres towards the breach, restrained by the same tether.

Seconds later, all sound died away and I could only hear Hodgson's breathing over the open comm. He confirmed that this section was in a vacuum and we repeated the venting operation on the other side of the hangar doors.

We worked out the details of our escape while we approached the flyby with the Rego vessel. The window was tight and we wouldn't be able to dock the two rapidly passing ships. Our only avenue was to launch the drop ship.

With the gravity field restored, we boarded the shuttle. While Hodgson prepped it for departure and laid in the docking maneuver with *Victorem*, I did a once over of the containment unit with the secured virus samples safely inside.

"This would be a lot easier if I didn't need this bulky space suit," I said.

"Like you said, best to keep everything in a vacuum. Anyway, the suits give us an extra layer of protection. Even at the higher flyby orbit, it's still pretty deadly out there."

"Maybe the radiation will fry any loose nanite that we may have tracked in."

"Maybe. It won't matter, though, if our timing is off. We only have one shot at this. If we miss our link up, we'll be cooked. This little ship can't take too much."

"Are you always so gloomy? After everything we've been through, I think the universe owes us one. Don't you?"

He didn't say anything, but I knew he smiled.

Despite Hodgson's concerns, the maneuver and docking went flawlessly according to plan. The only event that wasn't on the programme was the destruction of our ship. As we entered the massive hangar of *Victorem* I looked at the aft monitor to see

Helios explode in a brilliant flash like the *Fortuna*. It seemed our rescuers didn't want anyone else recovering a sample of the virus. I thought that a good idea, myself.

The next thirty days became a routine. Confined to our dropship, once a day two technicians in pressure suits approached and took bio-scans of the hull. We supplied interior scans three times a day to our hosts. They were gracious enough to connect us to power and air, and we had enough emergency rations to stay comfortable, but after that length of time, the smell inside our little cell started to become ripe.

On day thirty-one they pressurized the hangar and we were escorted to individual cabins. I couldn't believe the luxurious quarters they gave me and spent over an hour in the hot shower. When I emerged, I discovered that someone laid out a tasteful dinner dress for me on the bed, along with an engraved invitation to dine with our host.

I had a strange uneasiness about meeting with the person I talked into rescuing us. To this point, none of my claims were questioned, but I knew the time approached when I would be compelled to hold up my end of the bargain and let them poke and prod me for the anti-virus.

I had no problem with them taking as many samples as they needed. I worried, however, that they might want more of me than just samples. This was the same corporation that manipulated me into working for them.

Like the other rooms I'd seen, the *Victorem's* dining room appointments were more suitable for a luxury liner than a warship. I got the impression that we weren't dealing with middle management types anymore.

"I don't trust them," I whispered to Hodgson who joined me at the table. Our host had yet to arrive.

"That's probably wise. Do us both a favour and follow my lead."

I frowned at his comment. "I got us here, didn't I?"

"Yes, for which I will be eternally grateful, but at this point, you're operating out of your league."

I glared at him and my voice rose to a stage whisper. "What the hell do you mean by that?"

He didn't respond but nodded towards the door and stood as a man entered the room. I composed myself and rose as well.

His slight stature surprised me. I suppose I expected somebody in command of a ship like this to be built more like Hodgson. He wore a dark business suit and carried himself as a man who was comfortable holding authority.

"Good evening. I am Felix Altius." He motioned for us to sit while he took his place opposite us.

He was half a head taller than I and very slight of build. I could have picked him up. Except for his strange, milky blue eyes, his features were Mediterranean. He moved with a slightly effeminate grace, but his voice had a masculine and calming tone to it. I thought him to be charming.

We were treated to a lavishly prepared meal, and I'm afraid I ate far too much, having survived on emergency ration packs for the previous thirty-one days. Hodgson displayed a less vigorous appetite, choosing to mostly pick at and sample the contents of his plate. I wondered if he suspected the food to be poisoned until I noticed Altius eating from the same serving trays. Perhaps the ex-soldier preferred emergency rations.

When the plates were cleared, Altius wasted no time.

"Doctor Destin, I believe you understand that we must verify the claim you made over your transmission?"

He smiled pleasantly with his whole face, giving me the impression of an amicable old auntie who would not hesitate to slap me up the side of the head if I didn't live up to expectations.

"Naturally, Mister Altius, I would be pleased to submit myself for tests."

"Excellent." He continued to smile. "Would you be averse to beginning in the morning?"

"I'm more than eager, Sir."

"But before we get too carried away," interrupted Hodgson, "we need to establish the terms around the submission of samples."

Altius was as surprised as I.

"I beg your pardon? What exactly is your stake in all this, Mister Hodgson?"

"I have a prior claim to Doctor Destin. I am returning her to Mars under my protection."

Altius' smile slackened. He took a sip of wine while he regarded Hodgson in a new light.

"Why should that be of concern to us?"

"Because of your arrangements with certain parties on Mars. You've had thirty-one days to confirm my identity, Mister Altius. I'm sure you've discovered who I am and, more importantly, who I work for."

"Indeed." His smile gone, he placed his wine goblet firmly down. "I'm curious to learn why you think there are arrangements between Mars and ourselves."

I was curious too. What the hell was Hodgson doing? Trying to get us spaced? I kicked him discretely, but he ignored me.

"First, if you had any intentions of dealing with Terra, that opportunity existed while *Athena* was still in range. Second, given your escape velocity from the sun and the time we've been in transit, we passed the Terran and Lunar jurisdictions about ten days ago, suggesting you are en route to Mars. Third, as you are aware, I am a spy."

Hodgson smiled like a little boy who outsmarted the teacher. He leaned back in his chair and took a drink from his own goblet.

Altius stared at him, clearly weighing every point laid out before him. I began to compose something to say to salvage the situation when Altius again smiled and relaxed. He leaned forward on his elbows.

"What terms were you thinking of?"

"Nothing elaborate. Only that you limit yourselves to less than 500 millilitres of blood and five, non-life threatening internal tissue samples."

"Is that all? Anything else?"

"Oh, and Doctor Destin must be allowed to live and

accompany me to Mars."

I thought Hodgson's last demand paranoid and wanted to tell him so, but the longer Altius considered the terms without responding, the more I appreciated how much I underestimated the danger I was in.

Altius abruptly stood and offered his hand to Hodgson. "Agreed."

He then shook my hand. "The medical technicians will escort you both to the lab tomorrow. I understand it shouldn't take more than a few minutes of your time."

Halfway to the door, he turned back and said, "We will be arriving at Mars in two days. Is there a particular docking station you wish us to drop you at?"

Hodgson smiled. "I'll let you know."

Altius left and the room was eerily quiet until I finally spoke. "How the fuck did you know they didn't intend to let me live?"

"I've had lots of experience with these guys."

For the rest of the night, during breaks between our desperate coupling, I prompted him for more details. I couldn't pry anything more from him on the topic.

I decided it best to leave it alone. I was alive and finally going to Mars. Life looked pretty good and I wanted, for once, to savour the moment without worrying about why.

CHAPTER FORTY-SEVEN

My tattered old travel poster no longer hung in my bathroom, but on the wall of my reception room. I don't really comprehend why I kept it. Everything it advertised about Olympia had been exaggerated to the point of caricature. But it still made me smile when I came to work every morning.

Some of its claims were true. Olympia was a real, floating city over Mars though hardly a city of the clouds. In reality, it was an orbiting habitat and the largest settlement. Instead of the poster's promise of greening countryside split by blue rivers filling azure lakes, the rusty landscape below still appeared the same as it had for the past few billion years.

Except for the clouds. Sometimes blankets and pillows of clouds of every shape and texture from the terraforming effort obscured the red surface beneath Olympia. When that happened, I would spend as many hours as possible staring at them. At those times, I believed the promises of the poster were the closest to being fulfilled.

Felix Altius honoured my contract and paid me in full, every credit promised by Charlie. Though my deal with Dunn obviously was never mentioned, the corporation did reward me with a handsome finders' fee for the recovery of the virus. In a pique of greed, I tried to push for a royalty agreement for my 'invention' of the anti-virus, but after Rego's smarmy lawyer reminded me of their prior competing patent on the process, I dropped the whole subject. I earned enough to buy my citizenship, apartment and establish my medical practice. Cinderella lived in the palace, and couldn't be happier.

Almost a year to the day after *Victorem* deposited us here, I returned home to find that someone had broken into my apartment and set a candlelit table for two. Mouth watering aromas drifted from the kitchen, making my stomach grumble. I threw my things on the floor and rushed to embrace Dylan Hodgson for the first time in months.

"You're back early. Why didn't you tell me you were coming?"

"I wanted to surprise you." He handed me my favourite drink and led me by the hand into the sitting room.

"Dinner will be ready in half an hour. It would have been finished when you got here, but I needed to do some shopping. Honestly, Mel..."

"I'm not the domestic type, like some people." I took his hand and laid my head on his chest. I'd never felt more content than in that moment.

"I missed you. I worry about you when you're off doing spy stuff."

He kissed me on the top of my head.

"You might be glad of my job when you learn what I discovered."

He took both of my hands in his and gazed straight into my eyes. Perspiration shone on his forehead and he struggled to push the words out. My heart pounded in my throat.

Oh God, no, please don't ruin everything. Please don't propose.

"Mel, I found someone who knows what happened to Carlos."

I stared at him stupidly. "What?"

"The guy is here on Mars. In fact, he's been here for some time, hiding in one of the surface work settlements."

"Why is he hiding?"

"There are lots of people interested in seeing him dead."

"Hmph. He sound's like one of my old pals."

He didn't crack a smile at my joke.

"Okay, spill it all, Hodgson. Who the hell is he?"

He didn't answer right away but seemed to weigh a decision. Finally, he swallowed hard and blurted it out.

"Charlie Wong."

"Fuck me. No."

He nodded and moved back like he expected me to slap him.

"And you think that son-of-a-bitch knew about Carlos all these years?"

"My source tells me he has reliable intel. I don't know how long he's known."

"This is verified? It isn't another bullshit story of his?"

"It checked out, at least, the parts I could verify. That's where I've been for the last few weeks."

There was a sadness in Hodgson's eyes. Like the look of a little boy who found out his dog is going to die.

"Why are you telling me this, Dylan? You could pretend you didn't know anything. I was quite content to go on without knowing what happened to Carlos."

"For the moment you are. But, eventually, knowing that he hadn't died would eat at you and..." He looked at the floor.

"You didn't want Carlos to come between us?"

He gave me a sad smile. "If you love someone, let them go."

I hugged him tight. "You've been reading too many inspirational posters in the spy's lounge."

We both laughed at that, happy to break the tension.

"It's your call, Mel. If you want to meet with him, I can arrange it. If you don't, we can leave him to his fate."

"What do you mean?"

"He's being hunted by Felix Altius. He was part of Dunn's inner circle and the corporation is doing some house cleaning. He's been on the planet, posing as a medical technician and living pretty meanly. Conditions are not very nice down there."

I sighed. Did every world need to be built on the backs of others? Guilt tugged at my conscience until I recalled many of them were there by choice and didn't want to be found or rescued. I remembered surviving like that.

"He'll want something for the information," I said.

"He needs funds for a new ID, a new DNA profile, travel documents; the works."

"And he thinks I'll pay handsomely for something he may or may not possess?"

"I could find him and shake him down for the info and then tell Altius where he is."

"No, I'll meet with him."

"Are you sure?"

"Yeah, I am. Set it up. I want to see the look on his face when he's forced to admit everything to me."

I wanted to tell Dylan Hodgson he had nothing to fear from my learning what happened to Carlos. I let go of him a long time ago. Yes, the shock of hearing that he faked his death and vanished was tough to get over, but Carlos, for whatever the reason, chose to leave me. No way I would pursue this to rekindle an old flame between us. I had put that fire out with my tears long ago.

Someone went to a lot of trouble to help Carlos go away. They faked a DNA profile and substituted another body for his. The idea that a crook like Charlie would know about him and now try to extort me with it bugged me.

I would meet with Charlie and make him squirm. I would give him a deal. I would arrange for everything; the ID, the DNA, the travel docs. He would receive all he asked for, but with a caveat. If his information proved to be bullshit, I would inform Felix Altius who would be happy to hunt him down like a scared rabbit. My biggest question remained; what would I do with the information about Carlos?

CHAPTER FORTY-EIGHT

Three grave-faced men sat, one on each side of the triangular table. Records of this meeting would not be kept. The men themselves did not officially exist. Their true names were not supposed to be known though Primus was aware of the identities of his companions. He suspected they likewise knew as much about Talus Varr. Their mutual distrust ensured complete honesty, as previous attempts at deception proved fatal for more than one of their predecessors.

The room they occupied was unusually dark for late afternoon. The magnificent view of the red canyons of Mars below was blocked out by the drawn shades. The two others stared at Primus as he studied his copy of the document.

Finished, he looked up from the page. His appearance belying his fifty-eight Terran years, he sat ramrod straight and his muscular build filled out his crisply pressed bronze coloured tunic of the Martian military council.

"It would seem the mission you two were so reluctant to sanction turned out to be a success."

"Except for the complications around the woman, I would agree with you." Secundus, at forty-eight, was the youngest. Shorter than the others by a head, he possessed the stocky build of a career-long soldier, though he never served a day in the military. He was, by profession, a scientist and head of Mars' science council.

"They are inconveniences at the most. She is a valuable asset in her own right, according to her file." Primus would need to argue convincingly.

"She is unconventional and volatile, to say the least. There are key questions about her that make me uneasy," said the oldest man, Tertius. He alone of the three showed all of his eighty-four years. A career in public service weighed heavily on his thin, fragile frame.

"Yes, her history of independent and, I might say, antisocial behaviour could be a complication, but I do not believe it diminishes her value as an asset," replied Primus.

Secundus said, "Naturally if you insist on this course of action, she will require management."

"Yes, she will, especially if we are going to realize her full potential. We have an agent in place who has assumed that role."

"She will rebel against such controls. She must not suspect or the entire operation will be in jeopardy." As always, Tertius delivered a worried appearance with his warning.

"Yes, I agree with Tertius. We cannot risk initiating this if there is any significant chance of failure. It would be better to terminate the woman than begin this and fail," said Secundus.

"It will not fail. I have the utmost faith in our agent. As you gentlemen know, we will not accomplish our goals overnight. It will take some time to prepare the woman for her role, and the sooner we begin, the sooner we will be ready for what we know is coming. She is the most likely candidate to emerge in five years. If we reject her now because of a few, minor personality flaws, we must consider the possibility we will never find the right person in time."

The others sat in silence as they contemplated Primus' arguments. He looked from one of his colleagues to the next while he gave them the time they required. The decision must be unanimous.

"Very well. I vote in favour of proceeding with the plan as presented," said Secundus.

Two men now observed Tertius and waited patiently for him to decide. They would wait for hours if necessary.

"I too am favourable, with one condition."

A frown creased the brow of Primus, but it was the only sign of annoyance he would permit himself within the Triumvirate. "What is your caveat?"

"If a more suitable candidate can be found before the first critical juncture, then the woman will be terminated and replaced."

Secundus responded without hesitation. "That is acceptable."

Now two sets of eyes regarded Primus as he weighed the proposed modification to their plan. He had hoped to avoid such a complication. Tertius' caveat placed significant risk to his personal stakes. His partners in the Triumvirate were ignorant of his machinations; he paid good money to ensure so. Still, he couldn't shake the feeling they had found out more about the woman than he wished them to know. He would revisit his network and purge some of his agents as a future precaution. He would also put new measures in place to guarantee any search for an alternate candidate ended in failure.

"Of course. The condition is acceptable," he responded. "I will instruct our agent to begin the operation." He had, in fact, already done so.

Secundus rose from the table and went to the credenza along the wall. He returned with three glasses filled with amber liquor.

"A toast to our future success."

"Yes, a toast to the conquest," said Tertius, visibly relaxed with the crucial vote concluded.

The worried expression returned to Tertius. "I still have concerns over the fate of our friend. We must surely now allow him back into our good graces?"

Primus suppressed a sigh. He'd wondered when the subject of Regis Mundi would again be raised. He was surprised it took Tertius this long to resurrect the running debate about his old friend.

"Don't you think Mundi has outlived his usefulness,

Tertius?" asked Primus.

"Regis Mundi is the reason we have reached this stage. Without his aid, the Terrans would now have the Ares virus and we would be facing their invading armies." Tertius took any criticism of his friend to heart.

"Do not forget it was because of him that was ever a concern. He was merely fortunate matters resolved themselves in his apparent favour," said Primus, more firmly than he intended.

"Gentlemen, please! Your bickering is not helping me enjoy this fine whisky," said Secundus. "Primus, I understand your dislike for the man. He's done little to endear himself to us in the last number of years, I'll agree. But you must admit he redeemed himself and gave us, not only the virus but now the means to use it to its fullest potential."

Primus regarded both of his companions as they stood firm in their support of the one man he, as Talus Varr, hated more than any other. Tertius would ever be loyal to his oldest friend. Secundus would change his opinion once Mundi again failed. This was not a battle he would win here. He needed to allow Mundi enough rope to finally hang himself.

"I'm sure you are correct. My apologies for my critical comments. Of course, Regis Mundi must be given every opportunity to demonstrate his worthiness of reinstatement." He lifted his glass to support his insincere words.

Varr raised the blinds and admired the panoramic vista of Mars beneath them. The setting sun painted long ochre shadows across the canyon walls far below, where modern rivers would one day again flow. His comrades were right about one thing. Mundi had given them a key element in realizing the future of the Martian people. He was eager to begin the next phase of the operation to transform the dream into reality.

Do you want to read more?

If you liked this book, I am humbly gratified. If you liked this book enough to want to read more of my work, I am thrilled. Fortunately, there is a way for this to happen by joining my reader list. By signing up to my list you will also receive a **free ebook** containing a short story about one of Mel's early life exploits on Terra and a collection of other short stories, not available anywhere else. You will also receive advance notice of all future books, well in advance of publication, have opportunities to sign on as a member of my Advanced Review Team and receive a prepublication copy of the book for review purposes on Amazon.

Claim your free ebook by going to www.prudenauthor.com

Did you like this book?

Let everyone know by posting a review on Amazon.

Acknowledgements

Just as it takes a village to raise a child, writing a book requires a community of supporters. This work would not have been possible without the support, encouragement and critical eye of my wife, Colleen. I also want to give a special thanks to Pat and Paul Brown and Alex Avrio who all suffered through the beta reading of my work and offered helpful insights in how to make it better. To all my supportive family and friends on Facebook, your encouragement helped me along when I thought this project would never end. Finally, to all my readers, my most humble thanks. I hope this book was worth the time you made to read it.

About the Author

D.M.(Doug) Pruden is a professional geophysicist who worked for 35 years in the petroleum industry. For most of his life he has been plagued with stories banging around inside his head that demanded to be let out into the world. He currently spends his time as an empty nester in Calgary, Alberta, Canada with his long suffering wife of 34 years, Colleen. When he isn't writing science fiction stories, he likes to spend his time playing with his granddaughters and working on improving his golf handicap. He will also do geophysical work when requested.

Go to www.prudenauthor.com and sign up to the email list. You will receive a free, never before published ebook about Mel Destin's early life on Terra as well as a collection of short stories. List members will receive early publication notice of upcoming books, blog posts and other goodies from time to time.

Made in the USA
Charleston, SC
23 September 2016